Grimm's Last Fairytale

Also by Haydn Middleton

The People in the Picture
Son of Two Worlds
The Lie of the Land
The Collapsing Castle

The Mordred Cycle
The King's Evil
The Queen's Captive
The Knight's Vengeance

Grimm's Last Fairytale

A NOVEL

Haydn Middleton

THOMAS DUNNE BOOKS
ST. MARTIN'S GRIFFIN NEW YORK

THOMAS DUNNE BOOKS.
An imprint of St. Martin's Press.

www.stmartins.com

Library of Congress Cataloging-in-Publication Data

Middleton, Haydn.
Grimm's Last Fairytale : a novel / Haydn Middleton.
p. cm.
ISBN 0-312-27290-1 (hc)
ISBN 0-312-28858-1 (pbk)
1. Grimm, Wilhelm, 1786–1859—Fiction. 2. Grimm, Jacob, 1785–1863—Fiction. 3. Philologists—Fiction. 4. Fairy tales—Fiction. 5. Brothers—Fiction. 6. Germany—Fiction. I. Title.

PR6063.I248 G75 2001
823'.914—dc21 2001032557

First published in Great Britain by Abacus, a division of Little, Brown, and Company (U.K.)

First St. Martin's Griffin Edition: May 2002

10 9 8 7 6 5 4 3 2 1

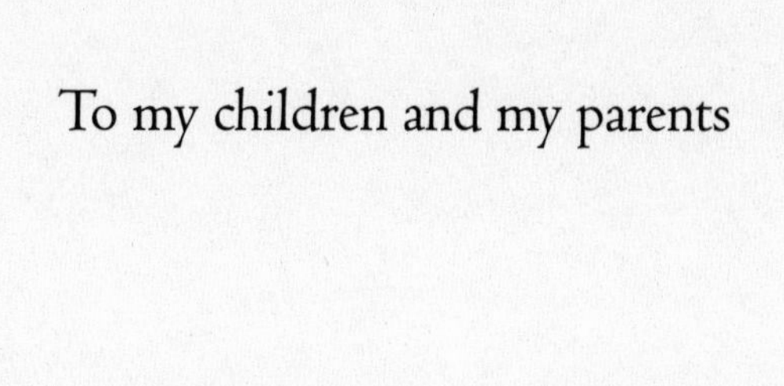

To my children and my parents

Once upon a time, there was no Germany.

For centuries the German people lived in a patchwork of principalities, duchies and kingdoms, some of them so small that one ruling prince was said to have accidentally dropped his realm from his pocket and lost it forever while out on an afternoon stroll. At the other end of the scale stood militaristic Prussia, with its capital at Berlin.

But as the age of the railway and the factory dawned, there lay beyond the map another Germany: a timeless land of the heart and mind, full of dark forests and sometimes even darker fairy-tales.

Prologue

From a distance the pines looked heather-blue, soaring away from the wall of his small town like a vast tilted ocean. On breezy moonlit nights he watched spellbound as they rippled in gently majestic tides, and afterwards he would see the elms outside the Rathaus, the beeches in the market square and the lone peach tree by his own window as sorry bits of jetsam swept in and left behind.

While still a child he was forbidden to go far into the forest, but often he went to gather brushwood at its fringes. He loved to be there when the sun sank low, and briefly its fireball brilliance was trapped beneath the canopy. No artist ever mixed colours quite like the ones he saw then.

Warm tendrils and tubers gleamed on fat beds of sphagnum. Opalescent shrubs caught the sparks from swaying creepers. In dank mulchy hollows, ochre turned to auburn, amber to copper, emerald to olive then darker into sage, until the black of night swallowed even these last shining embers.

But for all the forest's beauty, its siren call was silence. Further in, an old pedlar woman once said, it was so quiet you could hear a heart-string snap. Yet to him the trees' stillness was attentive, and this in turn encouraged him to listen harder, to believe only in what his own ears told him.

And that was how he picked up the first faint disturbance: a dry insistent clacking, far out in the depths of the needle-leaf sea. For a while it sounded like a clock's pendulum, though never quite so regular. Then it was more like a distant boot-heel coming down on stone – again, again, again – until finally the silence closed over it once more.

For years afterwards he did not hear the noise again. But from that evening on, however hard he tried to forget, he knew that it was there.

September
1863

ONE

They arrived in Hanau at dusk, but did not make straight for the inn. Kummel thought old Professor Grimm was eager to find their rooms as soon as possible. But with a girlish grin his niece led him down past the Rathaus then along a narrow street of pointed-gabled houses with huge wooden doors.

Kummel followed at ten paces, occasionally setting their portmanteaux down on the cobbles to improve his grip, or to adjust the straps of Fräulein Auguste's hat boxes, which he wore across each shoulder. The heavier, less valuable luggage had been carted on ahead to their night's lodgings. Even so, the twenty-five-year-old servant – craving tobacco – could have done without this detour.

The three of them stepped aside to let a bullock wagon pass from the opposite direction. Apart from a water-carrier and several smocked men returning from the fields, the streets were deserted in the bilious gloaming. As she walked on, the Fräulein turned to right and left like a crinolined clockwork doll, pointing, nodding, asking the Professor inaudible questions. In their usual fashion they stayed very close without actually touching, as if they feared a profound magnetic reaction should they so much as brush cuffs in public.

Finally the pair halted in front of a comfortable-looking, free-standing house, distinguished from all the others only by its garishly yellow front door. Since there were lights upstairs, Kummel expected one of them to step up and knock, then indicate to him whether to follow or wait. But when neither moved he put down the cases, rolled his shoulders in the dark grey morning coat that had once belonged to the Fräulein's dead father, and turned around in his hands her jewellery case, which was attached to his wrist by a chain.

Some hushed words passed between his temporary master and mistress, but mainly they stood in silence, staring up at the house as if it were preparing to perform a trick. Kummel sniffed the thick country smells of woodsmoke, sweet damp hay and animal dung and looked around as he waited. It was all a far cry from the arrow-straight thoroughfares of Berlin, with their promenading soldiery and the deafening clatter of *droshkies*, but he had been through many similar backwaters on his involuntary travels. All these houses would have a yard for domestic livestock: hens, geese, possibly pigs. If a cow fell sick here, a pastor was probably still called in to bless it.

The Professor was the first to turn and move on again. For a man of almost eighty he was very nimble. During the holiday with the rest of the family in the Harz Mountains over the previous fortnight, he had refused to use a cane even on the steepest walks. He walked hunched forward now, his right hand balled at the small of his back. The slender Fräulein was slower to peel herself away from the yellow-doored house. Then she glided back into step in her alpaca travelling coat, smiling almost apologetically back at Kummel as he set off again in their wake.

On reaching the modest half-timbered inn, its keeper – a moustachioed man built like a herring-barrel and very nearly as oily – had gathered his staff at the back of the foyer for a formal introduction to so honoured a guest. Kummel meanwhile was directed up to the higher storey, where the three of them had been given adjoining rooms. His own was a mere cubbyhole filled by a truckle bed and a sour latrine stink, but it would do for a single night.

Setting down the bags, he peered over the banister at the porters and grooms, some of whom gnawed on radishes while the keeper seemed to be listing every book the venerable Jacob Grimm had ever written. Works on language, literature, law and history, as well as the famous *Tales for Young and Old* in collaboration with his younger brother Wilhelm, and the still incomplete *Deutsches Wörterbuch*, a gargantuan dictionary that would finally contain every German word. It appeared he had also once been political: a member of the 'ill-fated' German National Assembly of 1848, and, a decade before that, one of the 'celebrated Göttingen Seven', who sounded to Kummel like the title of one of his fairytales.

The hawk-faced Professor listened patiently. Although he must have been used to this kind of acclaim, he looked as embarrassed as his audience looked bemused. From up above he also gave an impression of extreme fragility: small, stooped and skinny, with cotton-wafts of hair straggling down to his shoulders, his legs bowed but seeming to bear hardly any weight from his upper body and, for all the brains inside it, even his high-domed head with its Napoleonic nose and sunken cheeks looked light and deflatable.

Finally, after polite applause, his face broke into a warm smile. 'It's good to be back in my beloved Hesse,' he rasped, throwing back his coat-skirts from the waist and inspecting the Kurd rug at his feet. 'Thank you for your welcome.'

As the crowd dispersed the keeper asked if his guests cared to take dinner immediately. Kummel watched the Professor grin. '*Ach*, first I must wash and change. We've spent most of today inside clouds of locomotive steam and dust scuffed up by coach horses. If you'd be so good, I yearn for some hot water.'

The keeper called out instructions to his maids, and Kummel backed into the antechamber to the Professor's bedroom to secure the windows and close the coarse linen curtains. The old man certainly liked to keep clean; in the Harz he had often bathed himself twice a day. And Kummel had noticed that sometimes when he woke from dozing he would rub at the skin on his hands and even his cuffs, as if he could see stains.

By the light of a smoky candle lamp on the bureau, he began to unpack his master's clothes. Soon afterwards the Professor passed behind him. Kummel glanced up and watched him take off his frock coat, lay it on the turned-down bed, then stand rapt in front of an oval hinged mirror on a gilt occasional table. He did not seem altogether pleased with what he saw.

Ancient though he was, he did not miss much. Aware of being watched, his eyes darted to the doorway. 'I am quite shockingly filthy, Kummel,' he smiled, touching his fingertips to his cravat, inspecting them as if he expected to find soot then shaking his hoary head. '*Mein Gott*, you could almost take me for a Turk!'

From his tub on the floor Jacob could see the whole fuggy room. Marie had one jug, Gretchen another. While the first maid poured in heated water, the second slipped in small measures of green wine that stood warming in a pan on the stove. 'May I drink the wine, Mother?' Jacob shouted, attracted by its sweet smell, mixing it in with the flat of his hand, then putting his fingers to his lips and pretending to suck off the drops.

'Rub it on yourself, child,' she called back from her low stool by the stove, 'or do you want to end up like poor weak-chested Willi here?'

Jacob dropped his hand at once and waited for her to smile, dark-eyed, across at him. But her attention had already turned to his younger brother, often mistaken for his twin, freshly bathed and lodged between her fleshy knees. She unfastened his pigtail, dragged apart his hair with her fingernails then began to nip at his scalp for nits. The simple act of watching made Jacob's own head prickle. His turn would come later – a few days' blessed respite. 'More wine, Gretchen,' he shouted, drawing up his knees to his ribs. He watched the liquid splash in, then cried in delight as the maid ran the last of it down his shoulder.

'Story, story, story now,' little Wilhelm chanted in his hoarse, breathless way.

'Story, story, story,' their mother echoed in mock weariness.

'*Story!*' Jacob yelled from the tub. 'Oh please, Mother. Please Mother *Goose!*'

He glimpsed her teeth as she smiled behind her long tumble of thick, loosened hair. Teeth and tales, always teeth and tales. Jacob would watch her mouth so closely during the tellings that he almost felt sucked inside. 'Which story?' she asked.

'Butcher! Butcher! Butcher!' For Willi there was only ever one choice.

'Surely not Butcher again?' she teased, smearing tiny insect forms on to the leg of the stool under her skirts. 'I don't know that I *can* tell such a terrible tale again.'

'Yes, Butcher!' Jacob pleaded, smacking his palm against the tubwater. And as soon as he said it, and Willi ceased his racket, and even before their mother tossed back her hair and purred the first magical words up at the nursery ceiling, the room became different. Calmer, cooler, more spacious, older.

'A long time ago, when wishing was still of use . . .' She paused just to tantalize them. Jacob felt his own breath and that of his ailing brother rush out into the even deeper stillness, freezing the maids with the jugs, the nits in their hair, the collection of bird feathers on the desk by the window, everything, just for the length of time she needed to take them there and back. 'All that time ago,' she went on, with Jacob's eyes fastened on her lips, 'a man slaughtered a pig while his children were watching. Then later, when the children started playing, one child said to the other . . .'

Both brothers knew their cue: '"*You be the little pig and I'll be the butcher!*"'

'Whereupon,' she took both dimpled hands from Wilhelm's hair and folded them in her lap, 'the first child took an open blade and thrust it into the other's neck.'

'*Gottes Willen!*' gasped Gretchen, rushing a hand up to her throat, and at once the boys hissed at her to hush.

'And their mother, who was upstairs,' she widened her glinting eyes across the room at Jacob, 'bathing the youngest child in a tub, heard the cries and quickly she ran downstairs. And when she saw what had happened, she drew the knife out of the child's neck and – in a fierce rage – thrust it . . .'

'*Into the heart of the child who had been the butcher!*'

She nodded. 'Then she rushed back to the house to see what the other child was doing in the tub . . .'

'*Nein, ach nein,*' winced Marie.

'Ssh!' hissed the brothers, Jacob sliding a little lower in the tub-water.

'But in the meantime it had drowned in the water. And the woman was so horrified that she fell into a state of utter despair, refused to be consoled by the servants, and hanged herself. Then . . .'

She paused again, which surprised Jacob. The goosebumps were up on his shoulders and knees, ready for her final line, but again she was looking at him, so piercingly and with her lips so uncharacteristically pursed, that he opened his own mouth and heard himself finishing the story all by himself: 'Then when her husband returned home from the fields and he saw this, he was so distraught that he died shortly after.'

She nodded, solemn-eyed, satisfied. 'This is my story,' she concluded, 'I've told it, and in your hands I leave it.' Then her face broke apart in its loveliest, toothiest smile and poor panting Willi reached up and clasped both her hands, half in anxiety, half in elation.

Jacob needed more warmth in the tub. Although he grinned and his cheeks were flushed, the goosebumps had not gone down. Even another jugful made no difference. He clenched his teeth to stop his jaw from quivering. In speaking that last sentence on his own, the words had seemed to sweep through him from some other place entirely, leaving an unfamiliar, almost peaty flavour in his mouth.

'You spoke well there, Jacob,' his mother said. 'Soon you will be able to tell the stories to us, *ja*?'

'No, no, no!' Willi protested. 'Boys don't tell stories. Not men either. There's no *Father* Goose, is there? Only maids and mothers!' This little sally so overstrained him that he broke into the hacking cough which Jacob always felt ripping at his own chest too, in sympathy. Their mother chuckled, ruffled his deloused hair and drew him back tighter against her knees until the spasm passed.

Jacob curled smaller in the tub. 'Can I come out now, Mother?' he asked.

'Come out?' snorted Marie behind him. 'But you're still quite shockingly filthy, young man. If I didn't know who you were, I'd take you for a Turk!'

After dinner the Professor withdrew to his room to 'chop wood'.

This was how he always described his work on the great *Wörterbuch*, presumably to set it apart from the fine carving of his less monumental books. Back in Berlin Kummel had helped Grimm's besotted niece to pack the *Wörterbuch* papers and related legal documents, chapbooks and romances through which he trawled for words. Already, she said, he had been slaving at the project for twenty-five years and now he was supervising the work of over ninety contributors. 'Yet he takes such little pleasure in it!' she whispered with a fraught, embarrassed smile. 'He took it on originally, you see, only to secure a regular income for our family. My Apapa has always been *quite* the most selfless of men.'

The Fräulein went out on to the veranda alone for chicory coffee, and when Kummel arrived with the jug and glass, she quickly set aside the green gilt-edged book that she had been reading throughout their stay in the Harz.

'It's a pleasant evening,' she smiled at him in greeting, 'if a little humid. But at least we seem to have left the rain up in the mountains.' She had an almost English fascination with the weather. In the Harz Kummel had heard her discussing it at length with her mother, her brothers and her sister-in-law. She brought the same intensity to her chatter about the landscapes, the restorative quality of the air, even what clothes they might wear the next day. It seemed deliberately dull and impersonal to Kummel, but as a previous mistress had once loftily told him: *Servants talk about people, gentlefolk discuss things*. He poured the Fräulein's coffee, but she did not take up the glass.

'We must pray for no rain again tomorrow,' she told him. 'The Professor wishes to walk in the hills. I thought we might set out soon after breakfast, since we're scheduled to travel on to Steinau in mid-afternoon. You know, Kummel, there's some very beautiful country here in Hesse. I'm sure you'll like it.' She smiled more broadly, then went on as if reciting from one of the new *Baedekers*:

'Steinau, tomorrow, is smaller again than Hanau, and really quite lovely. Then Marburg, where we are due on Friday, is a splendid university town in the hills. And finally Cassel has the *most* magnificent castle and parks.'

She let her gaze wander past him to the silhouetted ridge of low hills where they would walk in the morning. Gustchen, her fond but undemonstrative uncle called her: Little Auguste. Although she had a shawl to hand, she was wearing the evening bodice to her best burgundy dress, which showed her slim arms under its short sleeves. Her chestnut hair was scraped back into a red crocheted chignon, which made her pale face look older.

To Kummel's way of thinking, her small, fine features – which by the light of this rapeseed-oil lamp softly recalled the Professor's – always seemed more fetching inside a spoon bonnet. But still she looked a good deal younger than she really was. Kummel had been quite startled to learn that the birthday she celebrated in the mountains had been her thirty-first.

Unsure if she wished him to go or stay, he glanced out at the forested hills, which seemed to press in so much closer in the starlit dark. High above, a bright sliver of moon played hide and seek behind thin clouds, and a scatter of stars shone like fragments of shattered crystal. Behind him, in the dining room, he heard the staff laying tables for breakfast. If they were to walk in the morning, he needed to return to the kitchens soon to make arrangements for a small refreshment hamper. And he himself had not eaten since midday. His glass of Weissbier, plate of leftover Schnitzels and pipe were still awaiting him inside.

'You do understand why we're here, Kummel, don't you?' the Fräulein suddenly asked.

He looked down and her almost perpetual doll's smile seemed a little vexed. There was also something nervous about the way she had asked the question, as if she had momentarily forgotten the reason herself and was looking to him to remind her.

'Why yes, Fräulein. You're bringing back the Professor to visit the places where he once lived.'

She nodded in her usual mechanical fashion, her eyes again on the faraway ridge, but now beginning to glisten. 'It's very important that my Apapa should enjoy this short tour. At his advanced age he deserves an agreeable few days and I'm determined that he should have them. Both you and I, Kummel, must ensure that he doesn't get bored – and some people *do* bore him, I'm afraid. But Hesse is his true home. For so long his work and his responsibilities to his family have forced him to live away, but this is where his heart has stayed. These are the places where he grew up, where he became the man he is today.'

'Yes, Fräulein, I see,' said Kummel, surprised to hear her speak so frankly to a male domestic. He had guessed, though, that someone as naturally garrulous as she would be at a loose end in the evenings, which for the past fortnight the Professor had insisted on devoting to his woodchopping. Perhaps that was why her mother, Frau Dortchen – a formidable little woman of seventy – had been so adamant that Kummel should accompany the smaller party into Hesse.

On the last night at the Harz spa he had overheard a very crisp exchange between the two women. There was nothing personal, Kummel was sure, in the Fräulein's declared preference to travel without him. She had treated him perfectly civilly ever since he had been loaned out to the Grimms for the summer vacation by his regular Charlottenburg employers. Yet she plainly wanted the Professor to herself for these five days, and Kummel could not help wondering why. He also kept noticing the way she looked at her 'Apapa' – longingly, almost hungrily – which rather suggested that she needed something from him.

She picked up her shawl and arranged it over her shoulders. 'We shall spend two nights in Cassel before returning to Berlin,' she said on a more practical note, immediately becoming more animated. 'On the second morning there, the Sunday, I shall require you to attend the Professor on your own. I am organizing a small surprise party for him, and I'll need you to make sure that he is occupied until it begins.' She looked more like the old man than ever as she thought ahead to this event. Her eyes seemed positively to dance, just as his did whenever he tracked down a particularly pleasing set of words amid his stacks of papers. But then her gaze wavered and she swallowed a little too quickly.

'That will be all now, Kummel,' she said. '*Wiedersehen*.'

The coffee remained untouched beside her small, elegant hands. For over a week Kummel had watched her eat virtually nothing too. With a freshly wound-up smile, she swung away from him to study the distant trees so intently that she could have been anticipating a signal.

TWO

There was once a poor woman with too many children. People believed her to be wise and came to her from all around for cures and advice. She was married to a nightwatchman who worked at the gatehouse to their little town. Often he did not come home at dawn, but gambled away the money he had earned or drank away any money he had won.

Although the woman now had eight children, she called none of them by their given names. 'Little One', 'Naughty One', 'Girl', she would say. The only child to which she referred by name was the first: Friedrich, the first-born and first-dead, snatched away even before she had given birth to the second. The townspeople whispered that after Friedrich she was afraid to become too familiar with the rest of her brood. It was as if by keeping them at arm's length she also hoped to keep them all alive. Even so, two more of the eight were taken. Ripped away like Friedrich, in the night without a trace.

Some of the six remaining children were more of a burden to

their mother than others. By far the most helpful was the eldest, the boy she called 'Old One'. Without her ever asking, he did all the work that their father should have done around the tiny home: making and mending furniture, haggling with creditors. He even herded the younger children together on Sundays and organized them into armies to fight out his intricately planned campaigns.

Old One was always the last to put his head down at night, always the first to rise in the crowded bedroom where the children slept in line like a hand of wooden pegs. Often the sighs and wheezings of the others disturbed him so much that he dressed while it was still night and went out into the yard to watch the sun rise over the forest.

The trees would then look flat and dense on the high horizon, a great glittering smudge in the sunlight. And he would always remember that somewhere out there, on a pine-covered crag, stood the Rose King's splendid palace. When he was small his mother had told him many times about a feast there. He was sure that she spoke of it only to him. Maybe even his father did not know. Only then did her face become as beautiful as he knew it could be. If her life was a mud-packed oyster, then that one day at the palace was the shining pearl at its centre, and even years afterwards the glow from it could light up her eyes.

When he asked how she came to be invited to the feast, she explained that a wise woman had been invited from each of the kingdom's cantons. Ignorant of the kingdom's traditions, Old One asked no more. His guess was that she had once broken bread with the best as of right and he had no wish to remind her how far she had fallen. Sometimes, while spinning flax into linen for a little extra income, she would sigh, 'There are other worlds than this, you know.'

But Old One knew almost nothing about the world. He did

not even know if the Rose King was still their sovereign. Rumours said that he had lost his mind with grief, and his court at the place where the sun rose had been abandoned, that now an ogre lured children to the deserted palace and ate them.

He was certain only that the great feast had been held to celebrate the birth of a daughter to the queen. And hours before the dancing was due to begin, the guests had sat down to a sumptuous meal at places personally set with thick gold caskets, each containing a knife, fork and spoon of gold too, all studded with diamonds and rubies and topped by dazzling emeralds.

He often wondered why his mother had not brought her casket away with her. By selling off just one of the precious stones she could have made life immeasurably easier for herself. At times it crossed his mind that she had made the visit only in her imagination. But he fiercely believed in his mother. And the look in her eye when she spoke of the feast touched him to the quick in much the same way as when she talked with regret of her poor lost Friedrich: 'Such a plump small child he was, Old One. So fat and pink and healthy. Oh, how it would please me to have him now.'

Years went by and although no more babies were born, life in the house became harder than ever. The children's father came home so seldom that the youngest sometimes failed to recognize him until he reminded them with a blow from his watchman's bugle as he stumbled among them, drunk and full of bile.

Old One now worked through many of the nights, completing the chores his exhausted mother had been unable to finish during the day. Meanwhile the five other children, whom he still saw as 'the babies', slumbered obliviously. And when he did snatch a few hours' sleep, it would be in a small niche in the town wall near the gatehouse, wrapped in a grimy horseblanket.

He liked to feel the tremors of the watchmen's boots as they patrolled the parapet overhead. It soothed him to know that his father was guarding him here, even if he treated his family so shabbily in their own home. Through gaps in the wall's mortar he could watch the sun bring the forest to life in the morning. At times he fancied that his father and the other watchmen were keeping their vigils purely to hold this mass of tangled nature at bay. Its fringes certainly seemed to have crept closer to the walls over the years, and the fall of the understorey's leaves each autumn left a crackling golden carpet ever more clearly visible when the gates swung back to admit a cart or a coach from another canton. As Old One gazed eastward, he thought less about the distant palace or the feast than what it might be like to enter the forest's depths, how it might sound and smell, even how it might *taste.*

It was when he came back from his niche in the wall one morning that his mother greeted him with the news. She was sitting, fully dressed, beside her spinning wheel, staring at the rag-stuffed window.

'I have fallen with another child,' she said.

Old One made no answer, but tried to smile. He knew there was no chance that their life could go on as before. There was simply not enough space in the house for another body. But his mother did not tell him exactly how things were going to change until a week after the new child was born.

THREE

Mercifully the weather held. Immediately after breakfast Auguste and her Apapa changed into sturdier shoes and stepped out into bright sunshine. Away to the west, over Frankfurt, the skies looked less settled, but Auguste was sure they would be safe for a couple of hours, so she handed Kummel her Chinese-style silk painted parasol to carry, rather than the umbrella.

Walking steadily, they soon passed beyond the little town. Since most of the men were out helping with the harvest, women dominated the lanes, strolling arm in arm to fetch their shopping or sitting on benches outside their homes. Time certainly moved more sluggishly here than back east. Away from her city, it was said, the Berliner is only half herself. Auguste already found herself missing the Prussian capital more than she had in the Harz: the steady round of waltzes, poetry readings and outings to the Philharmonic; the queues of laughably unsuitable suitors that were forever being lined up by her mother; the city's smoke, its speed, but most of all its constant, unadulterated din.

These sepulchral surroundings meant the world to her Apapa, but she herself could not have survived in them for long. They reminded her too strongly of that 'other Germany' he had told her about as a child, the land of dark forests and sometimes even darker fairytales. Untamed nature had always made Auguste shiver. She even recoiled from parts of central Berlin's gently landscaped Tiergarten.

The Professor was explicit about the route they should take. He said it was one that he and Wilhelm had used as boys, presumably very small boys, since they had moved from Hanau to Steinau when he was only six. Soon they were climbing a well-grassed slope. Now and then the old man pointed out fleabane or angelica, goldenrod or ironweed. Otherwise his silence was punctuated only by soft little cries of '*Heh!*' Sometimes these had the ring of 'I told you so!' and sometimes 'I do declare!' Either way, they suggested a running internal monologue – or, for all Auguste knew, a continuing form of dialogue with his late brother, her father, from whom he had been inseparable for seventy years.

Watching him forge on ahead, she could not help remembering the way he had stepped out at Wilhelm's funeral four years before, up the cemetery's incline, flanked by her brothers Herman and Rudolf. She recalled how he had stooped, unassisted, to claw at the snow-flecked crumbling earth, then dropped a handful down on the coffin. Briefly he had swayed, his face creased up in what looked like resentment. After seven decades of almost legendary stoicism he had seemed on the point of showing his deepest feelings. But like the servant in the fairytale who set three iron bands around his heart, he had kept his emotions under the strictest control, both then and in the four years since.

Auguste was thus under no illusions. She knew how hard a task she had set herself in organizing this sentimental journey, how resistant he would be to the almost impossibly delicate questions that she finally had to ask him. Talk can always wait, he liked to say. But time was running out, for Auguste herself as much as for this increasingly fragile old man.

He turned to look back at the town nestling below and indicated to Kummel, who had been following at his customary ten paces, that he should unpack the old rug and spread it out. Auguste sat first, the hoops under her walking skirt initially refusing to collapse. Then, as so often, her Apapa sat with his deafer right ear towards her.

Kummel – as prescient as ever – brought up her parasol, apples, some corners of dark bread, a flask of water and another of quite decent Schnapps. Eagerly Grimm poured some liquor on the bread to soften it before beginning to chew.

The sun, warm now on their hats under a cloudless sky, struck gold and amber from the jumble of roofs below. One could have said it was a fairytale village, although from here a dyeworks and a printing house gave the place a slightly less medieval air. And, like so many German towns that they had seen together in recent times, it had long since spilled beyond its original confines, with new streets appearing where the old fortifications had been allowed to crumble. This always seemed a hopeful sign to Auguste: no more walls and gatehouses, no more need for sieges and bombardments.

Under light prompting, Grimm identified some landmarks for her: that was his grandfather Zimmer's house; that one, Schürko the baker's; and that church in the market square had a gilt weathercock on its steeple. He even pointed out the yellow-doored house of his birth in Langgasse that she had taken him to see on their arrival the night before. More talkative now, he mentioned that a lone red peach tree had once bloomed in front of it.

'That must have looked pretty,' said Auguste, polishing an apple on her skirt, even though she had no appetite for it.

'*Ja*,' he replied after a thoughtful pause, 'but then again, no tree is really intended by Nature to stand alone.'

After that, they fell again into silent contemplation, batting away flies, listening to an insistent thrush above the more distant field cries, the church bell's tolling of the hour – and then to a hollow, almost inaudible clacking noise, which may well have been coming from inside Auguste's own tired head. She had not been sleeping well, and in growing drowsy her head became heavier. *Take her back now* . . . echoed between her ears as it always did when she let her defences drop. *You're* the *most precious person in my life* . . .

She tried to concentrate harder on the flimsy little chimneys below. It seemed incredible that they were sending smoke up into the same skies belched at by the Ruhr's great furnaces and the factory stacks of Berlin's 'Elektropolis'. They seemed to belong to entirely different worlds. Doubtless her Apapa saw it differently. For over half a century he had been calling for all the Germanies to be united. And, as far as Auguste could tell, his books all aimed at the same end, showing that since a unified German *Kultur* already existed, a nation state must follow, peacefully brought together by 'moral conquests'. But, to his ever increasing dismay, what he called his fatherland was still as broken up and vulnerable now as it had been fifty years before.

As the faint clacking began again, Auguste shook her head. Slowly the noise faded. She knew it was shallow not to be stirred by the German Question. 'History herself will know nothing of those who know nothing of history,' her Apapa would say, but that was a risk she was prepared to take. She simply could not feel haunted by the horrors suffered by the *Volk* during the Thirty Years War and the Napoleonic occupation. Even the recent restoration of the Bonapartes in France left her unmoved, as did the rumours of new French designs on the Rhine. Yet to her Apapa this was life itself. 'The grass will soon grow over me,' he had once declared in a public address. 'If there should be those who still think of me, I wish only that they will say what I say of myself – that in all my life I never loved anything more deeply than my fatherland.'

'*Heh*,' he murmured, nodding, and Auguste smiled. When the time was right she would turn him towards the issues that preoccupied her, and try at last to shatter those bands around his heart. She owed it to both of them to prove that there were far better things to love than a country. A country, after all, can never love you back.

Jacob liked writing letters and he knew he was good at it. Over the previous year, encouraged by his father, he had written many times to his grandfather back in Hanau. At first he filled his pages with descriptions of the Amtshaus, the family's palatial new home in Steinau, with its stables, turret stair and walled courtyard, that came with his father's job as district magistrate. Then after he and Wilhelm began their wider explorations he wrote detailed accounts of Steinau's brown and yellow houses, the old moated castle of the counts and the gardens so full of flowers that in high summer they burst over the gates and walls into the crooked little streets.

Now on this dark January afternoon as the 'babies' napped in the nursery, he sat at the window desk, penning his thanks for the present that Grandfather Zimmer had sent him for his eighth birthday: a pencil box with a good English pencil inside, along with some raven quills especially suitable for fine drawing. Stretched out beside him on the floor Willi was already using one to make specimen sketches of the latest additions to their collection of insects and butterflies. The stillness in the room, which their quills' scratching and the hum of the tea-urn from the sitting-room seemed only to deepen, was perfectly serene.

Moving on to his second sheet, having given all the local news, Jacob felt he had to share with his grandfather the recent report from France. This had so startled him that he was still not quite sure whether or not to believe it . . .

'So what are you telling your grandfather this time?' boomed a voice from the doorway.

Jacob looked up from his desk and reflected in the window glass he saw his father in full official regalia: blue frock coat, red collar, black leather breeches, silver-spurred boots. He was not a big man, but the uniform gave him such presence, as distinctive as his reek of pipe tobacco and wig powder. Even now his taller manservant Müller was behind him dressing his pigtail.

Jacob began to twist around in his chair and rise but in the glass he saw his father raise a hand. 'No child, never be distracted from the written word. Talk can always wait.'

Jacob lowered himself again into his seat. 'But I'd *like* to talk, Vati,' he told the smiling reflection. 'It would help me to continue. You see, I'm writing to grandfather about the King of France. I wonder if he's heard yet about the turn the Revolution has taken?'

'Alas, poor King Louis. Kings shouldn't lose their heads, now should they? They ought to be more careful.'

'The people just sliced it off like a wedge of cheese,' Willi croaked from the floor, then coughed, but without interrupting his sketching.

'So who will rule the French now, Vati?' Jacob asked the little man's image. 'Will they make someone else their king?'

'Kings and princes can't be made, my son. They are born. You can't make gold out of straw. No, they want no more kings for themselves in France. Or so at least they're telling us. The French are very good at telling the world what they want – and at telling the world what *it* should want too, at the point of a bayonet if needs be. But make no mistake, if our French friends have their way now, the rising tide of this Revolution will lift all boats.'

Jacob frowned. He loved the way his father talked to him, making so few concessions to his youth. Much of it still went over his head; he was not even certain what the word 'Revolution' meant. Yet this in no way detracted from the pleasure of being taken into the confidence of a man who *was* the law.

He stared back at his father's reflection as Müller made his final adjustments. But as if superimposed on it Jacob was imagining a hand holding up a disembodied head by a hank of its surely blameless hair, a head that looked strikingly similar to their own Elector's. And at once his father, as so often, seemed to see with his eldest son's eyes.

'Don't dwell on the execution, Jacob,' he called across warmly before departing once again to take justice into the Kinzig Valley. 'These are the French, remember. They're not like us. They had a single monarch and they all agreed to murder him. *We* have as many petty princes as there are days in the year, and *they* can't even agree on a common time of day!' He beamed. 'It all goes back to Nature. The French, you see, have their prim little gardens – but we, Jacob, what do *we* have? The *Wald* – our magnificent, gloriously untamed forest! Keep your concerns closer to home, I say.'

Jacob turned to bid his father farewell but already he had gone, calling out his goodbyes from the top of the stairway. He returned to his letter with a lighter heart, convinced that Philipp Grimm was the living proof of what he had just himself pointed out: that kings were born, not made.

Auguste did not quite fall asleep on the slope. But she gazed down for so long – daydreaming, losing track of time – that eventually she wondered if she and her Apapa had achieved a silent kind of communion.

For as long as she could remember, silence had been his favoured element. It had been her father's too, necessarily so, since all their lives they had shared a study or worked in adjoining rooms. Throughout her childhood, first in Göttingen and then in Berlin, she and her brothers had forever been tiptoeing past their desks, making even less sound than the noise the men made writing: Apapa bent so far forward that his eye seemed to touch the page as he formed his tiny, uncapitalized letters with his goose quills cut off short; her father taller, gaunter, apparently the more relaxed of the two, his quills left unplucked to their ends, his eyebrow often arched as he stared out into space. Yet Apapa had been the more tolerant of any disturbances, at least from the little Auguste.

She remembered one particular evening in the Lennéstrasse apartment, their first in Berlin, when she could have been no more than eight. On passing Apapa's study on her way to bed she had slipped and fallen on the passageway's lacquered floor. He came out to her, moving even then with that brisk old man's gait of his, like a beaver disturbed in its lodge. 'Story, story, story,' she sobbed, hardly expecting one. But squatting down, he picked up her small stuffed monkey, smiled, and launched into one of his cautionary tales.

'In the beginning,' he said, 'the Creator gave the same life span to all His creatures: thirty years. Not a day more, not a day less. But the ass came to Him and said, "Thirty years is too long for me to be carrying burdens," so the Creator took eighteen years off his span. Then the dog came and said, "Thirty years is too long for me, for what will I do when my legs give out and I can no longer bark?", and the Creator took twelve years from him. Then along came the monkey' – he shook the little cross-eyed toy close to his face – 'and the monkey said, "I don't need thirty years, for how can I hope to entertain folk with my tricks for all that time?" and the Creator took ten years away from him.

'Now man heard of all this, and unlike the animals he wanted to live *longer*, so he went to the Creator and said, "Oh give me the years you have taken from the others." And the Creator did just that, which means that now man lives for seventy years. The first thirty are his human years, when he is healthy and happy, but those years are soon gone. Then the next eighteen are the ass years, when one burden after another is laid on him, and all he gets for his faithful service are kicks and sticks. Then come the twelve dog years, when he drags himself from corner to corner and can only growl toothlessly. And finally the ten monkey years form the end of his life' – at this, he shook the toy again but more sombrely – 'when he is so weak-brained that he can only do silly things that make little children laugh at him.'

Auguste smiled inwardly at the memory. Like many of his stories it now unsettled her a little. And there he sat beside her, clasping his knees like a sprite and thinking God knew what as he looked out over his homeland, eight years past the monkey stage and still as sharp as ever. Too sharp, most of the time, for her. But she was, after all, now into the ass years herself.

'Fräulein Grimm,' murmured Kummel, bringing her back to herself, 'it's past noon now.'

She swung round to see that the servant had stepped across from a knoll where, with Grimm's permission, he had been smoking a series of pipes. He was holding out to her a fob watch from the waistband pocket of her father's old peg-topped trousers. 'If you wish to take a fuller lunch before leaving for Steinau, perhaps you should not linger here too much longer?'

She smiled, shielding her eyes from the sun, surprised that he had made the suggestion to her rather than to Grimm, but rather idiotically pleased to have been addressed at all on this already tense little expedition without having spoken first. 'Yes, of course, thank you.'

She rocked herself to her feet and saw only when it was too late that Kummel was offering a hand on which his dark diagonal hairline reached down almost to the knuckle. But that was so often the way with this footman whom her mother had borrowed from the Dresslers while they were away travelling in Umbria. Such was his knack of discreetly blending into his surroundings, both indoors and out, that at times he seemed no more noticeable than a coil of his own pipe smoke. In that respect her mother had been right to insist that his presence would not intrude on her time alone with Grimm – but on the other hand, Auguste's mother had no idea what she needed the time for.

Grimm too rose unaided. '*Weaving, we are weaving . . .*' Auguste heard him sing beneath his breath, but only to himself. Pushing back a swatch of soft white curls from his face, he narrowed his eyes at the eastern tree-lined horizon over which they would be travelling that afternoon.

'*Heh!*' he smiled after vigorously shuffling his shoulders until his coat sat as he wanted it to. 'Soon it will be time to leave home again.'

FOUR

Old One's mother called him to her bedroom late on the fifth night after the new child was born. 'It's time for you to go from here,' she said without lifting her eyes. She was standing in front of her spinning-wheel, absently rocking the cradle that he had hammered together for her a few weeks before. 'You're old enough now, a man in most senses. It's time for you to make your own way.'

Although it was so late, he thought that she meant him to go at once. And he was ready to leave; in his heart he always had been. But still it was a shock finally to hear the words. He leaned against the bedroom doorway, awaiting more detailed instructions.

'Perhaps you won't return home,' she said with a shrug. In rocking the newest baby she was half turned away from him. Her greying hair, unbound for bed, hid the expression on her face, but her voice sounded uneven. She could have been swallowing tears; she could have been biting back one of her bitter, toothy smiles.

Recently nothing with her had been predictable, and he was afraid that under all the strain her mind was beginning to suffer. 'Perhaps when you discover what's out there,' she went on, 'you won't ever want to come back.'

'No,' he told her, swallowing hard himself. 'This is my home. It will always be my home.' Unable to say more, he stared at the blue toughened skin on her heels under the frayed hem of her bed-gown. Her feet never looked warm enough, and her hands – as far as he could remember – were like cool slate to the touch. *There are other worlds than this, you know.* Again he could only think she had somehow slipped into this world from another and that, having known so much better, she simply did not know how to make her blood run warmly in such sadly shrunken circumstances.

'You're the Old One,' she said. 'It has to be you. If Friedrich had still been here, then of course it would have been him.'

'I know that. You don't have to explain.' It twisted up his stomach to hear the despair in her voice. She had lost so much on the night Friedrich died, for her first house had then burned down within hours too. 'I know there are too many of us here now. Truly, I understand.'

But he was saying this only for her sake. He took far less out of the household than he put into it. He was more like a servant at the hearth than a son in the home, and he was not even sure how all of them would manage without him. But his trust in his mother did not waver. She had her reasons; she had always wanted the best for him. And she had called him a man. That pleased him. 'Tell me Mother,' he said, 'tell me where I must go.'

'To the palace,' she replied at once, in a louder voice that disturbed the baby in the cradle and made it begin to whimper. He knew which palace she meant. There was only one: the Rose King's in the east. But he was thinking first of how he would have to get there – through the forest.

He watched his mother stoop, wearily scoop up the mewling bundle, and sit with it on her spinning stool, her face still turned away from him. She peeled back the baby's ragged blanket and fixed its tiny puckered mouth to her breast.

He could not help resenting this baby like all the rest. What was worse, he believed his mother had little love for it either. 'He looks like Friedrich,' was all she ever said. 'Yes, Friedrich.' She sighed as she tossed back her hair, then went on speaking as if to the treadle: 'You must go to see the king's daughter at the palace.'

'The one whose birth feast you went to?'

'Yes, yes. She should be ready now.'

'Ready?'

'For whoever comes, when the time is right.'

'And what then? What will I say? Do you have a message?'

'No. No message. I've said all that *I* have to say. But you'll know. When you arrive at the palace, it'll be clear what you have to do.' Her answer sounded so final, her expression looked so set as she studied the greedy baby, that Old One could only nod his head and idly wonder, without being quite sure why, if his father also knew that he was going.

'You needn't leave till morning. Stay in the house tonight.' The baby had fallen back to sleep. Carefully she lifted it back into the cradle before she had refastened her ties. 'You can be in here if you wish.'

'In here?'

She looked at him from under her hair as she bent over. The candle flame by her bed danced on the point of guttering in its own pool of tallow. It seemed to make her dance too, flickering across the room and all over him with her teeth and her feet and that bent little bone between her breasts. 'I can make a space,' she said, 'tonight.'

'No,' he told her after a moment's hesitation. 'I'll go now. I want to go now.'

'You're not afraid, Old One, are you?'

'What should I be afraid of?'

She lowered herself again on to her spinning stool and rested her hand on the high heap of flax. In the intermittently brilliant candle light, it gleamed like a pile of yellow straw or even tarnished gold. 'As you travel, think of yourself as a prince,' she said, 'a prince who could one day be a king.'

He smiled, and his heart started to pound. Was she at last about to tell him the truth about her past? That once, deep in the forest, she had not only known luxury and sophistication, but had actually been a queen herself? 'Why should I think that?' he asked.

'Why?' she chuckled. 'So that you will have a prince's courage.' She pressed the flat of her hand into the flax then raised it, leaving behind a clear impression. 'And, more important, so that you'll have a prince's good fortune.'

The flame at last ate up the wick and the room was scythed into darkness. Old One heard his mother chuckle now as if from a great distance. 'There,' she said, 'now you look for all the world like a prince to me. You *are* a prince – I hereby invest you – and you can be a king as well. Tell me what you are.'

'I'm a prince.'

'And what will you tell those who ask who you are?'

'That I am a prince. I promise I'll say so. I've changed. Already I'm no longer Old One.'

'Go then,' she laughed, 'and be a prince for me. And that will be prince enough for anyone else.'

FIVE

'*Weaving, we are weaving . . .*' Grimm was dreaming so deeply when Kummel entered with his shaving water that it took him several moments to recognize the lean young serving man. And even as he peered across from the pillow, his head began to pulse again with that tantalizingly unidentifiable line of verse.

Only after setting down the basin on the washstand did Kummel glance over at the narrow bed. Then he drew the curtains to unveil a square of ominously white Steinau sky before bowing and leaving.

Grimm's dream had been drearily predictable: burial alive, passing through to some other world as the dirt rained down on him from this one. It could hardly be called a nightmare any more. He felt almost relieved each time to be departing from a fatherland whose future now looked so bleak. But it left him more than usually unsteady as he cleaned himself up for the day, and also with the start of an all too familiar throbbing pain at both temples.

Gustchen was already at their window table when he arrived for breakfast. Most of the dozen other tables were occupied too, some by young families, and the level of noise was high but ill sorted. As Grimm sat he noticed several male guests leafing through newspapers while they sipped their tea and buttered their rolls. Breathing faster, he tried to gauge from their expressions how bad the news was from across the French border, or even from Berlin itself, where the new man Bismarck seemed barely more reliable than the latest Bonaparte.

'Rain is threatening,' Gustchen said as Kummel came to fill Grimm's cup. 'We may not be able to walk very far today.' She smiled the dazzling smile that she snapped open and shut like a pocket book when she was especially nervous. 'But could we instead visit the church where your grandfather was pastor? Father said you used to tell everyone you were going to be a clergyman yourself one day, and you gave sermons standing on a chair in the parlour.'

'*Ach* now, is that what he said?'

'But I *would* like to see the church, Apapa, since you've said you would prefer not to look at the Amtshaus.'

There was disappointment in her tone, and maybe even reproof. But if she wanted him to explain why he shrank from revisiting the old home where he had briefly been so happy, he could not bring himself to do it. To him the Amtshaus would always be a place of mourning and he needed no sharper reminder of that; for wherever he looked now in this wonderfully unspoiled country, bereavement and lost opportunities were all he seemed able to recall.

'So could we send Kummel to the pastor's lodgings for a key?' Auguste persisted.

Grimm nodded and turned to look at the street of low-slung shops and wine lodges. A muscular bearded drayman was unloading barrels with the help of a boy. They were working well together, saying nothing, each implicitly understanding what the other wanted: more leverage here, a little more play there, a brief pause to catch breath. It was almost like watching a couple dance, the kind of *pas de deux* that he and Willi had long ago mastered in their own life and work, before Dortchen had arrived to teach new steps to both of them.

When he drew back from the window, a short middle-aged woman with a very high colour was standing by his table, presenting a small girl in front of her like a criminal suspect. He started to struggle to his feet but the woman gestured for him to stay seated. 'Herr Professor, forgive me, but last evening after dinner I heard that we were staying in the same establishment as yourself,' she nodded towards Gustchen whose smile blazed back, 'and my daughter here is such an avid reader of your *Tales for Young and Old* – as in fact am I – that I felt we must come to tell you personally of our admiration.'

Grimm noted a stilling of the conversations all around. Kummel too paused on his way to the table with the plate of boiled oats. 'You are most kind,' he said.

'Tell the Professor now,' the woman urged her daughter with a shake, 'tell him which of all his stories you like the best.'

The pantalooned girl had to be shaken again before she opened her pert little mouth, but not out of nervousness. She was grinning at Grimm, marvelling first at his white drift of hair, then his soft, hoary hands on the red-checked tablecloth: their liver-spotted transparency and sheer uncalloused smoothness. 'I like the one about the miller's daughter,' she announced. 'The one whose father said she could spin straw into gold. And the king asked her to do it, and she couldn't, until the little old man came along and helped her. And in return she had to promise to give him her first-born child when she married the king. That's the one I like.'

A rustle of appreciation passed around the room. Still pinned by the girl's wide green eyes, Grimm ran his tongue across his lips.

'And how did it go on?' asked the mother with another shake. 'Tell us.'

'Oh, the queen had a baby and she didn't want to give it to the little man. And he said' – she drew in her chin to find a deeper tone – '"*I will give you three days' grace, and if you can guess my name then you can keep the baby.*" So for two days she guessed all the proper names she could – and then some mad names like Bandylegs and Crookshanks, but one of her messengers told her he had heard the little old man singing his real name and he told it to her. So when the little man came on the third day she said, "Could your name be *Rumpelstiltskin*?" and she was right and the little man tore himself in two.' Simpering, she added: '"This is my story, I've told it and in your hands I leave it."'

A handful of listeners at the nearer tables applauded. A newspaper reader further back cried '*Bravo!*' 'Splendidly told, little one,' said Auguste, reaching out to touch her arm. 'And what is *your* name?'

'Charlotte, Fräulein. Lotte.'

'I once had an aunt of that name,' Gustchen told her. 'Well, we are most impressed with you, Lotte.' Kummel then came forward with his master's breakfast and the child and her mother had to step back.

'We're so sorry to disturb your meal, Herr Professor,' the woman said, motioning her daughter away to their own fireside table, where a man and two small boys were looking on in delight. 'But your *Tales* are so very popular in our home: *Hansel and Gretel, Snow White, Little Red Riding Hood, Rapunzel . . .*'

Grimm smiled, relieved to hear the talk rekindling at the other tables. He could only repeat, 'You are most kind,' but the woman still seemed reluctant to leave. 'Your stories go so deep,' she went on. 'The pure good and pure evil – it's right for children to know about all that, and in such beautiful language too. Did you, perhaps, use to tell them to your own children, before you put them into the books?'

Grimm picked up a roll then returned it to the basket. 'No no. I never married.'

She glanced at Gustchen then back again at Grimm. 'Well, that only makes your work all the more marvellous.'

'The work was not just mine,' Grimm felt obliged to tell her with a smile. 'I collected the *Tales* with my late younger brother. And we were presented with such rich material too, in the stories told to us by the ordinary people of Hesse. All we really did was give back to the *Volk* what had belonged to them in the first place.'

At that, the woman became unsure of herself. '*Danke schön, danke schön*,' she nodded to Grimm and Gustchen, then bustled off to rejoin her family. Grimm, whose throat had begun to burn, returned his gaze to the street where a number of passers-by were now holding up umbrellas. 'Straw into gold, straw into gold . . .' he breathed, his attention taken by a prettily coloured array of bottles and boxes in the apothecary's shop window opposite. And then, again, the elusive line flitted through his mind: '*Weaving, we are weaving* . .'

'Do you think, *Liebchen*,' he said to Auguste after sniffing twice and finding his nose dispiritingly congested, 'that we might try to preserve our privacy for just a little while now?'

Both ornaments had stood on the nursery shelf ever since the Grimms had lived in the Amtshaus. Perhaps they had even belonged to the previous magistrate's family. In making up conversations between the two ceramic figures, Jacob always spoke in the voice of the man, even though his own voice had not yet broken. And when the moment came for them to perform their peculiar tricks, he would reach up with a single finger to make the man's tricorn-hatted head nod while Willi would set the woman's elaborate coiffure to shake. But never, before now, had either child been allowed to take one down. And to be holding the little man in his cold hands only made this day seem more profoundly unnatural to Jacob than it already was.

Beside him at the window stood Andreas, the old Amtshaus coachman who doubled as a butler. Jacob could smell the gingery preservative on his unaccustomed dark clothing, and he was still unsure if he liked it. He himself was wearing a coat of heavy grey cloth that reached down past his knees. It was to stop his obsessive fiddling with its large white buttons that his Aunt Zimmer had taken down the ornament and pushed it into his grip. Now he held the bearded figure in his left hand while with the forefinger of his right he kept it nodding incessantly at the snow-smeared windowpane: *Ja, ja, ja, ja.*

The snow had been cleared from the steps below, and a path swept out to the carriage, which was waiting by the stables. Once again, it amazed Jacob that the insatiable armies of France should be waging their campaigns across German soil at a time when most ordinary people could barely keep their feet on it. His eye caught the family sledge lying half in, half out of the nearest outbuilding, its gilt Hessian lion decoration now seeming rather forlorn. Andreas touched Jacob's shoulder, a sign that he should look directly down.

The procession moved more quickly than he had expected. Soon the black coffin was obscured from his sight by those who followed it. The mourners, carrying lemons and sprigs of rosemary, were hard to identify from above in their headgear. No one slipped. No one fell. Then the coffin was in the carriage, and another vehicle drew up behind to take in all the living. For a short period Jacob let his little man rest his head. When the horses of the leading carriage struck out on their journey to St Catherine's, he set it nodding again.

Although the big house was by no means empty, over the next hour and a half it was abnormally still. Jacob spent a good part of that time wandering slowly from room to room on the upper floor. It was unusual to be allowed to do just what he wanted, without being responsible for poor sick Willi's entertainment and welfare. He could not now remember a time when he was not his brother's keeper; perhaps there had never been one. He did not enter his parents' green-and-white bedroom. He just looked in to see his father's Polish cotton dressing-gown casually strewn across the foot of the great four-poster bed with its extravagant swagged curtains of grey and dark blue stripes.

Andreas finally came to find him in the nursery, where he was admiring Willi's latest arrangements of their butterflies, chestnuts and acorn cups. Jacob had already heard the rooms downstairs filling up again, the sombre clinking of the best blue Dresden china. It did not take so very long to dispose of a corpse. He knew, because this had not been his first death. In the year they had moved from Hanau, his mother gave birth to a son who had lived for only fourteen months. She, in turn, had lost an infant before: a first child who had come and gone even before Jacob. She never said a word about that now, but Jacob often tried to imagine how different life might have been if he himself had not been the eldest, or if he and Willi really had been twins, set on a truly even footing.

'They're waiting for you,' Andreas said from the nursery doorway. Jacob looked up then went across to where he stood. 'Shall I take that?' the old man asked, eyeing the nodding figure that Jacob held tightly against his stomach.

'Look,' said the boy. And slowly he drew up the head, showing the ceramic stick to which it was attached, then higher, higher until both head and stick came clear of the little striding body. He held it aloft for several moments, then deftly aimed it back down into the neck. When he had balanced it perfectly again, he handed it over and descended the stairs, wondering if they would have to leave the figures behind in the new move.

Everyone, Grimms and Zimmers alike, stood in the salon set aside for domestic devotion. For a moment Jacob felt tiny, insufficient, in the face of so many adults. Like the path through the snow to the carriages outside, a narrow way had been cleared for him to walk down to the mahogany eagle lectern, where the family Bible had been opened at the appropriate place. Not allowing his eyes to be drawn to right or left as he approached, he felt himself growing with each stride. Then he turned and stepped up to grip the tip of the eagle's wing with his left hand.

Some of the women were weeping, Willi too, held around the shoulders by their mother as he quaked with grief and asthma. Jacob smiled to reassure his dear brother, feeling just a brief sting of envy that he *could* cry. Picking up the long quill, he dipped it steadily in the inkwell. But then he hesitated as the handwritten names on the great wood-bound book's title page seemed to stand up in front of him.

His own name was there, recorded by his father with his birthdate: *4 January 1785*, almost eleven years ago to this day. Immediately below it, in the same hand: *Wilhelm, 24 February 1786*, and just above his own name, that of the unfortunate first son: Friedrich, born in 1783 and died in 1784. Diligently his father had inscribed all the later babies' births: Carl in 1787, Ferdinand in 1788, Ludwig in 1790, the second ill-fated Friedrich who had lived only from 1791 to 1792, and finally a girl, Charlotte Amalie, born just three years before.

Jacob moved his quill to the yellow space below Lotte's name and wrote in his small, firm, already adult hand:

Philipp Wilhelm Grimm, died 10 January 1796.

His late father had been forty-four years old. The pneumonia had cut him down so quickly that Jacob could still not fully believe he would never again pick up his dressing-gown from the canopied bed, nor read again to his doting family from the holy book on this lectern.

Jacob's mother stood closest to him, still too stupefied to cry. Higher than her on the lectern step, he looked only now at her unseeing eyes, proud nose and those even rows of teeth, revealed by what looked like a smile. In that moment he was shocked to feel almost as afraid of her as for her. His father's death had broken her as simply as Jacob had pulled the little ceramic man in two for Andreas. If the war with the French had spilled as far as the Amtshaus and raged through these rooms, the disruption could not have been greater for her. Never a stalwart woman, she had been left behind with no certain means of support, a house she would have to move out of and six children to care for.

No, Jacob thought as he replaced the quill and smiled down at her just as he had smiled before at poor racked Willi, only five children – and me.

In the pretty Gothic pile of St Catherine's, Gustchen counted the names of ten of her ancestors whose mortal remains lay beneath the church floor. There were, Grimm knew, four more that she had missed, but he did not make a point of tracking down all the inscriptions.

Shivering a little as his headchill took hold, huddling inside his *surtout,* he would probably have stayed outside altogether had it not been raining so hard. A handful of others were likewise taking shelter, one or two looking at Grimm as if in recognition. A man of around forty – side-whiskered, reliant on a cane, regularly kneeling to pray – caught the old man's eye several times and seemed to be on the verge of speaking, or at least of offering a greeting.

Kummel, for his part, looked uneasy from the moment he entered the building. Had he been a dog, his ears would have been flat and his belly close to the ground as he edged around the inner walls, never venturing into the openness of the aisles or nave. He could, thought Grimm, have been a Catholic, disarmed by the Reformed austerity all around, but he rather fancied not.

He was developing other doubts about young Kummel – not that he could fault him in any aspect of his work. His service was exemplary, far superior to that of the usual run of boys Dortchen plucked from the beetroot fields around Berlin. But one never knew as much about these people as one would like. And Kummel seemed almost too vigilant, too biddable, as if he were trying to hide himself behind all the duties he performed with such aplomb.

Out in the porch Grimm found a place to sit and wait for the rain to ease. *Weaving, we are weaving . . .* Gustchen was still ostensibly counting grave slabs near the altar. Kummel went on padding under the lofty windows, never letting his master out of his sight for a moment. In its way, it was amusing. For all the true regard the three of them were paying to anything but one another, they could have been circling in a game of children's tag. But it had been much the same story ever since they had left the Harz Mountains. Then he heard a voice:

'Professor Grimm, this must happen to you often and surely it must irk you, but may I introduce myself? My name is Quistorp. I travel for a firm that sells and hires marquees and tarpaulins, but my family is from Hanover. I was a child in Göttingen back in the thirties when you still taught at the university.'

Grimm tilted back his head and peered up at the pious man with the cane he had noticed earlier. Behind him both Kummel and Auguste took several steps towards the porch, the latter looking quite mortified and shaking her head at Grimm as if to disclaim any responsibility for the approach.

'I happen to be staying at your inn,' the intense businessman went on, perching next to Grimm on the bench. 'I was at breakfast when the child came to pay her respects. Delightful, quite delightful. Had I recognized you before then, I might well have come and taken the same liberty myself. But may I do so now? Not so much on account of your excellent stories, Herr Professor, as for the stand you took against the King of Hanover all those years ago. I was in the crowd, you see, running beside your coach when you and the other six Professors were exiled. My father even bought me the little model that was made of the coach's entry into Witzenhausen. And do you know – I still have it!'

He sat so close that the smell of their shared breakfast gusted at Grimm as he spoke. The man looked harmless enough, but Grimm liked being buttonholed by perfect strangers about as much as he had enjoyed trying to teach students. Inside the church Auguste retreated, still nervously shaking her head. There seemed to be nothing for it but to hear him out.

'And since then, Herr Professor, I have closely followed your arguments for unification. Your articles, your speeches. Like you, I fervently believe that it must come. The customs union has proved that the states *can* work together. And Prussia must take the lead – through force of arms if needs be. The Prussian way, *ja*?' He was getting louder. 'But do you not agree, Professor Grimm, that in Bismarck we at last have our man? *He* sees things as they are. The time for talk is over, he says. Now it's time for blood and iron. *Blood and iron . . .*'

'Excuse me, *mein Herr . . .*'

The businessman glanced up, then sprang to his feet despite his enfeebled leg. He completed the sudden manoeuvre by taking a single step back towards the rain and tossing his cane from hand to hand. Grimm frowned with both relief and surprise, since his withdrawal had been caused only by Kummel's arrival.

'Excuse me, *mein Herr*,' he solemnly repeated to his seated master. 'It's time for your medication. Would you care to return now to the inn?'

The businessman apologized for detaining Grimm and with a bow limped away into the churchyard, but not before turning on Kummel a lengthy, narrow-eyed look of feverish, even personal distaste. And Grimm felt almost as unnerved by this as by his repetition earlier of the brutal Bismarck's sinister phrase.

Staying seated, he said flatly to his servant, 'Medication? I don't have the first idea what you're talking about.'

Kummel's large, long-lashed eyes seemed to become opaque. 'The gentleman's attention appeared unwelcome to you, sir. And back in Hanau, Fräulein Auguste told me that I was to make sure you were never bored.'

'So you believe that I was being bored just now?'

'I imagined that if you were not, sir, then you would have waved me away.'

'I see. Yes, I see.'

But when Gustchen came up, strenuously smiling, Grimm was thinking less about Kummel's presumption than the disgusted way that the blood-and-iron businessman had shrunk away from him.

SIX

The newly invested prince had not been prepared for the forest's many faces. The scenery changed so often that for several days he felt that he was moving through a series of interlinked chambers and galleries. Some of these rooms were cool, still, willow-fringed lakes; others stretches of boulder-strewn heath; others still amphitheatres walled in by living pillars of fir.

But the further east he travelled through successive cantons, the less inclined he was to see architecture in the green, bronze and russet profusion. He began to appreciate the relentless hanging beechwoods and hazel groves for what they really were, the forest floor as a random tesselation of roots, shoots, grasses, herbs and decay, not some carefully contrived mosaic decoration. He even stopped thinking of the tangled majesty as a lapse from some long-lost order or a neat walled garden run horrifically to seed. This vast expanse had never been anything else and would never be shaped into anything different. To him, it was as old, as young and as pure as the world on the day of its birth.

He had expected, too, to find fewer people making a living there. Although he generally skirted the occasional clusters of cottages, the clapboard houses of lone woodmen or the tell-tale smoke spirals from charcoal-burners' fires, he was glad to know he was not entirely alone. But he was happy enough to sleep curled up in combes or hollowed oaks, to eat whatever he found on the branches, bushes and coverts, and let his ears feast on nothing but birdsong.

Other than to ask directions or exchange greetings, he came closest to a conversation when he crossed a clapper-bridge one day towards dusk.

'You walk very purposefully,' said a voice from below. On breaking step the prince looked down to see a young washer-woman. 'Where are you heading?'

'To the Rose King's palace.'

'The palace with the princess?'

'You know it? Am I far from it now? Whenever I ask, people will only point eastwards and say, "It's closer to where the sun rises."'

'Well, that's true enough.' She pursed her lips, then stood up straight and arched her back with both hands on her hips. With her calf-length dress pulled taut, her body was attractively slender; her heart-shaped face was pleasing too, especially when her eyes danced almost mischievously over him. 'So you'd be a prince, then?' He hesitated only briefly before nodding. The young woman finished her stretch, wrinkled her nose in a delightful smile, then bent back down to her twisted lengths of linen. 'Good luck to you. It'll take you a while yet. Ask again at the cottage of the three spinners.'

'And is that on this path?'

Again she straightened, leaving her biggest sheet – weighted down by a flat stone slab – to rustle in the shallow stream's current. She looked up at him then in a different way from before, as if some new truth had just struck her, and she dried her hands on her apron. 'Tell me this. Do you know what you're going to do when you reach the palace?' But instead of waiting for him to answer, she came up the rough steps on to the bridge itself.

'I intend to find a way of helping my mother and her children,' he answered, thinking of the thick gold caskets with the jewel-encrusted cutlery inside. At the very least he planned to bring back one for her to sell.

'Your mother? At the palace? Oh no, that's not right.' She did not stop short of him until he could smell her sweaty fragrance: warm, dank and sweet like the lakeside moss on which he had rested his head the night before. 'Oh, highness, isn't that your father's job?' she smiled, and again, he was enchanted by her prettiness. 'The *king*, would he be?'

'I have no father,' he surprised himself by snorting back.

She had taken hold of his shirtsleeve and was inspecting his filthy cuff with a professional eye. His jerkin and breeches were similarly muddied, and his boots riddled with holes. A less likely prince, he knew, could not have been standing before her. She began to inspect each of his cracked shirt buttons. As she did so, her fingertips slipped between the flaps of the fabric and brushed against his skin. On his own fingers he felt the kind of stickiness he often noticed after eating apples. The taste on his tongue now was appley too.

'There's more for you to do when you come to the palace,' she said. Her voice was little louder than a sigh, her lips so close to his throat that bumps rose on his skin. 'But will you be able to do it?' Her attentions were new to him. He quite forgot that they were standing together on open ground, with a mill just a shout away upstream, standing lopsided above six little cottages like a blowsy maid left to mind a brood of children.

Her fingers played at the top of his breeches, then she slid her hand inside and he swayed where he stood. '*Are* you a prince?' she whispered. He could only make a grunt of assent that sounded a little like '*Heh*'. Her grip on him tightened. 'You don't look like a prince. You don't *feel* like a prince.'

'Maybe not,' his voice was brutish under his breath, 'but I assure you that I am.' He reached in turn for her, drew up the hem of her thin skirt to the same place where she now held him, then higher again, and with his free hand he crammed her buttocks together. 'Believe me, I am.'

'Because if you *are* a prince,' she sang amid tiny gasps, 'then you're not for me.' And with a cry and a skip she dashed down both her own skirt and her handful of him and was grinning back dazzlingly from two paces away.

'Why?' He came forward but she retreated again to her washing.

'Oh cover yourself, highness,' she said with a curtsey. 'The trees have eyes as well as ears.' He looked up and saw three men coming down the path from the mill. One, walking in front of the other two, was gesticulating. 'Go on from here now,' the washerwoman urged, waving too. 'The miller is my husband. Go! Find the canton where there are no spindles.' She flexed her thumb at him.

'But didn't you say I should make for the cottage of the three spinners?'

'They're one and the same. Now *go!*'

SEVEN

'Please come in,' Auguste said. 'Sit down, won't you? I apologize for calling you away from your beer and cards. It's dreadfully late, I know.'

As Kummel stepped from the landing into her small panelled dressing-room, Auguste had to struggle not to cry. Still she was trembling from her Apapa's polite insistence after dinner that he did not require her company the next morning – the very morning when she had planned to take the bull by the horns and start her questioning. It was almost as if he had *known*.

Turning, she crossed to the window and closed the velvet drape. Night had long since fallen on the steep streets of Marburg. There seemed to be more steps on those streets than stairs inside the houses. Her Apapa had pointed out one building, close to this pension, which was actually entered through a door in the roof. Now she could see little more than a sprinkling of street lamps in the darkness, overlaid by her own reflection in the glass, and there, behind her, Kummel, without his coat and neck-cloth, still standing because if he used the ottoman there would be nowhere for her to sit.

Turning back to him, Auguste said quickly, 'I mentioned in Hanau that I would need you to attend the Professor alone on Sunday morning in Cassel. The small surprise party? Well, now I must make further arrangements for it from here. Telegrams to send and so forth. The Professor will therefore walk out alone tomorrow. He was a student here, you see, fifty years ago. The place holds many fond memories for him.' She broke off, glancing at her bedroom door.

'And you wish me to accompany him?' Kummel asked. The smell of tobacco smoke was very strong; it seemed to have impregnated his sober waistcoat.

'No. Not exactly. He wishes to be unaccompanied.' Flushing, Auguste put up a hand to her favourite wide dog-collar necklace. The look in the hired man's impossibly dark eyes was already too knowing. Were her white lies so utterly transparent? 'Oh dear, this is difficult. You will have noticed that Marburg is by no means an ideal place for a gentleman of seventy-eight to go walking. As a rule the Professor's health is marvellously sound, but there have been some serious bouts of breathlessness and quite possibly a fall, back in the Tiergarten. And now, as you know, he has unfortunately picked up a summer cold.'

Her eyes were fixed on the low mahogany table between them. Her father's green, gilt-edged original edition of the *Tales for Young and Old* lay there and to her it looked like a ripped-out, still-beating heart. 'My Apapa is a very capable man, Kummel. He has recently travelled alone in both Scandinavia and Italy. But at times he can overestimate his own strength.' She closed her eyes to steady herself. 'I am asking you to watch over him tomorrow – but from a discreet distance. Am I making myself clear?'

She turned her eyes on him, dizzy from drinking too much

anisette after Grimm had made his announcement and then left for his woodchopping.

'Yes Fräulein, I understand,' he answered. 'Whatever you wish.' There was something exotic about his impassive high cheekbones with that pointed, assertive chin. And although his ebony hair was cut to within a whisper of his skull, it somehow looked tousled that night. Auguste found herself wondering what he was like among men of his own sort. She almost wished she could watch him, unobserved, down there at his cigarillo-clouded card table.

She took two steps closer to the English-style hearth. A painting hung above it, quite an effective one too: a Romantic, billow-sleeved young man reclining with a book, surrounded by what looked like poplars, but rather surprisingly he was reading by pale moonlight.

'This will set my mind at rest considerably,' she went on. 'You should be able to keep yourself hidden among all the twists and turns of these little streets. And I know you have presence of mind, as you showed with that awful man at the church in Steinau.' She tried to smile and felt herself flush again. 'But please don't let my Apapa see you. His pride would be most dreadfully hurt. He's always taken such complete responsibility for himself, and for most of the rest of his family too, so it's very hard for him to accept that now in turn he has to be looked after by us.'

Kummel nodded. Auguste expected him to back away, but he stayed motionless. For a moment she was lost for words, yet the silence was suddenly too awkward for her to say nothing more. 'His family has always mattered so much to him, you see,' she wittered on. 'He left the university here without completing his degree, just to try to find work to support his widowed mother and her other children.'

To her surprise and relief, that seemed to catch his interest. 'I had thought there were only two children: the Professor and your own father.'

'Oh, far from it. There were six. Five boys and a girl. They're all dead now, the others. And from the age of eleven Apapa was like a little father to them all. To some of them, it has to be said, a better father than they deserved. Think of it, Kummel, taking on such a burden at so young an age. Imagine having to support a family in that way.' She smiled. 'Do *you* have a large family?'

His eyes slipped to an even deeper level of darkness. And he seemed to flinch, as if from an unexpected lick of flame. 'No, Fräulein. Not large.'

'My father of course was closest to the Professor, in academic interests as well as age, although he could never hope to match his intellect. But then, who could? He is, after all, a man with a law of language named after him! Grimm's Law, yes. It's all to do with the way consonants correspond in the Germanic and other Indo-European languages. He coined the term "sound shift" too . . .' She paused, sensing that this was going over the serving man's head. 'He is so passionate about Germany and the German tongue, yet he is expert in many others. If something is worth reading – the Professor says – it's worth learning to read the language it is written in. So when he was sent as a member of the Hessian delegation to the Congress of Vienna, he learned Serbian in his spare time!' She smiled to herself, tensely, looking up again at the painting. As a child she had grossly exaggerated her Apapa's role in the post-Napoleonic peace-making of 1815; to friends she would claim he had drawn up the new map of Europe single-handed, and more than half believed it herself. Then she added: 'My father, when not collaborating with the Professor, was in the main a translator.'

When she glanced back at Kummel, tears were starting in her eyes. But now he seemed to be staring at the area of her small bosom left uncovered by her evening dress's décolletage. Auguste was not quite as unpractised as she made out at reading the looks she received from the opposite sex. It was just that the young and not-so-young Biedermeier-men who gave them were generally so unthinkable. 'Again I apologize,' she sniffed, 'I'm keeping you from your game. Tell me, are you winning?'

For the first time that she could remember he smiled, broadly. It was as if he had let another man out of himself, someone flintier whom Auguste had perhaps suspected – even hoped – to be there all along. 'The other valets and batmen think they're better cheats than me,' he said. 'But they're wrong.'

Auguste smiled back. 'Do please keep a close watch on my Apapa tomorrow, won't you? I don't know what I should do if anything happened to him.'

Snow lay on the slope outside, but it was snug in Friedrich von Savigny's private study. For Jacob, the warmth came as much from the awesome array of German medieval texts as from the small black stove next to which Willi wheezed as he copied out another precious manuscript. And the elder brother's cup overflowed when, as now, von Savigny himself – their young but august law lecturer – sat in his clouds of pipesmoke working alongside them.

Here for a few hours each week Jacob could close the great oak doors not just on his family's money troubles but also on Napoleon's butchers in cocked hats, who were infesting the fatherland like lice in an otherwise healthy head of hair. He could even close his ears to Willi's ratchety breath and his memory to the promise he had made their mother that he would act as a father to his now chronically asthmatic younger brother. And here, only here, by turning page after page, he could dance to the rhythms of the old romantic troubadours.

The library doors opened inwards. It was Kunigunde, von Savigny's wife of just six months. Turning, she took a tray from Bake the footman and brought it inside herself, wrinkling her nose at the fug her husband had created. Jacob and Wilhelm both stood as she put down the cups of tea laced with red wine. Von Savigny smiled and mouthed an endearment, then worked on.

Jacob could not help liking the Professor's wife. Everyone did. As unaffected as she was pretty, she looked particularly striking that afternoon with her hair arranged in the Grecian style, and gowned in blue high-waisted muslin that accentuated her pregnant stomach. Even so, Jacob always felt a twist of resentment when she came in to break their almost monastic concentration.

'How dashing you look, Jacob,' she smiled, 'quite the dandy.'

'You are very kind,' he said, feebly shooting the cuff of his second-hand scarlet frock coat and shuffling from foot to foot in the spurred boots. He felt closer to nine than nineteen years of age: a boy caught dressed in a grown-up's clothes.

'Is there perhaps a pretty Marburg Fräulein who has prompted this new look?'

'In Marburg, no.' Jacob felt himself shrinking as her heavily painted mouth smiled wider. 'But my brother and I do have friends at home. Female friends.'

'Ah – friends at home. There are pleasures to be had here too, you know. *Thés dansants*, parties, concerts.' Standing behind her husband, she put a hand on his shoulder as he continued to make notes. 'But Friedrich tells me that the other students often comment on your ceaseless dedication to your work.'

Jacob put his head on one side. He knew what the other students said. They laughed at Willi and himself as a kind of composite creature unsatisfied by any company but each other's, and although there were only thirteen months between them they called Willi 'Little One' and himself 'Old One'.

Thankfully Kunigunde eased out from behind the Professor and went across to admire Wilhelm's beautiful script. Jacob heard his brother engage her more smoothly than he ever could in a discussion of the chivalric tale he was copying out, even managing to master his cough for a few blessed minutes. Then von Savigny called Jacob over, patting a place on the bench beside him.

'As you know, Jacob, Kunigunde and I must shortly travel to Paris,' he said. 'Many of the manuscripts I need to consult for my history of Roman Law can be found only in the Bibliothèque Nationale. With my other commitments this will take months and, of course, there will soon be the baby too. So perhaps at some stage I would benefit from assistance. Tracking down the relevant papers, distilling them into note form, maybe making copies. I wondered if you might be interested? The work wouldn't in itself be as stimulating as you might like, but there *would* be a good deal of free time . . .'

Jacob fluttered a hand behind him in the oblivious Wilhelm's direction. 'Herr Professor, we're honoured that you should consider us for such positions. Truly we are. But my brother's poor health prevents any kind of travel.'

'I was thinking, Jacob, of you alone. Wilhelm, valuable though he would be to me, is a year behind you and not so well placed to break from his studies.' He glanced away. 'I would also, naturally, need your mother's consent.'

'*Ach*, my mother.' Jacob gazed at the table top and the pipe that von Savigny had put out on his wife's arrival. The idea of spending even a week apart from his brother made his blood run in a different direction. Three years before, he had come to Marburg on his own, and for the first six months of their separation Willi had been bedridden with asthma. To leave him now for another country would be tantamount to passing on to him a new disease. But that was only the half of it. Jacob could not even think of how another separation might affect *him*. Those six months in Marburg had proved to him, if he needed proof, that without his brother's constant presence he lost the fullest sense of himself.

With no Willi to look out for at every turn, he barely knew where to look at all.

'There would be no question of you paying your own way in France. You would be our house guest, a most welcome one. And Paris is a fine city, Jacob. It might even persuade you to forgive the French for some of their other . . . abominations.' His eyes flashed. There was no truer patriot than Friedrich Carl von Savigny. It was he, after all, who had opened the Grimm brothers' eyes to the fatherland's rich yet neglected folk heritage. But unusually his love of Germany had never required an accompanying hatred of France. 'Drink your tea now, before it cools.'

Jacob obeyed. The delectable warm liquid passed his lips as if it were fuelling another person's body. Behind him Willi was chattering on to the lovely pregnant woman. 'I don't, of course, have Jacob's intellect,' he heard him say. 'But my brother is so patient with my sluggishness. At times he even deigns to listen to my own clumsy observations on the treasure house of texts that has been opened up to us here!'

Jacob stared with gratitude at their mentor's chiselled features, his hang of straight, shoulder-length hair. Not only had von Savigny shown the brothers the magnificent old manuscripts, he had also directed them to the wealth of traditional songs and stories preserved in the tellings of humble spinning women, maids and carters. And he had introduced them to scholar friends such as Clemens Brentano and Achim von Arnim, who were even now making literary records of them. 'Through men like these,' he had said, 'the first drops are watering the tree of German life from its fountain. By reminding our people of their own glorious past, we can begin to revive our nation's confidence. Not law but literature – spoken, written, shared, passed on – *that* is the common bond uniting the entire German *Volk*.'

Odd words, coming from a Professor of Law. But Jacob

already knew how true they were. He himself had no sense of vocation for the law. If he – not his mother – had made the final decision, he would now have been studying botany. But month by month it was becoming ever more obvious that the family did not have the finances for him to study at all. Able-bodied as he was, he knew that soon it would be his duty to replenish the coffers, not simply continue to drain them.

'You look distracted, Jacob,' smiled the Professor. 'But I hope you'll seriously consider what I've suggested. Paris might suit you well.' His expression grew more amused. 'Think of it – in that splendid city, just for a short while, you would not have to be "Old One".'

As far as Auguste could tell, Grimm's morning alone passed without incident. After lunch she was delighted when he suggested a stroll together around the lower town. Kummel, with whom she had not yet had a chance to speak in private, dutifully followed.

As in most of the towns and cities of her Apapa's 'fatherland' now, the place seemed to be overrun with the young: children batting hoops across their path, swinging from the low arched bridge, scampering up the stepped streets, all so brimful of zest and purpose. The strutting-peacock students looked especially sure of where they were going, or else enviably unconcerned about what lay ahead.

Grimm, beside her, seemed preoccupied. He said little, although sometimes his lips moved as if he were reciting verse to himself or, more likely, trying to frame new answers to the perennial German Question. It was hard to imagine him as a callow student here. Hard to imagine him young at all. *A long time ago,* Auguste remembered from the *Tales, when wishing was still of use . . .*

Her own father by contrast had never lost a childlike wonder at the world. To Auguste he had never really seemed to grow up.

But perhaps, she thought as they passed a sweet-smelling bakery, some people become their truest selves only in old age, when it is too late for any more choice. In this she was thinking of her mother as much as her Apapa. If she tried to picture either of them in their prime, she could only ever see them straining – usually together – for the safety of the twilight, racing away from their own intractable present, craving age in a way that Auguste was now beginning to find sadly familiar herself.

Just before they entered the twin-steepled church of St Elisabeth, Grimm sent Kummel off to the Postamt with some letters. For a few heady minutes Auguste wondered if a miracle had happened: that independently he had decided to talk about the things that she still lacked the nerve to raise with him herself. But once they were inside he spoke only – if interestingly – about the church's fabric, its many fine monuments and frescoes.

At the end of one aisle they briefly stood in silence below a fifteenth-century statue of St Elisabeth. Her medieval cult had apparently been so influential once that her relics had attracted pilgrims from all over Europe. The saint, richly robed and wearing a princess's crown, stood above Grimm and Auguste holding a model of her own church. 'For an ascetic Franciscan nun,' Auguste could not help remarking with a smile, 'she looks extremely shapely.'

'Indeed,' Grimm nodded. 'She herself would doubtless have abhorred an image like this. But she was, by origin, a princess – a daughter to the King of Hungary. The statue was probably commissioned by her aristocratic descendants . . .' He went on to mention a number of self-sacrificing legends attached to her name. But the longer Auguste looked up past the nubile body to the lovely frozen face, the less she saw of the later saint and the more of the former princess, trapped still in this towering mausoleum, waiting for the day when a prince would come to kiss her back to life. And then she would smile, gladly set down her little model church on the floor, and walk out on the arm of her rescuer into her first shaft of sunlight in centuries.

Outside the church Kummel was waiting to fall into step behind them. '*Weaving, we are weaving* . . .' Auguste distinctly heard her Apapa mutter once again. It was starting to bother her.

'Ah,' she smiled. 'Heine.'

'*Heine!*' the little man exploded, swinging around briefly to face her. 'His *Song of the Silesian Weavers,* no? Now how could I have forgotten that? The line's been plaguing me for days. Thank you, *Liebchen,* thank you.'

'*Old Germany, we are weaving your shroud,*' Auguste quoted in a mock ominous tone. '*We are weaving into it the threefold curse* . . .' and then Grimm joined in: '*We are weaving, we are weaving* . . . *Heh!* Whatever is happening to my memory?'

They walked on with Auguste sensing that for him another ghost had just been raised, not laid. 'I always preferred that other verse of his that you taught me,' she volunteered brightly:

> '*Russia and France control the land.*
> *Great Britain rules the sea.*
> *Ours is the cloudy realm of dreams*
> *Where there's no rivalry* . . .'

'Yes,' he smiled. 'That, too, was Heine.' But he was years away from her now. Centuries. Away from a desk, Jacob Grimm was only a tenth himself.

Back at the pension they took coffee together before he announced that he had letters to write. The *Wörterbuch* had always generated such a mass of correspondence. Since its scope was so broad – embracing technical vocabularies, popular rhymes and even obscenities, as well as the literature of several centuries – and since examples of usage were required to provide a 'natural history' of individual words in their context, he had needed collaborators from the outset. But because many of them were so undisciplined or whimsical in collecting and collating material, he often complained that he spent more time writing to them than on his own research. Auguste returned to Reimer's first edition of the *Tales* while her Apapa covered page after page at a bureau in the drawing-room, raising his eyes at intervals to smile wanly at the wall.

He may well have been writing to her mother too – back now in their Berlin apartment – asking why she had let her daughter drag him around on this apparently aimless tour. *The most precious person in my life,* she thought as she kept snatching glimpses of him and her eyes filled up. It is better to learn without travelling, he had always used to say, than to travel without learning.

It must have been so different eleven summers before, when her father and mother had made this same little journey, seeing the same sights, putting up at the same lodgings. Her father could never have been so reticent about it all. Faced by that child at the breakfast table in Steinau, for example, he would have set her on his knee and made her tell him more stories. Here in Marburg he would have taken her mother to see his tiny student rooms, the great von Savigny's home, the lecture halls, the castle. But her Apapa did not have a Dortchen to show these things to. There was the problem's beginning and its end.

After dinner Grimm went to chop wood and Auguste curled up again with the *Tales.* Her father had made handwritten notes in many of the margins, usually to remind himself where, and from whom, a particular story had been collected. The tale she was reading, *The Singing Bone,* was marked *Dortchen 19 January 1812, by the stove in the summer house.* The tale itself was about fratricidal rivalry: one brother kills another for his own selfish ends but a bone from the dead body then sings out loud what has happened, so the killer is duly sewn into a sack and drowned in retribution.

Not for the first time, Auguste found herself blanching. She had not read the book so closely or continuously for years. Taken as a whole, the tales' range of raw emotion was almost overwhelming. Spite, envy, malice, dread, obsession, love: they all roiled up off the pages like steam. And it seemed more and more incongruous to her that her little uncle – so fastidiously, constantly, faultlessly formal – should have set this pot to boil more than fifty years before. For back in 1812 he had been the originator, even if her father had supervised subsequent editions until the very end of his life, systematically prettifying the contents to lure in ever more readers.

As usual she could think only disparagingly of the younger 'fairytale brother'. True, he had always been ill, but her Apapa had surely suffered more. The warmonger in St Catherine's Steinau had reminded her of that: both brothers had defied the King of Hanover when she was a child, but only Jacob had been driven out. And Jacob alone had then gone to find new work to keep them, to set up a new life in a new city: not just for his brother but his brother's family too.

She was even beginning to blame the dead man – unjustifiably, absurdly – for leaving her behind unmarried. It must have been the *Tales'* influence: all those fathers giving away their daughters to the first hero who could kill a boar. But it was the stories' unmitigated action that compelled her, in spite of their grisliness. The way that so much *happened.* No boredom, no hedging, no holding back. And she wondered whether, deep inside, her Apapa had ever hankered to slip into such an untamed forest world too, to live inside Nature, not hover at its edges identifying the plants and trees for everybody else.

The brisk knock at the door so surprised her that she went to answer it with the book still open between her fingers. Kummel stood outside.

'Forgive me for interrupting your evening, Fräulein. I thought you might like to know that the Professor had no problems this morning. He went to a shop to look at shawls. Then he walked up to a coffee house below the castle and spent virtually the whole time there, writing for the most part.' He hesitated and his eyes dropped to Auguste's book. 'I just thought you might like to know.'

'I do, oh I do. Thank you. Shawls, you say?' That had an old resonance. But now that she felt calmer, she thought she better understood her Apapa's sudden need for solitude. She often felt it herself, even while appearing to be lost without company. It was just as she kept thinking: under the skin they were the same.

She smiled, noticing a new air about Kummel. Although he stood still in the shadows, his whole body appeared to be craning forward where usually it seemed to slink irretrievably back. Auguste saw too that his dense stubble had grown in black whorls even since that afternoon. He continued to stare at the book, which she now clutched to her breast in both hands. She had no idea if he could read, but he could well have been trying to decipher the words on the binding. 'It's a volume of the fairytales that the Professor and my father collected in Cassel,' she explained, 'after their college days.'

'Ah,' he said, apparently indifferent, before quickly going on. 'And as far as I'm aware, the Professor didn't notice me watching him. In fact, I'm sure he didn't.'

'Good. I really am most grateful. *Danke schön*.'

She was about to ask him the outcome of the previous evening's card game when he stepped back. It was as if a ribbon running from Auguste's shoulder to his upper chest had been snipped in two, so abruptly that for an instant she felt thrown off balance. He bowed, said goodnight and was gone.

Auguste closed her door thoughtfully. There had been little enough reason for Kummel to come up to her in the first place, but none at all for him to have left again so suddenly.

EIGHT

After the incident on the clapper-bridge, the prince took care to say no more than a polite good day to any of the women who greeted him further along his route. But there were few enough of them in these more overgrown regions of the forest. The evergreens themselves seemed to have turned their high shoulders towards him to mark his passing; when fronds brushed against him, fondly, almost sensuously, it was as if they were continuing the exploration which the miller's wife had begun. And where the warm sunlight filtered through so unpredictably he often lost track of the hours. The trees around him seemed to be warping time, or at least creating a variety of times. Here it seemed to rush past, there to flow more sinuously. But never did he have the sense that had always haunted him in his hometown – that time was simply plodding on.

The miller's wife had told him to head for the place with no spindles, but as far as he could see, there were no spinning wheels in any of the cottages he passed. Finally late one afternoon, after beating his way through a thicket that drew blood from his hands, arms and forehead, he came to a lake surrounded by hazelnut trees and blackberry bushes. Two seagulls swooped down out of the sun, followed by a dozen others that silently circled the lake at no great height then flew across the treetops behind him, setting off a chorus of cawing rooks. The rays of the dying sun seemed to strike sparks off the water's surface as the clean light caught small bursting bubbles blown up from below.

He stood for a while, mesmerized, then could not resist undressing and slipping into the coolness. He did not see a young woman come up to sit on the bole of a severely lopped cherry tree nearby, her golden hair tied in a green muslin kerchief that matched her ankle-length dress. As he splashed and ducked, she patiently folded his shirt, breeches and jerkin. And when he finally turned her way, standing erect in the calf-deep water, she stood too, and smiled prettily at his attempt to cover himself.

'We can give you better clothes than these,' she said. 'Better suited to your station.'

And in a single graceful movement she scooped up the pile and vanished through the wild apple trees behind her. He followed, calling, feeling less embarrassed than amused at his own nakedness – even taking an unfamiliar pleasure in his lean, supple, almost golden figure in the late sunshine.

She did not stay unseen for long. The grove of trees thinned into a shady clearing, overarched on three sides by poplars and larches. A spacious timber cottage – two-storeyed, shingle-roofed and impressively gabled – stood towards its rear. In the centre hung a pot on a trivet over a crackling cook-fire, which rose from a specially dug pit. Slivers of smoke drifted in all directions around the area and the smell from the pot was delicious.

Not one woman but three turned to face him. The nearest was scattering feed to a troupe of orange-breasted hens. A second sat on a ladderback indoor chair, preparing lentils. The third was the girl with his armful of clothing. They were all attractive but each – he saw on stepping further forward – had a glaring and unusual impediment. The hen-feeder moved awkwardly, since her right foot was both enlarged and flattened. The left-hand thumb of the lentil-preparer was similarly outsized and misshapen. And the lower lip of the clothes-snatcher had become so swollen that earlier he had mistaken it for a salaciously lolling tongue. As he looked with pity and curiosity from one to the other, they exchanged knowing glances then explained in turn:

'From treading. From treading.'

'From twisting thread – twisting and twisting.'

'From licking the thread.'

Still baffled, he frowned. The girl with his clothes elaborated, nodding to her companion who limped: 'She used to draw the thread and ply the treadle, do you see? While I would moisten the thread,' she put a finger to her mouth to demonstrate before pointing at the third who sat, 'and she would twist it, and strike the table with it, and each time the table was struck, a stretch of fine yarn would fall to the floor – oh, millions and millions and millions of times.'

'You all work at the same wheel?' he asked, the lake water drying on him.

They laughed. '*Worked*, not work. There have been no wheels here, no spindles, for as long as anyone can remember.'

'Why not?'

'Well, would *you* want to spin and spin, all the hours of the day and night, if it left you spoiled like this?' In the course of answering, the third girl wandered over to the trivet and absently dropped all the prince's clothes into the fire in the pit. She kept hold of his boots but, on inspecting their soles, threw them into the climbing flames too. He began to feel very cold. The hen-feeder came close enough delicately to finger the goosebumps at his elbow and upper arm.

'All the spindles in these cantons were destroyed,' she said, addressing his question more seriously. 'The king's men came to gather them up, then there were bonfires all through the forest. We believe that they were trying to stop something from happening. It was so long ago now.'

'But you all look my age. You must have been babies when you last spun.'

She smiled at his innocence, but her answer was gentle. 'Perhaps a year where you come from lasts for longer than a year here? Doesn't every canton have its way, its own kind of time?'

He chewed on this, unable to answer. 'So why were the spindles destroyed? What did the king not want to happen?'

'No one told us,' said the lip-girl, drifting closer to the cottage doorway. 'And we weren't going to stop and ask questions. For us – for all the girls and women – it was an end to the drudgery. It was like a miracle, an answer to our prayers and dreams.' She paused under the porch and beckoned, so far away from him now that he could see no blemish. 'Come inside.'

Obediently, keenly, he crossed the clearing, glancing down at the charred fragments of his clothes. Behind him the evening began to spread itself out like more of the smoke. A stair led up directly from the cottage's entrance, and the girl bent down around the newel post at its first return. 'Please come up.'

It was warm inside, perfumed with what smelled like juniper and unseasonal winter heliotrope. The stairs, well made, were silent under his bare feet. There were maybe only twenty steps in all, but he felt as if he were rising for hours, even days. The higher he rose, the further he seemed to be moving beyond town-time. His mother became a distant memory. Virtually all he could remember of that earlier period of his life was the slightly eerie clack-clack-clacking of the spindle that bobbed at night in her upstairs room. *Perhaps when you discover what's out there,* she had said, *you won't ever want to come back.* And now he could not tell whether, in arriving at this cottage and feeling so much at home, he was fulfilling her dearest wish or deepest dread.

On reaching the long gallery at the stair-head, he steadied himself on the deftly carved ash banister. Below him the entire downstairs storey was laid out as invitingly as any room he had ever seen.

'Here,' she called from inside one of the rooms off the gallery up ahead. He went at once and stepped into what appeared to be a dressing-room. Along the facing wall hung a startling array of piped, fluted and bejewelled jackets – waist-length, knee-length, calf-length – in every shade of blue, green, saffron and red. Under them on wooden hangers were just as many breeches – satin, leather, velvet – and beneath them in turn stood a cobbler-shop display of pairs of shoes – buckled, laced, buttoned, wooden. It was dark in the room. The girl in green muslin had lit a candle lamp and stood behind it. He wanted her to put it down but she held it in front of her like a shield. 'All these outfits once belonged to princes,' she said.

'So where are the princes now?' He pretended to look into the room's corners. 'What did you do with them?'

'We? Nothing. The clothes were passed on to us when they were no longer needed.'

He shrugged and shook his head good-naturedly. Behind her on the wall was a painting of a young man reading by moonlight. It could have been him, out in the forest. It certainly looked like him, dressed in the clothes he had worn before coming here. He reached out and fingered the red velvet collar of the blue coat nearest to him. Leather breeches hung below it, and boots with silver spurs. A wig was attached on a loop of thread, freshly powdered and smelling a little of old tobacco smoke. He noticed that several rips in the coat's fabric had been carefully sewn back together. The boots, too, looked scratched and scuffed, despite a sheen from vigorous recent polishing.

'Is that the outfit you would like?' she asked from behind her light, edging towards the doorway. 'Try it on.'

'And then what?' he asked. This was not what he had been expecting.

'Then you will travel on, more properly dressed, to the Rose King's palace.'

'You know where I'm going?'

She indicated the roomful of clothing. 'It was where they all went.' And anticipating his next question she went on, 'They reached a certain point, then they could go no further. Please, dress yourself.' She sounded almost irritated by his nakedness now, where before he had sensed both interest and admiration. 'Then before you go, you can eat with us.' She put the lamp on the chest and left the room. Again, more vividly still, he remembered that noisome clacking from his mother's room.

It took him a good while to feel satisfied with his appearance. The wig in particular felt tight and cumbersome. Before taking up the lamp and descending the stairs he took a last look in the floor-length oval mirror. The clothes undeniably gave him greater authority and made even his facial expressions seem less boyish. Yet something was missing and he could not decide what.

The three spinners had set a place for him at a trestle-table outside. When he sat none of them commented on his new appearance, nor did anyone speak as they drank their white-bean soup and ate the bread and fruit. Each girl sat so that her disfigurement was hidden from him, and he found them all so beautiful that he could barely swallow a mouthful of the food or a sip of their cool apple wine. 'I'm most grateful to you,' he said as night fell on the debris of the meal.

'You're welcome,' smiled the lip-girl, settling the dishes among the hot coals to clean. 'We would give you more help if we could. But what goes on at the palace is largely unknown to us. It isn't easy to get through to it, that much we do know.'

He nodded, not wanting to ask if the princes whose clothes now hung upstairs had died in making their failed attempts. *She should be ready now,* he remembered his mother saying. *For whoever comes, when the time is right.* 'Then should I not go armed?' he asked, aware as soon as he said it that a sword was what had been missing from his reflection in the glass.

'Yes, we can arm you,' the three replied, 'if that's what you want.'

The foot-girl hobbled back to the cottage and promptly returned with a scabbarded sword on a plain leather belt. She drew it out so he could test the blade, and it seemed sharp enough to draw tears from the wind. He stood for her to buckle it on. When she had finished her adjustments, she ran her hand lightly across the front of his buttoned breeches, and the prince felt such longing. But then the three stepped back towards their cottage.

'You're not afraid, are you?' asked the girl who had led him here.

'What should I be afraid of?'

'It's all a question of time, of whether the time is right. For you, for anyone.'

He smiled. But as he turned to stride away the memory of his mother's distant clacking resurfaced so loudly in his head that he was glad when the mournful song of the doves on their beech branches drowned it out.

NINE

Before leaving Marburg Kummel had arranged for an afternoon-tea hamper to be prepared for the Professor and the Fräulein. With their train half an hour short of Cassel, he left his billet near the guard's van to serve the light meal in their otherwise unoccupied compartment. On arriving he found the old man lying back whey-faced in his seat – mouth wide open, eyes rolling – while the Fräulein stood trying to fan him with her flattened-out book.

'It's nothing,' the Professor breathed through his blocked nose when he noticed Kummel. 'A touch of travel sickness. *Gar nichts.* Nothing.'

'It came on so suddenly,' the Fräulein gabbled. 'One moment he was happily reading, the next this. I've let him do too much. I should have been far more cautious. Should we use smelling-salts, do you think?'

Kummel sat next to his master and loosened his cravat. 'I suggest, sir, that we take you into the corridor for some air. There's a window we can open. I think that'll revive you better.'

The Fräulein still fretted. 'You think he should be moved? Will his legs carry him?' Kummel was already easing him to his feet, taking most of the minimal weight on himself, then edging him out of the compartment. He glanced back before supporting the Professor down to the carriages' coupling, and saw his mistress slump back in her seat then stare up glassily at the luggage racks.

By the time Kummel managed to wind down the window, Grimm courteously said that he could stand unassisted in the smoky breeze. Kummel stepped away, still vigilant, watching some colour seep back into his sunken cheeks. Finally he smiled ruefully at his servant.

He was not, to be fair, a hard old fellow to serve. He did not ask for his shoelaces to be ironed every morning, nor was he forever spewing out biblical saws and improving moral epigrams. He rather seemed embarrassed to be served at all, seldom speaking and giving the impression when spoken back to that he was listening less to what was said than to the way in which the various word-sounds were being fitted together. Which was perhaps only natural in a man with an international law of language named after him.

'This is unlike me,' he said to Kummel's surprise, while gazing out at a row of terraced cottages for a new workers' colony. 'I normally travel well. I have done for years.' He took out a handkerchief and blew his nose, but then seemed to swallow back most of the catarrh.

Both men watched golden fields and vineyards slip past. There were still medieval-looking harvesters and carters in these parts, wearing soft, wide-brimmed bullycock hats. They paused from their work to wave at trains, and twice Grimm raised a hand in response. Sleepy little settlements with whitewashed walls and rutted, dusty market squares flashed by, shadowed in the distance by occasional bristling smokestacks and collieries then, way beyond those again, the forest's faint stain along the skyline. And there seemed to be children everywhere he looked, as if they were this region's staple crop. To Kummel the land looked serene yet at the same time out of kilter with itself, neither ancient nor modern, no longer sure perhaps in which world it truly belonged. And observed from aboard this train, it was all so strangely silent; not one sound filtered through, not even the age-old peal of the hourly church bell.

'This country,' said the old man, pushing back his hair, 'once it was under the French. They turned it into a kingdom in its own right. The Kingdom of Westphalia. Its king was a brother to Napoleon Bonaparte.'

'I didn't know that, sir,' Kummel replied. 'I presumed the land had always been German.'

An odd cast came over Grimm's profile. 'German it always was, my friend, and German it always will be. Only its occupiers were French.'

Kummel nodded, utterly incurious as to where one country ended and the next began, where one language stopped and another started. For what was national pride but a hollow form of ancestor-worship? And what did national differences really mean? Take those precious German forests out there. The loud-mouthed patriots, sighing for what they called their *Waldeinsamkeit* – 'forest-solitude' – seemed to find some deep moral significance in them. But Kummel had heard in the Harz that many were now stocked with imported, quick-growing Douglas firs. For his part, he had always been far more struck by the similarities that ran so predictably across every frontier.

After asking for the window to be wound up a little way, Grimm stared less at the fields than at his own reflection, just like he had in Hanau, as if he might find a clue there as to why he felt so bad. He did look poorly, though. The deterioration of his skin's tone and texture since arriving in Hesse was shocking; at times he truly did look stained, grubby, soiled – and quite alarmingly tired. It occurred to Kummel now that his biblical namesake might have looked rather like this after his night of wrestling with the angel.

At last the Fräulein reappeared. Kummel stood straighter at her approach, watching her laboriously reconstruct her smile. She was wearing a blue silk day-dress with a crinoline whose contours did not show from the front, which greatly enhanced the fluidity of her figure. Above the smile, her eyes were still bright with alarm and she pressed her open book to her breast with both slim-fingered hands, like a child holding a raggedy monkey for comfort.

'You look better now, Apapa,' she said, glancing at Kummel for corroboration.

Grimm shifted stiffly towards her. At that moment the carriage jolted over a point and he staggered. Kummel was too far back to steady him. The Fräulein thrust out her own hand to catch his elbow; the book slipped down her dress and almost out of her grasp. Kummel stepped forward and the Fräulein, still holding her uncle, was glad to pass the book across to him before turning the old man with both hands and guiding him back down to their compartment.

Once inside, she closed the door without looking back. Although she had gone, her subtle cologne lingered pleasingly. Uncertain whether she wanted him to remain on call, and to save himself from standing about looking like a soaked poodle, Kummel took a look at the book. She was in the middle of a tale called *The Three Sons of Fortune*. Kummel read a little of it and smiled. A man had come to a land where the scythe had not yet been invented. When the corn was ripe, they took cannons out into the fields and shot it down.

Then he turned back to the contents page. Attracted by the title of one of the tales, he flicked on ahead to it.

Jacob paused outside von Savigny's Paris house. Its front door was open and a trap waited outside. The walk back from the Bibliothèque Nationale had taken longer than usual on that April afternoon. Much longer. Von Savigny had said that in France Jacob would not have to be the Old One. But for all his host's generosity and all the visits to the uproarious theatre and well-stocked picture galleries, he now felt three times older than his twenty years.

After four months he had still received no word from his mother in Steinau, although according to Willi's last letter she was planning to move house, with the babies, to be closer to them both in Marburg. But when Jacob went back home he would not be continuing his studies. That morning in the library he had finally made up his mind, and now he wanted von Savigny to be the first to know.

On entering the house he found no maids but heard chatter upstairs. Von Savigny would be waiting in his study for Jacob's notes. Then for several hours they would work on them together. But at the head of the stairs, the Professor's door was wide open and the room empty. Still preoccupied, Jacob continued along the corridor to his small panelled study-bedroom, where Kunigunde had placed on his desk a pretty new purple wallflower plant.

He lifted a crystal fragment which he used as a paperweight and riffled through the sheaf of Wilhelm's letters. Phrases swam up at him: *Are the young women as beautiful as we are led to believe? . . . Have you missed me as much as, dear brother, I continue to find myself missing you? . . . Mother writes often of difficulties in affording clothes for the young ones . . .*

Mother . . . Why did she not send even a page of trivial gossip? Why had she been so silent since curtly permitting him to leave German soil? Was it a criticism of his absence – of his abandonment, however temporary, of *her?*

A kitchen girl rushed past his room, slowing only to grin at

Jacob as he turned from the desk. 'What is it?' he asked in the perfect French in which he had effortlessly begun to think as well as speak. 'Where is the master, please?'

'It's happened,' was all she called back over her shoulder. 'It's wonderful.'

Jacob followed her out and slowly headed towards where he had heard the voices before. It was absurd of him not to have guessed. The high double-doors to von Savigny's bedroom were flung back and it seemed as if half the population of the enemy city were inside. Most had gathered around the canopied bed, where Jacob glimpsed Kunigunde lying propped up, flushed and happy, with a small, swaddled bundle in her lap. It had happened. It was wonderful. It was always wonderful. But it was not for him to share. He turned and reached his room again with an unfamiliar sense of fullness in his face.

He had to write to Willi – had to talk with *him*, if only by way of pen on paper. For that, too, was a part of his torment. He did miss his brother, badly, even though he could not express such strong emotion in so many words. If this second separation had taught him anything, it was that he and Willi were two halves of a whole; not perhaps the only whole there would ever be in either of their lives, nor perhaps even the most important, but a whole none the less. For the time being at least – and this surprised Jacob as much as the thought of it could warm his heart – they still completed each other.

'Jacob, Jacob!' Von Savigny had seen him in the doorway and come out. '*Komm*, Jacob. It's a girl. A baby girl.'

Jacob felt a hand at his elbow and turned with a smile but kept his eyes down. 'I congratulate you, Herr Professor. It's quite marvellous. You're a father. Please accept our heartfelt congratulations. My own and all my family's.'

Von Savigny's hold on his elbow grew firmer. 'Are you well,

Jacob?' he asked, craning his neck down to meet his eye. 'You look pale. And your voice – it's different.'

Jacob shook his head. He could not speak – afraid that if he started, the words would never stop: words and maybe tears as well. It was so long since he had cried and the tears dammed up behind his eyes felt far from fresh.

'Are you homesick, perhaps? You can tell me, man.'

Man. 'No,' Jacob managed. 'Not homesick. I'm very happy here.'

'Too happy?'

Jacob swallowed. This was not so far from the mark. The longer he stayed away from Hesse, the more seduced he became. To be again in the bosom of a family – any family, so close-knit and now growing as well – was almost too much for his heart to bear. But the scent of the wallflower gave him strength. And although this could not have been a less suitable time and place, he went to his desk, turned and said: 'I can't stay with the law. I can't afford to keep up my studies, and even if I qualify I would then have to practise far away from my family. And that wouldn't do. They need me with them. My mother, brothers and sister. They all need me.'

'Your mind is made up? But the law was your father's profession.'

'Indeed, God rest him. But it was my mother who set me to follow him.'

'And now she has suggested that you reconsider?'

Jacob's eye wavered. 'I know that she needs me. When we return, I should be with her. She depends on me. She's needed me ever since my father died.'

'And how will you support yourself and your family? With administrative work?'

Jacob nodded. He would get work; he was able, willing, industrious. A position as assessor or secretary to the government in

Cassel should not be beyond him. Besides, his fluency in French would be invaluable, given the current volume of traffic between Napoleon's France and the various German states within its orbit.

'And Wilhelm? Will he too look for employment?'

Old One stared down at the stack of letters. 'My brother's uncertain health would make that difficult. No, one of us should complete his studies. But in the meantime, while I work in Cassel and he serves out his time in Marburg, we shall still collaborate in collecting and editing the old German songs and stories – perhaps with a view, in time, to seeing them published.'

Von Savigny's face brightened. '*Gut. Gut!* In that field you have a rare insight, Jacob. Let's hope that the law's loss will be the gain of German literature!' He offered his hand and Jacob came to take it. The two men's eyes met. Von Savigny had invited him to France as a form of escape and maybe, after all, he *was* now escaping, not to some different country, but further back inside his own.

'Come now,' said von Savigny, leading Jacob by the hand and clapping his free hand around his shoulder as they stepped out of the room. 'Come and see that there can be more to a man's life than law books, account books, or even – dare I say it? – books of traditional tales. It's hard to believe that now, I know. But you'll see for yourself one day. I promise, you will see.'

. . . So then the judge had the Jew taken to the gallows and hanged as a thief.

Chuckling, Kummel lowered the green-bound book when he finished the story. He was seeing flames, a fearsome old blaze, feeling its searing heat all over his face. Putting the book under one arm, he pressed himself back to let a self-important governess brandishing a lorgnette pass with three small boys. Then he leafed again through the four terse pages of *The Jew in the Brambles.*

A rich man once had an honest servant, it began. This honest servant amused himself one day by sending a Jew with a long goatee into a thicket of brambles, then making him dance uncontrollably to the sound of his magic violin. The brambles ripped his clothes and cut and scratched him all over, but the servant was unrepentant. '*You've skinned plenty of people in your time,*' he laughed, '*now the brambles can skin you!*' The Jew promised him a bag of gold if he would stop his playing. He duly paid up, but when later he tried to recover his money he was forced to admit – after more manic dancing – that he had stolen it himself anyway. So he received his just deserts on the gallows.

'Ah,' came a voice from his right, which led Kummel to snap the book shut, 'I see I have left the *Tales* in interested hands.'

He had not heard the Fräulein approach. She stood close to him, looking less fraught, but with the characteristic smile fixed across her face. (Sometimes Kummel imagined it as a mask, whose cracks from overuse she had to sit up mending late into each night.) Her arms were folded and she seemed not to want to take back the book, although this was presumably why she had come out to him. Still Kummel's face was full of the fire – *such* heat, although from where he had crouched, hidden, he was safe from it himself.

He held out the book and she took it, her smile flickering only briefly. 'There are two volumes,' she said. 'If you promise to take great care of it, I'd be happy to let you borrow one.' Her eyes looked Kummel's way, yet seemed to stop short of him, perhaps at his heavy old-fashioned coat that she must often have seen on her own father. He was fairly sure she had not noticed the colour rise in his cheeks, as if the fire were not just roaring in his memory but crackling there between them in the corridor.

'I don't read well,' he replied, making no move to take back the book. 'I haven't read – not properly – for many years. I'm not sure that I'm suited to it.' He could not keep back all the other images indefinitely. Now they reared up as vividly as ever: two dozen neighbours almost casually feeding the flames with armfuls of books; the air alive with plumes of smoke and swirling flecks of ash; the raw, rasping taste of others' burnt words in his throat as he looked on from his hidey-hole; then suddenly the screams and the more indescribable savour still of burning limbs.

But when he managed to press them back down, for several moments his head echoed to an inexplicable low clacking noise, like the repeated crack of a flag in a stiff breeze, or even a brisk distant bootstep.

The Fräulein's gaze warmed. 'That's a shame. For you, a great shame. Books make such a difference to a life. I can't imagine where my own family would be without them. Especially, of course, my Apapa.'

Kummel was glad she had steered the conversation away to the inevitable subject of her uncle. *Apapa, Apapa.* This now would put him completely beyond the fire's reach. 'Fräulein, I've been wondering,' he said, 'why do you call the Professor by that name?'

'"Apapa"?' She smiled, quite beautifully, in a way that softened all her face's angles. 'Oh, it's a family name, made up by one of my brothers when we were all small children. It was meant to distinguish our uncle from our father, "Apapa" from "Papa", although they were like twin fathers to us anyway. Apapa has always lived with us, you see. We've always been together.'

'Wasn't that sometimes confusing? When you were small children, I mean?'

The look she then gave him was acute yet vulnerably open, surprised but in a way she appeared to welcome. It seemed to have surfaced from an entirely different face. No clockwork doll's at all, but that of an eager child on the brink of young womanhood. 'Well, yes, in certain respects. Yes, you could say that.' And she looked away quickly, as if her answer too had fallen from another person's lips.

'And now he's fully recovered, the Professor?'

'From his turn? Yes, I believe so. *Danke schön,* Kummel. Thank you for your assistance. I truly am glad you're here with us.' She glanced at him as if to admit that originally she had been less convinced. 'Last summer I travelled with the Professor to a historical convention in Munich and I think he found my constant companionship . . . restricting.' She stoked up her smile's brightness, hiding once again behind its fierce but empty dazzle. 'This time, it's been good for him to mix my company with a little of yours.'

'I doubt, Fräulein, that he ever wants that. If I may say so, he's fortunate to have so devoted a niece.'

Her smile then became so brilliantly hollow that in another world Kummel would have gripped both her cheeks and shaken it out. 'He deserves any good fortune he might have,' she said. 'Over the years, he's worked so hard for it. He is a good man, Kummel, not just a great one.' Lightly she rapped on the book with her unringed finger, and the sound was jarringly similar to the odd tocking in Kummel's head just moments before. 'It's we who are lucky to have him. But we can all be of service to one another, *ja*? Each in our own little way?'

Her line of vision was now running past his shoulder, through the window, out into the fields and hedgerows over which the sun was spilling its last syrupy rays. Her look was so keen that Kummel glanced behind himself.

A short way up the line a town was gathering into view. Briefly it had the appearance of a little forest itself, sprawled across a sudden shoulder of land in front of a streaming crimson sunset that made it look more like a picture-book plate than a view through smoky glass.

'Cassel – my mother's home,' said the Fräulein, in a tone stretched so flat by her smile that she could have been identifying the next station of the cross.

TEN

After the prince left the three spinners' cottage, the forest changed. The sun's warmth and then its light diminished. He seemed to be moving through a region of perpetual murk, even though the tree line here was not especially high, nor was the sky exceptionally cloudy. It was as if a veil had been slung between heaven and earth, and had he not been marching ahead with such zest he might have found the new atmosphere forbidding.

Not wanting to rip his fine new clothing on undergrowth, he kept to clearly defined cinder tracks. At nights he took off his coat, folded it and put it in a sheltered place, determined to look his best when he arrived at the palace, for he had no doubt that his appearance then would matter. But the deeper into the east he travelled, the harder he found it to rouse himself each morning. He could not say why. The gradients were no steeper than in the west, and he felt as full of energy as ever. The tiredness seemed rather to steal up from the outside, swarming all over him like a blast of cool air from the heights ahead, stilling him from his skin inwards until he felt numbed to the core. And every time he woke he would feel more reprieved than refreshed.

The higher he climbed, the more worn the track became. He could see that once it had been wider, but still it bore marks of recent use: deep hoof-prints, dried-out cartwheel ruts. Occasionally when he hacked at clumps of wild grass he found roadside stones inscribed with numbers and eastward-pointing arrows. The small carved crowns told him that this had been a major highway, leading to and from a royal court. This had to be his road.

But although some of the trails were fresh, there were fewer people in this canton than anywhere else on his travels, fewer signs of any kind of life. Even the budding branches looked arrested in their growth, and the flowering shrubs were cobwebbed. The air itself tasted stale and thin. From the forest floor to the highest point in the canopy there were seldom birdcalls or rustlings.

It was as if the Creator had pressed a finger to His lips to show that He wanted this part of His garden to take a deep collective breath. And as the prince headed towards a great shoulder of rock, the highest point of which was obscured by tangled overgrowth, he found himself taking softer, more measured footsteps for fear of disturbing the deep, unnatural calm.

The track ran to the base of a smooth, almost sheer blue-grey rock face. As he drew closer he saw that steps had been cut into it, switchbacking upward to left then right then left again, disappearing altogether where they were overhung by conifers. Just looking at the climb made his bones ache, and with dusk about to fall he decided to bed down, then go up at sunrise.

The region's peculiar stillness thickened as he eased off his top clothes and settled into a mossy niche. Fatigue swept down the steps towards him like a gust of spores. Squinting up, he caught his first glimpse of the rock face's summit: crowned not, as he had anticipated, by a palace's turrets but by dense growths of what looked like briar, picked out in silhouette against the darkening sky like an enormous crown of thorns.

He closed his eyes and lost consciousness in peacefully easy stages, as if some soft-footed old retainer were edging around inside the shuttered room of his mind, carefully draping the darkest dustsheets over one piece of furniture after another until, finally, nothing at all was left on view.

He slept for what felt like weeks, aware of the sun rising and setting but unable to shift himself. The Creator's finger was no longer pressed to His lips but was pinning down the sleeper himself. Then, without warning – as if the finger had snapped against its thumb – it was over.

The prince's eyes opened on a mellow, golden morning and where, before, all his limbs had felt heavier than iron, now he was supple again and ready to spring to his feet. But before he could even look up at the crag, he heard a low cry of '*Heh*' and swung around to find that he was not alone.

A small, stooped man in a wig stood poised over the pile of prince's clothing and the sword on its belt. 'You!' cried the prince, leaping up and grabbing him by his velvet collar. 'Steal my property, would you?'

The man gave a strangled cry. His wig fell off to reveal a mass of unkempt white hair. He looked so ancient and afraid, the prince knew at once that he himself had nothing to fear. But something in the man's eyes kept his anger hot, and he went on holding him by the collar like a child's rag monkey.

'No, you misunderstand!' he protested. 'I'm no thief. I'm the palace chamberlain, like my father and grandfather before me – or I would be if the palace were still occupied. I mean neither you nor your property any harm. Quite the opposite!'

The prince let him go with a frown, then turned aside and

quickly stepped into his clothes. The chamberlain meanwhile fetched his wig but kneaded it between his fingers instead of putting it back on. 'Forgive me for running the risk of angering you again,' he stammered, 'but you're intending to climb up to the Rose King's palace in these fine clothes?'

'What if I am?' The prince kept his eyes on his swordbelt as he buckled it back on, then carefully fitted his own wig into place. This was even less easy than before. His hair had grown to a great length since he had fallen asleep. His jaw, too, was now covered by a thick beard.

'They will be quite ruined,' the chamberlain replied. 'It has happened so many times before.'

'Again, what business is that of yours?' And when he then glared at the man, he realized how much he looked like his own father, the watchman. His dark coat and breeches also reminded him of his father's uniform. It went some way to explaining why the mere sight of him was so irritating.

'The way up to the palace is impassable. It has been for more years than anyone remembers. No one can get through. I've buried the bones of so many princes who died in the attempt.'

'Then patched up their clothing and sold it on?'

'It's not the kind of living I would choose. I swear I had no designs on your own clothes. It simply saddened me to see yet another young man about to waste himself. I wish only to dissuade you from trying to climb any higher. The palace is surrounded by a species of briar that blunts even the sharpest sword.'

The prince drew himself up, his hand clamped on his sword-hilt. He did not have the slightest doubt that – by his own lights – this chamberlain was telling the truth. But it was no kind of truth he wanted to recognize. *It's all a question of time,* the lip-girl had told him. *She should be ready,* his mother had said, *for whoever comes when the time is right.*

'You say that the palace is deserted?' he asked. 'But what of the Rose King's daughter?'

The chamberlain went on helplessly twisting his wig in his hands, his head tilted like a bird's, presumably to hear with his better ear. 'There is a princess, yes, but she sleeps, just as this whole region sleeps. For years she has slept in the palace's oldest watchtower, ever since the wise woman cast her spell.'

'Spell?'

'To avert the princess's death after pricking her finger on the poisoned spindle.'

'Spells, poisons,' laughed the prince, stroking his beard, enjoying the new sound of authority in his voice, coupled with a new confidence in himself and his powers. 'You make it sound like a children's game. It's only ever a question of time, of whether the time is right. And this is my time now.'

The chamberlain peered up at him. 'How far have you come?' he asked in a different tone. 'From which canton?'

The prince described where it lay as he made some final adjustments to his lapels and ruff. It was a bright day full of the perfumes of spring and the air bristled with birdsong. I am a prince, he told himself, and it was true.

'So you heard in the west of the enchantment?' the chamberlain persisted. 'Of the princess whose sentence of death was commuted to this term of sleep? Who told you these things? Who sent you? Was it a woman?'

Instead of answering, the prince strode past him to the place where the steps began. '*Term*, you say,' he called over his shoulder. '*Term*. All terms come to an end, don't they?'

The chamberlain, still worrying at his wig, followed closely behind to keep him within hearing range. Disregarding his own safety, he plucked at the prince's coat and stopped him in his tracks. 'Think again, I beg you. You have come as far as you need to. You can go on from here to any number of other places. Why throw your life away? And maybe not only your own?'

The younger man swung around so abruptly that the chamberlain lost his balance and fell to the rutted ground. 'What do you know of my life?' he shouted, 'Or of how far I *need* to go? I would rather lose my life this way than keep it and end up like you, picking the clothes off dead men's backs. What kind of a life is that? Have *you* never dreamed of going all the way up to the princess?'

The little man rested back on his elbows in the dust, shameless now in defeat. 'The palace,' he said levelly, 'has always been beyond my reach. I accepted that many years ago. Go up then if you must, but you will not come down with that same smile on your face. For even if you find your way unobstructed, my friend, you will still be far from the end of your journey.'

Then he did an odd thing. With his rheumy eyes fixed on the prince's, he took a small clay pipe from his pocket and began to tap it, hard but irregularly, on the buckle of his shoe. The sound echoed around them both, seeming for a moment to silence the birdsong. And it was uncannily similar to the noise that came from the prince's mother's room at nights when she was spinning.

Disconcerted, he turned away, set his boot on the first step in the switchback, then began his climb up to where the princess waited.

ELEVEN

Gustchen came earlier that night than in Hanau, Steinau or Marburg. After his seizure on the train, Grimm was surprised she had let him out of her sight at all since dinner. He stayed at his table when she entered, swinging around in his chair to face her. As usual, he had changed into his grey cotton dressing-gown and Oriental curl-toed slippers after rigorously washing. Now he put down his pen next to the heap of *Wörterbuch* slips.

Auguste closed the door behind her with a soft click, her pale skin translucent in the light of the dresser lamp. She was clutching Willi's old Christmas edition of the *Tales for Young and Old*. 'You look more like yourself,' she said. 'Your colour. Your eyes. Have you felt quite well this evening? No more giddiness?'

'Gustchen, my dear, you mustn't worry yourself so. It was travel sickness. Nothing more than that.'

'But you still refuse to let a doctor come and verify it?'

'Absolutely! Why should I waste his time?' Or, thought Grimm, put himself at the mercy of some underqualified quack who would probably relieve him of litres of blood and prescribe a regimen of quite unnecessary laxatives?

As Gustchen made herself smile, he sneezed messily, then sneezed again. He turned away to blow his nose, wondering why she came to him like this every evening. As a child she had used to call in on him too, far more often than either of her brothers. But even then, once she was in his company, she seemed to lose her tongue, or perhaps the need to speak.

'Are you satisfied with the room?' she asked earnestly.

He waved at the restrained soft brown walls and impressive lion's-head door handles. Doubtless on Dortchen's advice, she had chosen the inn well, at the edge of the Wilhelmshöhe forest park to the west of the noisy town with its wine parlours and tobacco shops. He had even seen swans from the lake flying past his window. '*Gemütlich*,' he nodded. 'Oh, entirely *gemütlich*.'

Easing himself to his feet, feeling a new battered numbness in his right arm and side, he crossed to the high-backed chair beside the brass bed. It was covered in red velvet that had run a little shabby and he pointed out an indelible white patch. 'See,' he went on, sitting and pressing the back of his head directly against it, 'they have even been letting out the room to men of precisely my own height! And look at this.'

Again he stood, pausing to gather himself before stepping over to the dresser. On top of it stood two small ceramic figures in eighteenth-century dress. 'We had a pair of ornaments like these, your father and I.' As he spoke, he took the little man's head between his thumb and forefinger and to Gustchen's evident surprise plucked it up out of its neck socket. On setting it back down, he tapped it so that it nodded for several moments. *Weaving, we are weaving*, he thought as dizzily he watched it lose momentum. That old line of verse seemed not to want to leave him.

He returned to his desk and tried to hide his fresh discomfort as he sat. It was as if someone had been methodically punching and kicking his side for hours without him noticing. Gustchen's glazed smile suggested unease of her own, and she showed no intention of saying good night and leaving. 'I've almost finished reading the *Tales* now,' she said in a small voice.

'*Ach*, that must be a relief to you.'

She looked past him at the velvet-covered chair. 'They intrigue me. They're so passionate. So full of quite savage . . . emotion.' She smiled, as if puzzled. 'And I must admit that I find some of them very frightening, in ways that I didn't when I was younger. The imagery: it's often so *barbarous*.'

'It's the way they were told to us,' Grimm shrugged, and her wide-eyed expression encouraged him to go on. 'Sometimes, perhaps, we mightn't have liked what we heard, but we had to record it faithfully. What a people says is, after all, essentially what that people *is*. But of course, our German versions of some of the stories are nowhere near as "barbarous" as they might have been.'

This seemed to be news to her. 'Really? Which ones?'

'Oh, *Dornröschen* is an example. Sleeping Beauty.' Again she widened her eyes at him. 'Ours ended with the prince's arrival: the awakening and the marriage. In other versions this was no more than the mid-point in a much more grisly tale. Look at Perrault the Frenchman's variant, *La Belle au bois dormant*.' Grimm's lips twitched as he recalled it himself: the war, the prince's enforced absence, the hideous appetites of the figure who then took the reins of power . . .

Gustchen did not reply. Her averted gaze had become fixed. 'Why have you gone back to the *Tales* now, Gustchen?' Grimm asked her.

She looked at him as if she had forgotten he was there; she could almost have sleepwalked into the room. 'I was interested in reading them in the place where you collected them. I thought it might make me look at them differently.'

'It was a long time ago, Gustchen. Another world.'

'But isn't that time still very vivid to you?' The colour rose so high in her cheeks that she looked overheated. And then to his consternation he saw her lower lip tremble.

'In certain respects, *ja*.'

'And returning to these places – doesn't it stir more memories? Of how it was for you then? Perhaps of the passions that you, yourself, felt?'

He held her eye and thought hard. Her lip still shook. Her pretty fingers were locked so tight around the book that she could have been trying to keep all the dwarves and ogres and fairies inside from spilling out. Obviously this mattered a great deal to her, but Grimm had no clear idea what she wanted him to say, and on trawling his mind all he could summon up were headwords from his *Wörterbuch* slips: compound nouns with the root *Familie-*. In the German dictionary he had used as a boy, and still kept in his Berlin study, there had been only five of them; now he was dealing with almost ninety.

Before he could speak a knock came from outside. With some relief Grimm nodded and Gustchen stepped back to open the door.

'What are you writing there?'

Jacob started as his mother spoke behind him. By instinct he angled an arm around his letter, taking care not to smudge the damp ink, but when he heard no sound of her entering the room with her stick, he pushed back his chair from the bureau and stood to face her in the doorway. 'Only a letter to von Savigny, Mother.' He smiled. 'So, you feel well enough to rise today. That's excellent.'

She nodded and pulled her dressing-gown tighter at the neck, half turning with a squint from the bright morning sunlight that filled Jacob's bedroom. 'Von Savigny?' she repeated, as if by saying the name she could match it to a face somewhere in her increasingly clouded memory. And she succeeded. 'He's well connected, yes? He should be able to put work your way.'

Jacob smiled. Now he half turned too, away from her towards the brilliant window, so that – not for the first time during these difficult months – they faced opposite directions as they spoke. 'I'm not asking him for help of that sort.'

'I see.'

'I know that he would do whatever he could, Mother, but we live in a different world now.' Jacob was still not sure that she fully grasped why: because the old Reich had been swept away and the Hessians no longer had an Elector but a Corsican puppet king. ('Kings, Electors, Woodchoppers,' she would say. 'What's the difference?') But he wished she understood why he had resigned indignantly from the Hessian War College on its transformation into the commissariat through which Bonaparte's troops of occupation were carrying out their official depradations. By the time those vultures were finished, there would scarcely be a gilt candlestick left in all Hesse.

'So what are you telling your von Savigny? There's little enough news from here.'

The neighbour's quail, kept in a cage hanging from a lower window, started up its haunting cry. 'I'm sending him some copies of old stories. He has asked for them, partly to entertain his little three-year-old daughter, but also because we often discuss the possibility of Willi and I making a collection and getting them published.'

He was glad he could not see her expression as he said this. She had little patience with the brothers' interest in antiquarianism, and less than ever now that she depended on charity from relatives to keep her own family solvent. She had even stopped drinking tea because she could no longer afford the sugar to make it palatable.

'And which stories are you so conscientiously copying out for three-year-old girls?'

'Oh, *The Moon and his Mother*, *Rumpelstiltskin*, *The Juniper Tree* . . . all well known to you.'

'I should think they are! It was I who first told them to *you*! But do you really think anyone would publish such things, or pay good thalers to read them? Aren't they just the product of idle minds, women sitting spinning, mothers whiling away long hours with their infants? Isn't that right? *Isn't it*?'

Struck mute by her vehemence, Jacob glanced at her haggard profile. She had once been such a fleshy, large-eyed woman but the bones of her face seemed to have been pared away, leaving no shape for the folds of greying skin to follow. At fifty-three she had already endured twelve sorry years without a husband, and still she faced a future with six grown children, not one of whom was settled. After so much disillusionment, what could Jacob say about his little *Tales*? It had never been easy for him to speak with his mother as she wanted to be spoken with. Now it had become well nigh impossible. But, thanks be to God, he did not have to negotiate with her on his own . . .

'You do both yourself and the tales an injustice, *Mutti*,' said a breezy new voice from along the corridor.

Reprieved, Jacob watched his mother turn that way as the smiling Willi loped into view, still bleary from sleep and tightening the cord to their father's old dressing-gown. 'In all the Germanies the stories that used to pass from generation to generation are no longer so current. Unless they're saved – in the way that Jacob wants to save them: precisely as they are told – then our precious heritage might be lost altogether.'

'And would that matter?' She turned to fire the question levelly at Jacob.

'Yes Mother, I believe it would.'

'Even though your beloved "Germanies" themselves are being wiped off the map, as you never seem to tire of reminding us?'

Jacob could only flush at that, but Willi chuckled and cleared his throat to suppress a cough. 'Oh, then all the more so, *Mutti!*' he said. 'The tales contain our *völkisch* spirit, our vital soul. The fact that we share them helps to make us a *Volk* in the first place. Isn't that what you say, Old One?' He beamed at his brother with just a flicker of anxiety, as ready as ever to stand corrected.

Jacob gave him a grateful nod, but in the moments that followed he and his mother continued to stare past each other as the quail piped outside above the rush of traps and carts in the Marktgasse. Is this, Jacob could almost hear her thinking, why he gave up the law, gave up his job? For Dorothea Zimmer Grimm, it was always a matter of 'good thalers'. And while it was true that he had never found a way of talking with her, she too had never found a way of speaking to him, at least not since telling him all her wondrous tales.

'I apologize for disturbing you,' she said at last, then clattered back down the corridor towards her own bedroom.

As Willi stepped aside, Jacob crossed to the doorway. 'Is there anything you wish me to fetch?' he called to her hunched back, suddenly hating to see her so reduced by losing the one person she had loved best, and appalled at the thought that one day he might be similarly diminished. 'Is there anything at all that I can do for you?'

She appeared not to hear him before she entered her room and firmly closed the door behind her. Willi at once laid a hand on his sleeve. 'Go on with your letter,' he said softly. 'I'll go in to her presently. Don't fret yourself now.'

Jacob stared down at the pale claw of a hand, so fragile that he hardly felt its weight. Just days before, his invalid brother had told him of a recurrent dream he had, no more than a tableau really: night after night he would picture the two of them and their mother back in the Steinau Amtshaus, but he himself would always feel like an intruder alongside them. That was all. Beginning, middle and end. Poor, dear Willi. How could he not know how vital he was?

'Your letter,' Jacob's younger brother urged him again, and then he added in a chesty approximation of their dead father's voice, '*Never be distracted from the written word!*' They both gave a rueful laugh then went their separate ways.

Auguste drew back the door to let Kummel in, carrying his master's nightcap of warm beer mixed with egg, sugar and nutmeg. The old man smiled appreciatively as he put it down, then watched him cross to the window to close the looped muslin curtains.

Gustchen too followed the serving man with her eyes. Grimm wondered if she was going to stand like a rather wan statue through all the time it took Kummel to turn down his bed and lay out his clothes for the morning. Gingerly he picked up his glass and sipped from the potion's foaming head. Immediately it soothed the clawing in his throat, but did nothing for the pins-and-needles ache that now burned down the length of his right arm.

'Sir,' asked Kummel from the window, 'shall I prepare your best coat and boots for church tomorrow?'

'Church? Ah yes. *Bitte schön.*'

'Apapa,' Gustchen burst into life. 'About tomorrow. Would you excuse me from accompanying you in the morning? I'll worship later in the day. There are some matters I have to attend to, arrangements to make for the last part of our journey . . .' Her tremulous voice faded to a whisper. Grimm could not imagine what kind of travel arrangements she might need to make on a Sunday but her mood was so uncertain that he simply nodded his head.

'Of course I don't mind. Whatever suits you best, *Liebchen*.'

'I am sure that Kummel,' she added, causing the servant to pause and turn on the point of drawing back the drape that marked off the dressing-room, 'will be willing to escort you.'

Grimm did not miss the momentary widening of Kummel's eyes, as if he had been bitten simultaneously by two fleas, before he obediently tilted his close-cropped head. 'I won't trouble Kummel unless he wants to come with me,' said the old man, remembering how cowed he had been inside St Catherine's at Steinau. 'I'm quite capable of making my own way into town and back.' Again he noticed Kummel's eyes enlarge, this time at Auguste. Not for the first time, she reminded Grimm very powerfully indeed of her own mother when Dortchen had been no more than thirty.

'No,' she insisted, with some of Dortchen's stubbornness too. 'I should feel *much* happier if you weren't alone, Apapa.'

'*Ach*, we'll see.' Grimm was not going to argue in front of the servant, but her anxiety about him seemed to be increasing by the minute, and she did not even know yet about the numbness. He took another sip of the mixture, listening to Kummel brushing down his coat behind the drape. Still Gustchen stood as if nailed to the linoleum, like a child holding out for a promised bedtime story.

'You look tired,' he told her. 'You need a good night's rest.'

'It's true that I'm not sleeping well,' she admitted as Kummel re-emerged, carrying Grimm's shoes for cleaning. He hesitated to cross between them while they still spoke. 'But you should rest more too, not stay up woodchopping all through the night.'

'Ah, only the young need to sleep. The young and the beautiful!'

'Fräulein,' Kummel murmured, 'if you're not sleeping well, then would you like me to bring you a nightcap too? Some warm milk, perhaps? I could bring it up when I return the Professor's shoes.'

Grimm watched her wrench her gaze around. Her smile flickered but her eyes stayed anxious. 'Yes,' she wavered. 'Yes, some milk would be good. *Danke.*'

With a nod of his head, the servant effectively indicated that she should turn and precede him out of the room. Blinking, as if she really had just sleepwalked in and now found herself waking up in unfamiliar surroundings, she meekly did for the younger man what she had seemed so reluctant to do for the older.

TWELVE

The climb was easier than the prince had expected. The higher he went, the less overgrown the switchback path became, and the air grew sweeter with every step. All the old sluggishness was gone. And as for the impenetrable barrier of thorns, he never had to draw his sword. All he passed were particoloured acanthus, hyacinths and primulas.

The palace lay some way back from the edge of the bluff. He saw it for the first time only after reaching the top of the steps, and he paused to marvel at its beauty in the clear, warm sunlight. Sprawling yet delicate, it stood frost-white with towers at each corner, adorned by golden cupolas, encircled by linden avenues and terraces of vines. Summer fragrances threaded the air, but no scent was as deliciously strong now as that of fully formed roses.

Crossing the sun-striped courtyard he heard the echoes of his footsteps linger as if the sweet, starved air were caressing them. Sound had been gone from here for so long – sound, heat, colour, movement. The old man below had talked of a term, but more than just a princess had served the sentence. As she had slept, so had all the world around her. Now there was a grateful awakening, matched inside the prince by a hunger sharper than he had felt for any of the forest women.

He sensed the palace sigh as he entered it, from the great marble atrium's ceiling to the base of each intricately inlaid pillar. In the feasting hall his eye was caught at once by a sparkling array of jewellery on a tall dresser. Looking closer, he recognized twelve golden caskets, each with its lid thrown back to show a cutlery set encrusted with precious stones.

Smiling, he moved on. As he passed through the concert room, the gaming hall, the day rooms and guest suites, the sunlight seemed to trail behind him like a cloak, stirring each stone corner into life, each oaken beam and embroidered drape – until he reached the stairway to the oldest tower.

He had thought his climbing was over but the stair wound higher and higher, ringing under his spit-wiped hussar's boots. He considered all the princes who had set out hoping to make this final climb. So many men over so many years; so many victims of the thickets of thorn. They would not have smelled these roses. It was as if he was being showered with countless petals, swimming through their perfume where before he had tried to swim against sleep.

He came to where the steps all stopped. To his right a window let in light through an age-worn lattice of lead. To his left a narrow passage ran down to a shadowy spinning garret, its door ajar, a tarnished key in its lock. *When you arrive at the palace, it'll be clear what you have to do.* From his mother's darkened little room to the top of this tower, his route had seemed to be measured out in spindles. He looked through the glass.

The valley sheered away as if from the crest of a wave, verdant, sunlit, silent. At his coming, the Rose King's inner realm had been kissed back to life, right down to the flies that looped and circled outside this window. The full term, he told himself; surely this was the full term now. He turned from the window and strode down the passage.

When he pushed back the garret's door, sunshine speared in from a high oriel window, dappling a huge pile of flax beside a narrow bed, striking silver from a spinning wheel's polished spokes. He felt the princess's presence before he saw her.

Still in the doorway he let his eyes fall. He could see her only from behind, and her sinuous line made him shiver. Down on the tiled floor, where she lay with such grace amid thin scatters of straw, the new warmth played on her upper hip and shoulder. Her unbound hair was as golden as the flax, shot through with silver flashes like those struck from the wheel.

And it was just as the chamberlain had told him: thrust behind her was one slender arm and on stepping closer he saw the ancient flakes of blood turned to dust on her thumb where the poisoned spindle had pricked her. He unbuckled his swordbelt then silently sank to his knees.

Leaning forward, until his lips were almost touching her skin, with a tiny puff of breath he blew away every last rust-coloured grain. The wound in her flesh had healed over; her thumb was as smooth, alabaster-white and unblemished as the rest of her arm below the short sleeve of her ivory nightgown.

The garret was so cramped that he had to stand before stepping across her to a space on the floor, beside the wheel, where he could kneel again and look at her face. His breathing was shallow, erratic. She, by contrast, breathed to a deep and regular rhythm, like the babies at his mother's house when they finally stopped their night-time snorting and thrashing.

Back down on his knees, he put out a hand, drew aside a hank of her fine, straight hair with his fingertips and hooked it behind her ear. He was profoundly glad then that she was still asleep. If she had returned his gaze, he would not have dared to feast his eyes for so long. She seemed in truth more like an exquisite tomb effigy than a living, breathing young woman. Her face in repose, resting on an outstretched arm, was small and symmetrical. And under a freckled nose and apple cheekbones, her parted lips curved up so rose-red and full that, quite without thinking, he stooped lower and fastened his mouth on to hers.

It was as if the thorns and bushes that had grabbed the other princes like hands had become this lovely girl's flesh and held him. She seemed to be all around him, although just their lips were touching, and only chastely, lightly. His heart rose to all the life trapped inside her.

She should be ready now . . . Not once had it crossed his mind since beginning his ascent that she would not be his, nor he hers. With their lips resting gently together, he looked at the mauve semi-spheres of her eyelids and again he was thrilled by her stillness: the lack of any need for him to smile, speak, excuse himself, explain. He wanted no kind of language but this.

He drew his face away and kissed her languid arm. The taste of her was different there, fresh-cut grass where her lips had been dew-soaked roses. It was strange to feel the hair of his new beard and moustache fold down against her flesh, but her scents now clung to him more closely than if he had stayed clean-shaven. He eased himself back until his feet were against the wall below the oriel, so he could run his lips across her shin and the faint line of shadow at the hem of her gown.

In kissing her he touched her for the first time with the flat of his hand, soothing the backs of her slim legs as if to rub away all her sleep from the ankles upwards. His hand moved to her outer thigh, her waist, her ribs; the fabric of her gown lay almost weightless against the backs of his fingers. He came to the swell of her breast. Her gown was loose and had risen with his arm. He ducked his head to the place where his fingers had reached and, when his tongue brushed her there, she sighed.

He did not pull away as she stirred. The small sounds she made, her limbs' slight easy shiftings, were those of a woman still deeply asleep. But then she slid a little way from him, on to her back.

The sun streamed in hotter through the oriel. The prince watched her legs straighten. There was room now to stretch himself beside her in the straw. Briefly letting her go, he tore off the wig that had never fitted him properly and tossed it into the flax. Then he shrugged off the blue beaded coat and threw that behind him too.

His mouth searched out her lips again, running his tongue between them, pressing against the shield of her teeth. His steady hand snaked down to her flat belly. Once more she shuffled herself: pushing up her face in sleep until his tongue was rough against hers.

The floor was hardly softened by the straw. Still she slept, when he was sure that she would have woken. Two paces away stood a bed, but it was too far. The thorns and bushes of her held him too fast. The chamberlain's words rushed back – *You will not come down with that same smile on your face* – and then he forgot them again as he arched himself above her.

THIRTEEN

Through an oversight the innkeeper had given Auguste a better appointed room than her Apapa: a separate dressing-room, a broader bed, some rather fine Turkish rugs on the floorboards and a small wooden balcony from which, earlier that evening, she had watched the sun set over Wilhelmshöhe park.

Seated outside again on the wrought-iron chair, blowing the ink dry on the square of paper on which she had been writing, she failed to hear Kummel's discreet knock when he returned from below stairs with her glass of milk.

If he had hit the oak with a cudgel she might have been just as oblivious. Nor was she noticing any of the silhouetted alders against the pale moonlit sky. All she saw was Grimm's elfin grin as he sat in that stained velvet chair and played around with those silly little figures. She knew he did not become so skittish by accident. He could not fool her now. This had always been one of his ways of fortifying the emotional frontier between himself and the rest of the world, and all along its length he could have posted hand-scrawled placards: *Verboten! Verboten! Verboten!*

Tears welled in her eyes. Plainly he was suffering from more than mere travel sickness or a headchill. He had shuffled so feebly from desk to chair to dresser: his skin almost transparent, eyes rheumy, lips pinched. He looked less like a man at the end of a month's vacation than one in need of weeks of bedrest. And although he gamely tried to hide his discomfort she still wanted more from him. *The most precious . . . I've only ever been looking after her for you.* What did it mean? Earlier she had vowed to edge him at last towards the question. But her botched attempt had been about as subtle as cutting down corn with cannons. Her own crass selfishness revolted her. She bowed her head in the cool freesia-scented air and cried so hard that when Kummel knocked a second time, again she did not hear. But at the click of the door opening, she sprang to her feet to face it.

'Forgive me, Fräulein, I knocked twice . . .'

He looked taken aback, less by the fact that she was inside, framed by the doorway to the balcony, than by the way she continued to weep, with her free hand clasped over the fist that held the now crumpled square of paper. But he was discreet. Unimpeachably discreet. He seemed on the point of backing out again with the glass of milk still on its salver.

Auguste could neither speak nor make a gesture. She stood up straight but felt her shoulders heave as her head bobbed blindly like one of the figurines on her Apapa's dresser. And down below her balcony, although it was so late, voices wafted up in the dark: more children – always these children – two small boys bitterly squabbling.

She heard Kummel put down the salver, but through the blur of tears she could not be quite sure where. She waited for him to speak, excuse himself, maybe even question her, but no sound came. She half turned away, back to the balcony and the children's quarrel, raising a hand to her eyes as the tears flooded on, tears not just for herself but to be seen and heard.

Yet here – now – she had no audience. She heard the door click gently shut and once again she was left alone. The model male servant was, of course, too tactful even to notice her distress.

With a tiny sigh she sank to the carpeted floor, first to her knees and then, keeling over, on to her side, starting to crush her crinoline. But she did not fall completely.

She felt his hand from behind, taking her lower elbow, then his other hand gripping her upper, bared arm.

He was strong – stronger than she had imagined from his relatively slight build. In one smooth movement he twisted her around, but instead of raising her he dropped down to be with her, and the bodice of her dress came across his raised knee and her face pressed into the coat that had once been her father's. Its camphor smell sobered her but even that could not stop the tears.

'I'm ridiculous . . . So *dumm!* . . . So full of pity for myself . . .'

He did not speak, but lodging her against him he took his hand from her arm. She felt his fingers at the low chignon at the back of her head, pushing up through the hair above it, drawing her even closer.

'He won't *speak* to me . . . He won't let me near . . . And I need to be near . . . I need so badly to *know* . . .'

Her crying, more than the pressure of his hands as she shuddered, forced her to stop trying to talk. She gripped the back of his coat and felt him hoist her higher. As her face came away from the fabric, she smelled tobacco, then the oily, musky scent of the skin on his neck. Her mouth came against his thickly stubbled cheek, lips parted in her fight for breath.

Still he said nothing. No soothing, no coaxing, no sympathy. It was as if her wretchedness did not matter to him, as if it were no more significant a part of her than the crinoline that moments before she had felt crack and splinter. Here on the floor he was holding only her, not her unhappiness, and this so astonished her that when he shifted her again to bring their mouths together, his kiss seemed almost the lesser liberty.

Leloup, the gentleman usher, led Jacob through a succession of day rooms to a terrace above a beautiful sweep of the park they were now calling Napoleonshöhe. Immediately below lay the swan lake, its calm surface glistening under a hot spring midday sun.

'Your librarian, Majesty,' Leloup announced, standing aside to let Jacob pass. Beside King Jérôme Bonaparte of Westphalia – unshaven and wrapped in a gorgeous Oriental red silk dressing-gown – Simeon, Beugnot and two royal secretaries sat at the green baize table, poring over financial papers and murmuring among themselves. The young king turned.

'Monsieur Grimm,' he declared (he spoke no word of German). 'I have an additional post for you, if you want it. Auditor to the Council of State? There would, of course, be more cash. Your combined annual salary should as a result then amount to some thousand thalers. You'll take it, *oui*?'

Oui. Jacob's lips parted but he could not immediately speak. The raise would be paid for by more crippling taxes than ever on his fellow Hessians, yet he could not afford to make a stand. 'You are very kind, Majesty,' he said, in a French more formally correct than his master's.

A thousand thalers. How his mother would have clapped her hands. For the first time since leaving Steinau, the cheeseparing could end. And Jacob already guessed that his new responsibilities would be no more demanding than those he had taken up as the king's private librarian only weeks after his poor mother's death. Since then his chief duty had lain in breaking in this infernally embroidered court uniform.

'I dare say the extra income will be useful,' Bonaparte's improvident younger brother went on, in no hurry to return to his discussions as to how to bleed Westphalia drier still. 'I hear your brother is currently in poor health.'

'Yes, Majesty. But with him the condition is almost permanent. His heart isn't strong, he has problems with his breathing.' Already Jacob had worked out that he could now send Wilhelm for the cure at Halle. Suddenly all the mercury ointments and magnetic amulets were no longer beyond his budget, and with enormous pleasure he pictured his brother's smile when he heard the news. 'He depends very largely on me.'

'*Eh bien*, but isn't that the way – the elder brother looking after the younger?' There spoke a man who had been looked after by his own elder brother to the tune of a kingdom, ten million francs a year and the delightful Catherine von Württemberg for a wife. 'So do you now collect up all your old fairytales alone?'

'When my brother is indisposed, yes.'

'You collect them from the local ale wives, I understand.'

'From whoever remembers them best, Majesty. They've been told for centuries in all the Germanies. They are an important part of our nation's heritage.'

The king's eyes glinted at that. 'Ah now, do correct my error, but I rather thought these tales belonged to us *all*. Aren't they part of a more universal heritage? *Snow White, La Belle au bois dormant* . . . I distinctly recall our own Monsieur Perrault including these in his collection.'

'With respect, each people tells a story in its own way, suppressing some elements, elaborating on others.'

'Yes?'

'For example, *Dornröschen* – our Cassel version of *La Belle* – ends, unlike Monsieur Perrault's, when the princess wakes and marries her prince. Thus the evil principle – which might have been said to have caused all the trouble in the first place – goes unpunished.'

'And does that make your story better?'

'Neither better nor worse, Majesty. But it is ours. All these tales are our own. They have, as it were, the pure fragrance of the German forest.'

At that, the king's grin cracked his handsome face. Jacob knew he was being patronized, but he was glad to have spoken out. The least he could do was show pride in his fatherland, a land from which thousands less lucky than himself had already been conscripted to march east in the Corsican Emperor's ever advancing Grande Armée, just as all the treasured manuscripts and paintings travelled west.

'You're a Romantic, Monsieur Grimm,' the king nodded. 'I admire your passion.' Since his own passions ran to his hundred carriages and scarcely smaller number of mistresses, Jacob again saw this as gentle mockery. 'But you mentioned "an evil principle". That interests me. You mean the evil which caused the princess to sleep for so long?' Grimm nodded. 'So what happens in *your* story when this evil principle remains, as it were, at large?'

'That's where our story ends, Majesty. With the awakening. We know no more than that.'

'But where does the evil *go*? What becomes of it? Does it, perhaps, slink deeper into your fragrant German forest?'

Jacob frowned and was glad when Jérôme was distracted by a query from one of his secretaries. Straw out of straw, Jacob thought as he waited on the newly minted king; he was a pleasant enough fellow, but he spoke about evil as blithely as his brother talked of prosperity, liberty and equality. And although some of his 'modernizing' reforms – such as the emancipation of the Jews – were long overdue, they were carried out in an atmosphere of such dread and repression that no German could now drop a candy wrapper on Cassel's streets without a French policeman snatching it up to search for a subversive message. To all intents and purposes, the *Volk* here were living under a dictatorship.

'You may start work as Auditor next week,' Jérôme Bonaparte said, turning his attention back to the green baize table and effectively dismissing his librarian.

Jacob strode away through the castle to the library hall, his boots raising a louder echo than usual from the floors, until finally the tock-tock-tocking echo seemed to become an independent, irregular sound that made him feel quite nauseous. And as he went he ran his tongue restlessly over his teeth, scouring away the slick aftertaste of the language of occupation.

After the first searching kiss Auguste was too stunned to push herself away from Kummel. She was far from sure that she even wanted to, although she knew it was what she had to do.

Uncertain how long the kiss had lasted, she had stopped crying and was now fighting for breath against his coat's shoulder. His right hand still supported her neck, his fingers having dislodged two of the small combs in her hair. Since she was clinging to him with her right hand and her right side was lodged against his knee, his left hand had been free for some while to explore her shoulder, waist and bust.

He continued to pass his hand deftly across her as she gasped. She felt the coolness of his fingers through the linen of her high-necked dress: the coolness, the callouses, apparently even the contours of the skin whorls at his fingertips. 'Fool,' she breathed at last. 'I'm such a *fool* . . .'

But before she could whip herself further he wrenched her up, and again his lips dashed against hers, already open, and she pushed herself deep into the kiss.

Now his hand was at her thigh, screwing up the folds of her dress to find his way underneath. In the first of two almost overlapping instants Auguste greeted this by pressing her tongue so far into him that their teeth jarred. In the second she felt him slide her backwards off his knee and down on to the Turkish rug. She ripped away her mouth and cried out to redefine the frontier between them.

Twisting, she felt his grip on her tighten, then at once it loosened. Athletically she rolled to her knees and sprang to her feet, facing the balcony, the noise of the bickering children, the heavy scent of freesias. Closing her eyes, she gritted her teeth and stood motionless, as if all the scales of his touch might drop away, like her own inhibitions only moments before.

She heard him clamber to his feet and expected him to come up behind her. But he stayed his distance. Then he spoke, in a tone and with an accent that could have been another man's. 'Tell me,' he said. 'What is it you need to ask him?'

She smiled, her eyes still shut tight. *Him*. Incredibly Grimm had been out of her thoughts for more than a few moments. The man who would not speak. The man who had surely *never* wept. Slowly, she shook her head, unable to speak herself. Nor did she want to hear Kummel's steady, measured words. If he had stepped up and fastened a hand to each of her elbows she would have sunk back into him. Had an arm snaked around her waist, she would have turned.

'I could help you,' he said, from as far away as the wrong man can be from a woman. 'If you told me, could I not help?'

The frontier between them was now so clear again that she could shout back across it, without turning, without even trying to address him as an equal. 'I spoke out of turn,' she declared. 'Forget that I spoke. *Bitte schön,* forget what I said.'

She smoothed down her skirts with the flat of one hand and the balled fist of the other. With a pang she realized that he was waiting for her to speak again. To dismiss him? She thrust her left hand behind her, proffering the crumpled square of paper. 'Take it,' she ordered, wondering how his eyes looked as she felt his fingertips brush hers in obeying. 'It's an address. After church tomorrow, you are to escort the Professor to this house in the old town. He knows nothing about it yet, but the house is easy to find. Many years ago the Professor lived there. Say to him that I have asked you to escort him. I shall be there, waiting.' She heard him unfold then refold the paper. 'Thank you, Kummel.'

'And before that?' he asked. 'Do you wish me to shadow him again?'

Shadow sounded wrong, underhand, but it was precisely what she had forgotten to ask. 'I would be most grateful. After what happened on the train, most obliged.'

There was a pause. 'I wish you good night then,' a briefer pause, 'Fräulein.'

'Good night, Kummel. And thank you.'

At the click of the door she rushed forward to the balcony, as if catapulted, and came up hard against the white-painted balustrade that stood as high as her stomach. Gasping again for breath she stared directly down into a small rutted ash-and-earthen yard, enclosed by a coalhouse and several other lean-tos. The ground was littered with painted wooden toys – a clown, a hussar, a little steam engine lying on its side – but the quarrelling children were out of sight. All she could now hear was the sound of one of them crying, inconsolably.

Auguste stepped back and sank on to the cold wrought-iron chair. A bat rustled by at the edge of her vision. Somewhere out in the park a bird was piercing the sweet, smoky air with unsoothing regularity. Although her lips were parched, she could not put her tongue to them. She tilted back her head. Very soon, as if in answer to her own command, she felt the day's first spits of rain.

Half an hour later, drenched, she stood up and re-entered her room, able at last to hear her own thoughts again above the pulsing of her blood.

FOURTEEN

When it was over, he slid down beside her on the tiled floor and gazed up at the dazzling oriel window.

The sunlight seemed to mock all his earlier expectations. He had felt sure the princess was rising through her stupor towards him, that finally his own urgency would be matched sigh for sigh and gasp for gasp. But it had not happened. Now she lay beside him, as inert as when he had first seen her, her colour neither higher nor lower, the set of her lovely lips giving no hint of the part his tongue had played behind them. Ashamed, he rearranged her nightgown.

When you arrive at the palace, it'll be clear what you have to do. In his mind he retraced his steps down the tower's circling stairs, then back through the rooms that had all seemed to be stirring into life at his coming. He paused in his imaginary journey at the doorway to the feasting hall. There, on the dresser, stood the twelve golden caskets. That, at least, was as he had expected. That, perhaps, was all he should have laid his hands on.

He pushed himself up and drew his knees to his chest. Then, twisting away, he hurled himself into the pile of flax, burying his face. When he pulled back, he saw he had left an impression of his features, even to the texture of his beard.

The floor was cracked and uneven; he could not leave her lying there. He knelt beside her again, slipped one arm under her shoulders, another beneath her knees, then lifted her to the bed. She was so light that he remembered with a pang how, at the very end, he had let her take his full weight. Her bones seemed flat inside her flawless skin, which itself seemed no more substantial than the shaped patches of sunlight across this floor.

Reverently he laid her on the counterpane, and when he had plumped up the pillows he adjusted her position until she lay exactly as he had first seen her – on her side, knees slightly raised, with one arm trailing behind – facing the bare stone wall. Seeing her that way again, his interest returned. Afraid of becoming enmeshed a second time, he tore himself away without even stooping for a final kiss.

He was descending the stair when he remembered he had left his wig, fine coat and sword behind. It was not within him to go back and fetch them. If, without them, he no longer had the presence of a prince, then so be it.

Before leaving the palace he paused only to snatch up the first of the golden caskets. Like the princess, it was lighter and more delicate than he had anticipated. Snapping the lid shut on the jewel-encrusted cutlery, he swept out into the courtyard and strode past the vines and lindens to the steps in the bluff.

Already he was feeling time run faster at his departure than on his arrival. It was as if he had found his way through the labyrinthine forest with a spun thread tied to his ankle. And now – countless leagues away, in his cramped little home – the thread had been pulled tight to draw him back, through time and from this high forest crag.

At the foot of the steps he looked around in vain for the chamberlain. Instead a fresh white gelding waited, saddled and reined, with two bags strapped across its haunches. One contained bread and flasks, the other was empty, but when the prince slipped the casket inside, it fitted perfectly. As soon as he mounted the horse, it set off at great speed in the direction he needed.

Within the first hour he thundered past the lake near the three spinners' cottage. The horse's blistering pace did not slacken in all the time that followed.

Keeping to good forest highways it took him halfway home in twelve unbroken hours. He ate, drank and slept in the saddle. Each time he woke, the horse's hooves drummed on until, as the sun began to go down, he found himself within striking distance of the small walled town again.

They covered the last few leagues more slowly. At times he had been travelling so fast that he had not even been sure of the season. Now, at the great forest's outskirts, he saw the deep auburns and oranges of autumn, and through his silk shirt he felt a wind colder than any raised by the gelding's speed.

Lamps burned at the town's gatehouse, where the saddlesore rider dismounted. A watchman leaned out through a high barred window and began to demand identification, then fell silent on recognizing him. A second man unbolted and drew back a gate to admit both rider and horse. Then a third – as deferential as the others, perhaps on account of the visible changes in him – came up to lead the horse to the stables. But first the prince unfastened the nearer saddlebag and took out the golden casket, which sparkled in the light of the wall torches.

'Your father,' said the man at the window, 'has died in your absence.'

'Your mother's new child too,' put in the second.

'Both ripped away in the night, without a trace.'

He made no reply but headed directly for his home. Its outward appearance had not changed. The door at the front still hung loosely ajar from its perished upper hinge. First he went to the babies' bedroom, where all those left alive lay peacefully asleep.

The thin light of a candle showed under the door to his mother's room. He hesitated before knocking, since no sound came from inside.

'Why have you come back?' she called to him, neither irritably nor warmly, while he was still preparing himself to face her. He nudged back the door with the toe of his calf-leather boot. It swung away with a creak to show her sitting by the empty cradle. Hopefully, he held out in both hands the closed golden casket. Her eyes flashed in the candle light. For a moment her face looked bloated, misshapen. Her seated body too seemed heavier than he remembered, but then she smiled, sat straighter, and her old burdened beauty shone through again.

'I've brought it back for you, Mother,' he said, coming in and setting it down on the bed within her reach. 'It's yours by right. It will make all the difference. By selling just one of the jewels, you need never be poor again.'

She went on smiling at the casket, doubtless recalling the day when she had last seen it, but her hands stayed clasped in her lap.

'They told me about my father and the baby,' he said. 'I'm sorry.'

She gave no sign that she heard this. Her eyes were fixed on the casket, but her smile began to fade. 'What did you give for it?' she asked.

'How do you mean?'

She turned her level gaze on him. He had surely not been

wrong before. It was not just the comparison with the bird-boned sleeping princess; his mother *was* rounder, fuller-figured, somehow more swollen than she used to be. 'You brought away this casket, but what did you leave in its place?'

The question surprised him but an answer came at once, the only answer he could make, and the one that he believed his mother was looking for: 'I gave the princess my love.'

She nodded, satisfied. 'As a prince?'

'As a prince.'

'And so she let you bring the casket to me? As a token?'

He stared back. With its spinning wheel and heap of flax, the arrangement of his mother's room was almost exactly the same as the princess's garret, only here the bed was rather wider. He did not know what to say next. A token? He could not tell a bare-faced lie. Wordlessly he met his mother's eye, and it was she who lowered her gaze, ostensibly to admire his exquisite clothing.

'Didn't I tell you,' she said, 'that you were a prince?'

'You did.'

'I'm proud of you. Very proud. I trust that you, in turn, will be as proud of your own children.' She studied him hard in the next long silence. Then she relaxed, took the casket on to her lap, opened it and feasted her eyes. Her face could not have been any less bright or shining than the glittering knife, fork and spoon. 'So will you travel back to the palace immediately?' she asked without looking up. 'Or spend the night here first?'

The questions were startling enough, but the way she dwelt on the word 'here' reminded him so powerfully of her previous invitation to share her room with him that he found himself answering, 'Now. I'll go now. There's no space for me here.'

She said nothing. The trinket in her lap still seemed to mesmerize her. Yet, in spite of its huge significance, he had the impression she was even more thrilled that he had loved the princess. He could only presume that now, as always, she was putting him before herself, spurring him on to achieve the best that he could.

'I look forward,' she said, 'to the day of your wedding. When that time comes, you needn't come back to fetch us yourself. Send a coach. A coach will do perfectly well.'

'I will,' he said, swallowing.

'Travel safely,' she said, smiling at her baubles. And as soon as he left the house he saw the third watchman holding his tireless horse ready at the opened gate. Beyond it the now familiar sea of forest lapped and rippled in the moonlight, waiting to take him back in.

FIFTEEN

Kummel paused among the lakeside strollers to allow Grimm to amble on up to the baroque ornamental garden. Instead of spending the morning in church, the old man had been walking for two hours around the Wilhelmshöhe's follies, mock ruins and fountains, and still he showed no signs of flagging.

Kummel spat out his chew of tobacco and watched him climb closer to the monstrous statue of Herkules. The sun was warm on the backs of the park's many visitors, but the air in this quarter was cooled by the cascade that roared down a thousand steps to a fountain from the floodgates under the statue.

Before Grimm passed out of sight, Kummel set off again in pursuit. He was well hidden by other walkers parading up and down. Like the Fräulein and thousands of her fellow countrymen in this new machine age, they seemed almost mechanical themselves in their movements, wound up and set to march towards some even more impersonal future; a sea of sober, respectable faces, most of them indistinguishable from the faces he had grown up trusting. But even now one or two narrowed their eyes at him as they passed, just like that warmonger salesman in Steinau. They thought they knew, merely from the look of him. And they were right. They would always in the end be right.

As he climbed the gravelled path he played with the Fräulein's slip of paper. She had not come down for breakfast and when Kummel asked the Professor if he should wait on her in her rooms, he had virtually snapped back, 'That will not be necessary.' Still wondering what – if anything – might have changed between them, he came to the statue's massive base. On turning its first corner he pulled up short.

He had to, otherwise he would have collided with his little beige-faced master. Grimm stood facing him like a prize fighter squaring up: sideways on, knees bent, head lowered. But his left hand was placed as ever at the small of his back and he did not look wholly defiant.

'*Ach so*,' he panted, his nose and throat so clogged that it sounded as if a pillow were pressed to his face, 'this must be the medication hour?'

'Herr Professor . . .' Kummel began with a shrug.

'I couldn't shake you off in Marburg, and now I appear to be faring no better here.'

'Herr Professor, I can explain . . .'

'Ah, I *understand* well enough. You don't follow me out of any personal inclination. It's my dear Gustchen, *ja*? You put your heads together last night?' A glint in his eye suggested that he had chosen the words with his customary care.

'The Fräulein is extremely concerned about your welfare, sir. She simply asked me to make sure that you got into no difficulties . . .'

'She's terrified that I am going to *die*, Kummel. It gives her fancies.'

Again, the searching look. Then he wheeled around to continue on his way, gesturing to Kummel to walk alongside him now. The younger man fell in, the pace slowing as Grimm enjoyed the panoramic views of the parkland below.

'I like to seek out the high places,' he said, nodding, 'to see the frontiers between things.' He coughed, lengthily, and when he had finished Kummel decided to take a risk. Not such a huge risk, perhaps, given that the Professor seemed as well disposed as ever towards him that morning.

'Isn't it natural though, sir,' he asked, 'that the Fräulein should wish to look out for you?' The old man said nothing. 'She is so devoted to you, more like a daughter than a niece. And she does look to you for guidance . . .'

'Guidance?'

Kummel swallowed. He had come this far; there seemed no reason to go back. 'I know there are questions which she believes that only you can answer.'

'She's said this to you?'

He sounded so startled that Kummel shook his head. 'Forgive me, Herr Professor, if I speak out of turn. It's only what I see. What I notice.' They separated to let a young woman pass between them with her wide parasol, followed by two small boys dressed in hot-looking woollen Sunday suits.

Grimm glanced down again at the fountain outside the castle, took a long breath, then walked on. Kummel was glad to have spoken up for the Fräulein, but the old man's mood was hard to read.

'Well,' he said finally, biting back on another cough, 'you seem to know a good deal about us. Why don't you tell me now about yourself?'

'Myself?'

'Your origins. Your background. Notable events in your life. Everyone has a story.'

'In my case, there's little to tell, I'm afraid.'

'You have a family?' Although the Professor was expressing keen interest, Kummel again had the strongest impression that, when he himself spoke, he was being listened to purely as a source of sound, not for what he was saying.

'A family? Why, yes. In the east of Berlin. Near St Hedwig's.'

'In service too?'

'No. My father makes locomotive parts. For the Borsig works.'

They passed a knot of promenaders gazing in awe at the club of Herkules. All ten of them could quite easily have stood together on it. Grimm glanced up and shared a grin with his servant. 'Your people are Berliners by birth?'

'On both sides.'

The Professor's step quickened. At the same time he began to shake his head, vigorously, as if a cloud of midges from the lake had followed him up the hill and was playing around his face.

'I'm afraid, my young friend,' he said after clearing his throat, 'that I simply don't believe you.'

Kummel saw flames. The core of him felt scalding hot, while a chill crept over his skin, and the curious noise he had heard on the train from Marburg echoed again in his head – that irregular dry tock-tock-tocking, which now sounded more unnerving, ominous even, like the bones of a lynched man knocking together in the wind. 'Herr Professor?'

'I could be mistaken but I think not. I know little enough of life beyond the four walls of a study, do you see, but I do have an ear for accent and dialect. And while you generally affect an East Berliner accent ,with its soft Gs, I notice other sounds in your speech that suggest to me that you've not always lived in the city, nor indeed in Brandenburg or Prussia. If pressed, I would place you somewhere even further west than here?'

Kummel, saying nothing, looked dead ahead at the scintillating roofs of the Wilhelmshöhe castle. 'It's in the vowels,' Grimm went on, like a botanist remarking on a relatively interesting weed. 'They change when you speak with feeling. I've noticed this, most particularly, when you mention my niece.' He coughed again, possibly without needing to. 'Your reasons for inventing yourself anew are, of course, none of my business – and in any case, we are to enjoy your services for only a short while longer now before you return to the Dresslers. But naturally, I have my own suspicions.'

Already Kummel had fallen a half-step behind. It was as if the furnace inside him had burned up all possible words, however they might be pronounced.

'In your own time, *mein Freund*,' Grimm said. 'Or not at all, if that suits you better. Now: to more immediate concerns. My niece must have been organizing an event of some kind for me this morning. Is it to take place at the inn, or are we scheduled to meet her elsewhere? I presume that she has briefed you?'

Dumbly Kummel opened up his fist and held out the slip of paper to his master. Grimm glanced at the address and for a moment he looked mortified. 'The Fräulein asked me to take you there,' murmured Kummel, 'to meet her for lunch.'

'Yes. I understand.' He pocketed the paper and tottered on. 'We shall, I think, need to take a carriage once we regain the lower ground. Maybe you should go on ahead and collar one?' Kummel bowed and made to slip away down the slope.

'Please remember,' the Professor called after him, so that the younger man had to turn and meet his exhausted eyes, 'I mean you no harm – just as I trust you mean no harm to us.'

Jacob poured a full measure of coffee into the Dresden cup and took it through to the study. On the way he smiled at Willi, who was taking the vegetable-seller's carrot-heavy basket out into the kitchen. The brothers usually bought a few potatoes or peas whenever Frau Viehmann paid them a visit. Along with giving her coffee that they could ill afford themselves, it seemed the least they could do.

She had already taken her usual hard, upright chair in the corner where the bookshelves met, directly under the portrait of Jacob's mother in her buxom, stern-eyed prime. As he sat down behind his desk, she began to sip. She always needed a few minutes to recuperate by the time she made her afternoon calls at the upper-storey apartment on the Marktgasse. Fifty-seven was really too great an age to be peddling vegetables around Cassel's busy streets, but out on her little farm in Zwehrn she had a daughter and six grandchildren to support, and even at twenty-seven Jacob knew as well as anyone what a burr that could put under a person's saddle.

Willi took a while to come back. Jacob heard him chatting to Ludwig and Ferdinand about a problem with the kitchen stove, explaining that there were simply no funds available at present to fix it. Despite King Jérôme's continuing generosity to Jacob, the cost of living in his kingdom was still prohibitively high, and there was a limit to how far a single salary could be stretched.

Meanwhile in the drawing-room he could hear Lotte entertaining her pretty young friend Dortchen Wild. Had he been unoccupied, Jacob might well have found a reason to stroll past the drawing-room doorway in the hope that Lotte would ask him in to join them for half an hour. His liking for Dortchen, the apothecary's daughter from along the street, had steadily grown. They had rarely spoken in more than formalities, but she seemed to invest even these with a shy-eyed intensity that had begun to make him wonder if she might like him in return. Jacob did not have Willi's confidence or instinct with young women, but he did admire Dortchen's unaffected poise, her refusal to appear modishly 'delicate', and he was sorry he had to miss her now.

Frau Viehmann continued obliviously to drink her coffee. Her overdress looked dusty on that August day and, under the tight-fitting cap, her glimpse of scraped-back grey hair was slick with perspiration. Jacob saw a good deal of his mother in her mannerisms: the same stillness without quietness, the knowing way she studied him from her corner. Sometimes, when he glanced from her to the portrait above, it seemed as if the same set of teeth was about to be bared, the same pair of eyes was watching and forever finding him wanting.

'Don't you have enough tales for your book now?' she asked when she finally set down the cup.

Jacob smiled. '*Ja*, we have enough for *one* book, Frau Viehmann, and soon it will be published – by Christmas, God willing. But the stories that *you're* so kindly telling us will be part of a second volume.'

Her smile was sweet but not without condescension. Like his mother, she found it hard to equate tales with good thalers. But Jacob also knew she liked the attention he and Wilhelm gave her, and that – whatever she told the housewives of Zwehrn about the smooth-handed bachelors in town who sat scribbling down her every burp and sigh – she took care never to miss an appointment. 'But my stories are for the very young,' she said. 'How will they be able to read them?'

'Ah, then the *Mutti* – or indeed the father – will read them aloud, do you see?'

Smiling sceptically she shook her head. Jacob picked up his writing block then set it down. He glanced at the doorway, wishing Willi would come. Without his milder brother, whose presence seemed to soften the edges of any room and set at ease every person inside it, this whole procedure would have been so different. Jacob was well aware that on his own he could never have coaxed such treasure out of the tellers. The truest tales had to unfold calmly, quite without emotion, in much the same way as one might mete out punishment to a child. And time after time bluff Willi had the knack of making that happen.

'So, Frau Viehmann,' Willi declared on finally arriving, closing the door behind him and sitting at his own desk, 'what do you have for us today? As ever, we can barely contain our anticipation. "Story, story, story", eh?'

'I shall begin with something small,' she smiled at the moulding below the ceiling in the room's opposite corner. Jacob heard the new and necessary fluency. It was as if, by coming in, Willi had quite literally loosened her tongue.

'*Gut,* splendid.' Wilhelm sat straighter, tugging at his yellow waistcoat: a tall, luxuriantly maned, soft-featured man of twenty-six, whose ruined health made him look maybe ten years older, although still not as old as the brother who sat across from him, quill poised to note down as much detail as possible during the first, usually fairly rapid, telling.

'I know it as *The Naughty Child,*' she told them, her Niederzwehren accent becoming more pronounced. 'Once there was a naughty child who didn't do what his mother told him.' She grinned and her eyes brightened, as if only now did she remember the story's ending and could hardly wait to reach it. 'God was displeased with him and made him fall sick. No doctor could help him and soon he lay on his deathbed.' Here she paused, and when Jacob looked up from his noting, she briefly fixed her eyes on his.

'After he was lowered into his grave, and covered with earth, his arm suddenly came out and stood upright. They pushed it down and shovelled in fresh earth, but that didn't help. It kept springing out.' Again she paused, and when Jacob glanced up she looked back in a sorry kind of triumph. 'The child's mother had to go to the grave and whip the arm with a switch. When she had done that, the child pulled in his arm, and at last he had peace under the ground.'

A fat silence fell. 'Well!' Willi announced, softly clapping his hands just once but looking to his brother for a more measured response. Jacob – still to record the little tale's last sentence – kept his eyes down because he knew that the old woman was looking at him again and he did not yet know how to look back.

All Frau Viehmann's stories thrilled him, whether with their rhythms, her choice of words or the way she conjured up another time entirely, another time in his own life that seemed far more ancient than any that he could remember. And this tale touched him on the quick. He felt at once as if he knew the boy, knew the mother and – oddest of all – knew too that the buried child was still not dead but had just slipped through to somewhere else; some other world perhaps where its wickedness more properly belonged.

'*Gemütlich*,' he said, moving his quill again. The apartment's front door slammed as pretty little Dortchen left to go home and Jacob barely noticed. 'Yes, I don't need a second telling of this one.' *And at last he had peace under the ground.* His hand trembled, his lip too as he leaned closer to blow the ink dry.

'Will you put it in your book?' Frau Viehmann asked. It sounded like a taunt. Jacob glanced only now at Willi, who smiled back without committing himself. Unlike Jacob, he would doubtless want to dress the tale up: give the boy a name, describe the graveyard, bulk the thing out until its stark white bones were hidden from view. The brothers had begun to have their differences over these things.

'Oh, we will use it,' Jacob said, 'And in this case – I sincerely hope – in just the way that you've told it to us.'

Wilhelm heard how much this mattered to Jacob and graciously smiled his assent. Then he coughed, a soft rattle rising quickly to a crescendo that made him apologize and turn away. Meanwhile outside raised voices floated up to the study's opened window. Jacob rose and went to look down.

A carriage driver had pulled up his horses in the middle of the narrow winding street, which grew narrower still as the four- and five-storeyed houses teetered up to their high tiled roofs. Two boys, who must have run too close to the vehicle, raced away whooping, while the driver shook his fist and spat oaths.

Then the carriage door opened and a crop-headed servant stepped down on to the cobbles. Turning, he offered up his hand to a small white-haired master.

'Did my niece say we were to knock?' the Professor asked, standing with his back to the shopfront, which occupied the lowest storey of the half-timbered house.

'She said she would meet us, sir,' Kummel replied. 'That was all.'

Theatrically the Professor looked right and left down the cramped thoroughfare, which on trading days was probably impassable and even today was far from empty. At Grimm's request their carriage from the Wilhelmshöhe waited where it had suddenly pulled up short to avoid hitting the boys. Did he suspect that this rendezvous with the Fräulein was not genuine? His expression gave little away. But the lopsided hunch of his shoulders and the unusual hang of his mouth suggested that his walk in the park had taken a heavy toll.

'Would you care to sit in the carriage, sir?' Kummel asked. 'The Fräulein must have been delayed. I'm sure she won't be long.'

The Professor shrank further into himself. The street's pervasive reek of boiled cabbage could not have been making him feel any better. 'Yes, I think I will. Wait here, please, will you?' He seemed to be losing ground by the moment, and Kummel was struck by an unexpected pang of genuine concern for him.

Grimm edged over to the vehicle, shared a word with the driver, who had stepped down from the platform to stretch his legs, and let himself back inside. It was now Kummel's turn to look along the street for a sign of the Fräulein. The strollers, though, were almost all male, battalions of dark-coated church-goers whose excessively pious expressions and measured gait made them look to him like so many children dressed in adult clothing to ape their fathers. He could not see clearly through the carriage's window across the street, but he doubted that the Professor was watching him. Glad of the respite, the old man had probably shut his eyes.

This, Kummel knew, was his second perfectly good chance within half an hour to slip away. On descending the slope at the Wilhelmshöhe to call a carriage, he had planned to keep walking until he left all Cassel behind, along with Grimm and his cool curiosity. But he had stayed, and now he was sticking to his post outside this towering house too. Why? He was hardly worried about forfeiting a week's wages. The money mattered far less than the exposure that would surely result from his remaining, because, alerted by Grimm, the Dresslers were bound to confront him eventually, even if he managed to keep the old fellow at bay for another day. But still he could not go.

The door behind him rocked as it was unbolted from the inside. Kummel turned to find a consumptive-looking maid of around fifty. Beyond her shoulder the Fräulein stood bobbing. As soon as the latter caught his eye she blushed extravagantly, but did not smile, confirming at once to Kummel that all the frontiers in Europe were more bridgeable than the one she had now placed between the two of them.

She eased out from behind the maid and stepped on to the street.

'Have you been waiting long? I do apologize. I've been so busy arranging the reception inside.' She looked past him towards the carriage in which she must have guessed that her uncle was sitting.

'Shall I go up and say that the gentleman is about to arrive?' asked the maid.

'*Bitte schön*,' nodded the Fräulein.

The older woman bustled back up the lamp-lit stairs and the Fräulein glanced Kummel's way. Then, with an almost visible effort, she made herself look at him more frankly. The colour in her cheeks was still high but at least she now attempted a smile, which only succeeded in making Kummel think she had thus put an ocean as well as all Europe between them. It was over. He was free to go, free to wander on and leave behind his purely fictional family in Berlin. Another city, another situation. There was no shortage of work to be found for a 'steady, active, single man', as the advertisements always phrased it. Or perhaps he would even go back to the forests for a while. *Waldeinsamkeit* indeed.

'Thank you for your help,' she said softly, as if she knew she would not be seeing him again. 'Thank you.' *We can all be of service to one another*, she had said as their train steamed into this town, *each in our own little way*.

'The Professor is in the carriage,' he explained. 'He rather tired himself this morning, I'm afraid, in the park . . .'

He paused, but had he intended to say more, he was stopped by a loud shout from across the street. He turned to find the carriage driver gesticulating, while with his other hand he held his carriage door wide open.

'Here, boy!' he yelled at Kummel. '*Komm her! Komm!* Your master's collapsed!'

SIXTEEN

The horse, like its rider, sensed a longer journey ahead. The prince was glad of the slower progress. He knew that his mother was right to send him out again, but he was worried almost as much by what he was leaving behind as by what he was going back to. Her disproportioned look still haunted him: she seemed to have been pumped up like a pig's bladder, with different parts of her inflating to different degrees. If she had not been his mother, he would have found her grotesque. And still he was unsure whether it was she who had changed, or just his view of her.

Whenever she came into his thoughts as the horse led him on along paths he had not seen before, he tried to think only of the svelte princess. Even this did no good. His shame at the way he had treated the king's daughter now confused him so much that at times he imagined her bloated out of all recognition too, there on her bed in the garret.

Days went by. For all he knew the horse was leading him in circles. The forest was so dense that he was rarely able to glimpse the sun to work out his direction. But however slow his journey seemed, he sensed time racing past. He felt afloat on the horse's back, swept along by sudden currents over which he had no control. And although he had not planned to break his journey, in the end he had to stop and try to find out why he had become so disorientated.

Towards dusk he reined in the horse in a lumber yard at the edge of a sprawl of pines. The easy-going woodman was just a little older than himself. He was happy to take in a traveller for the night, share his solitary supper by the trivet over his outdoor fire, then talk good-naturedly afterwards.

'Tell me what you know of the Rose King,' the prince said after a while.

'Ah, there's no Rose King now, not since the enchantment.' The woodman smiled, as if he were joking. 'Or not since the enchantment took effect.'

'Tell me about that.'

'You probably know it better than I do. The story has been around for as long as I can remember. The king and queen had a daughter, and they invited twelve wise women to the celebratory feast, to bless her with their gifts.'

'Wise women?' The prince had never pressed his mother on exactly what that meant.

He shrugged. 'Guardian spirits? It was a long time ago. The language of these things changes. Some people, as I understand it, used to call them fairies. And twelve were invited, but a thirteenth arrived, and when she saw that no place had been laid for her at the feast, she cursed the princess.' He held up a thumb to show where the poisoned spindle would eventually prick her. There were odd little nicks on his hand, and also on his neck, cheek and arm. From where the prince sat they looked, rather forbiddingly, like very old toothmarks.

'And then one of the others softened the curse to a term of sleep?'

'As you say. After the feast the Rose King tried to have all the spindles in the land destroyed. But it did no good, because the one spindle that mattered stayed undiscovered in the palace. In due course the princess found it, was drawn to it, and the inevitable accident fulfilled the beginning of the evil prophecy.'

He grinned across the fire, and in the light of the low embers his long face and dark, close-cropped hair suddenly looked well-known to the prince. Then the woodman narrowed his eyes and softly said, as if reciting, 'She fell down in a deep sleep. And the king and queen, who just then came home, fell asleep too. And the horses slept in the stables, and the dogs in the courtyard, the pigeons on the roofs and the flies on the walls. Even the fire in the hearth left off blazing and went to sleep. And so everything stood still and slept soundly – which was when the hedge of thorns began to rise up around the palace . . .'

He broke off with a smile, nodding his scarred, somehow familiar head. But his fey little embellishments had struck a wrong note, and the prince sensed that they were talking at cross purposes. 'Excuse me,' he said, settling his emptied beer tankard on the stone beside him, 'but the palace isn't like that. There's no king, no queen. Only the princess. Even the hedge of thorns isn't there.'

'Then you've heard it told differently. Each part of the fatherland has its own version, I imagine.'

'You think it's a *story?*'

The woodman's gentle eyes widened in surprise, anxious if he had caused offence. He showed the palms of both hands. 'Forgive me. I'm nothing but a woodchopper. This is my patch. Beyond it I'm ignorant.'

'You really thought that what you were telling me was a tale?'

'That was how I heard it. How it was always told to me. But I'm ready to stand corrected. Please don't take what I've said the wrong way.'

'No please, forgive *me*,' the prince countered, not wanting to appear ungracious after so much hospitality. He listened to the bubbling of a pot on a smaller fire behind him, where deer hooves had been set to boil down for glue, but as his gaze fell on the nearer embers, all he could think of was his earlier disorientation. And then it began to dawn on him.

He had not just taken a new route to come to this place, but travelled sideways in time, so that whatever happened at the palace was no more than a distant legend here. Again his mother's shape loomed. *There are other worlds than this, you know* . . . Along these paths, beneath these trees, he seemed in his aimlessness to have slipped through a crack in the map into a place of wholly different possibilities, where even his own former life echoed like a story for children.

Other worlds . . . He peered more closely at his host through the smoke. A prickly chill crept up his right side, briefly numbing his arm and cheek. In everything except his peculiar scars, this woodman was physically similar to himself and all the babies. The family likeness was so strong, he could quite easily have passed as an elder brother. 'What is your name?' the prince asked, but he already knew the answer.

'Friedrich.'

Involuntarily, the prince nodded his head. 'And in your story,' he stammered, 'how did it all end? Did the princess wake up? Did everything come back to life?'

For a moment he looked reluctant to answer. 'A king's son arrived as the term of the enchantment was ending. He kissed her, she woke, and all was restored.'

'And they married?'

'Yes, they married.'

'And what of the evil fairy?'

'I don't understand.'

'What happened to the woman who had caused all the trouble? Was she punished?'

'That's where our story ends in this region. With the awakening, the marriage.'

The prince, bearded chin on knee, played with a twig that finally he tossed onto the ash-fringed carcass of a glowing log. 'If it hadn't been just a story,' he asked quietly, 'would *you* have wished to wake the princess?'

The woodman laughed. 'I chop logs. It was only kings' sons who tried to get through the barrier of thorn. And besides, it was not the *prince* who woke her. He was just the one who came at the right time.' He heaved himself to his feet. 'I have to get up early. Shall I show you to your bed now? It's not much – usually it's my own – but you're very welcome to it. You can stay here for as long as you like. Really, you can.'

'You're very kind.' The prince rose too. 'But I think I'll continue my journey. I've let my horse have his head for long enough and drifted too far from the paths I should be taking. But thank you. Thank you so much.'

With that he became aware of a distant, swelling rush of sound accompanied by bells and a mechanical whistle, apparently breaking up out of the ground, which shook a little under his feet. 'Whatever is that?' he asked as it faded.

'Only a locomotive. A livestock train, heading for Karlsruhe. I've come to find the noise comforting. And the railroad makes my job easier too: I only have to cart my logs as far as the depot now. From there they're transported all over Hanover and Württemberg.'

The prince had no idea what he was talking about. The names

meant nothing to him; these places figured in no world that he knew. But full of fresh purpose now, he wanted to lose no more time.

'Could you direct me back to the highway, please?' he asked, studying this Friedrich's toothmarked face in shadows that seemed, moment by moment, to be eating more deeply into it.

The woodman did not speak. In the fast gathering dark his hand rose, looking disembodied at the end of his umber sleeve, and pointed straight ahead, past the place where the chamberlain's horse stood tethered. The prince turned, climbed into the splendid saddle and saw through a break in the trees the lights of another cottage. Neither gap nor building had been visible on his arrival.

'Thank you again,' he called back as the horse awaited his guidance. But there was no sign now of the woodman or his fire. The prince knew that he himself had slipped back across a frontier, perhaps from a 'fatherland' into the land he had always regarded as his mother's. He had been offered a chance to escape, to avoid whatever might be waiting for him at the palace, but he had chosen not to take it.

He headed the horse towards the lighted windows. Soon he came to a small lake, and from its shore he recognized the facade of the three spinners' cottage. Now at last he was back on course. This was his own true country.

Hunkering lower in the saddle, he drummed along a well-remembered path that stretched on up to the heights.

SEVENTEEN

It was like riding. Grimm felt few breaks in the rhythm. He imagined himself drumming along a straight country track on a horse so reliable that he could let his eyes linger on the passing scenery, though just as a rider forms a full impression only of the far or middle distance, so the closer detail here was all but lost to him – everything, that was, except the palpable anxiety all around.

He dearly wished that the carriage driver had not seen him topple from his seat. After a moment or two he would surely have righted himself again and no one would have been the wiser. (He had, after all, fallen unseen before.) At no time did he lose consciousness. But as soon as the carriage began to fill up, this strange galloping fancy began: and it went on for some time.

Nothing close to him had substance, although he knew he was on a busy street overhung by wood-boned houses, and then that he was being eased up a flight of stairs he had climbed many times before. He recognized the smell of the coat of the person whose hand was constantly at his elbow, even after they entered the apartment to find a group of people who could have been mourners at a wake. To begin with he could not tell the men from the women. The hand at his elbow guided him down the corridor to a bedroom, unlaced his shoes, then swung him on to the bed.

Grimm, still burning up ground, watched the blur of his helper's face. The coat's frowsty smell told him that this was his brother, but he could not remember what he was called. Then, as the man reached out to plump up a pillow, a name came with such force that Grimm exclaimed it under his breath. 'Friedrich!'

A soothing voice floated back down to him, seeming to say yes. Others were in the room, but too far away to hear or to speak to him themselves. 'Friedrich!' Grimm repeated, louder, finding his nose and throat badly blocked and the whole of his right side feeling oddly muffled, as if a weight of earth lay on it.

The whisper from above sounded again: 'You know me . . .'

Then the phantom horse whisked Grimm on too fast for any of his subsequent conversations to make proper sense, although his own answers seemed perfectly well received. Twice he was turned and felt strong and confident hands on him, not those of his brother now. Cool fingers probed, his lips were drawn apart, his throat inspected. The nearby hubbub sounded less agitated. He heard quiet, rueful laughter. Whether his eyes were open or closed he saw only the high horizon, and along it the cupolas of a distant palace, threatening to dissolve before he arrived. Male and female voices became distinct. He followed the strings of words that crossed to and fro above him like bunting.

Once when he raised his head to look, there were only two people. The man was young with close-cropped hair, his back to the bed. The woman was his sister Lotte – no, not Lotte but her friend from the Sun Pharmacy, the girl to whom Grimm had taken such a private liking: Dorothea Wild. She saw him looking her way, and drew the man aside before gliding to the bed. 'Rest' and 'sleep' were the only words Grimm heard from her. She seemed to be trembling but deftly, lovingly, she touched his hair away from his forehead. This was not, after all, Dortchen. More beautiful, perhaps, but not her.

He shut his eyes, and when he looked again he was alone, and this time completely at rest. He felt dirty, though no more so than usual. Through the opened window he saw no cupolas but the roofs of the houses opposite against a pale afternoon sky. There was a washstand to the side of the bed's footboard, a framed daguerrotype of a jowly child by the window's pink sashed curtains, a large bowl of dark red geraniums. The room was awesomely clean, but still it smelled of damp grain and mildew, just as it had done more than thirty years before, when Grimm had last been inside it.

He pushed himself into a sitting position, which immediately eased the blockage in his nose and throat and more slowly brought his right side back to life. Earlier it had crossed his mind that he had died in the carriage and been translated to some sort of parallel life, although whether as a punishment or a reward, he had not had the time to decide. It amused him now to think he had confused Kummel with both Willi and their dead infant brother, less so that he had mistaken Auguste for Dortchen. *Ach*, dear Gustchen, presumably presiding now in the withdrawing room over a party without its guest of honour.

He swung his legs off the bed and managed to stand with only a slight tremor in his knees. Even if they were no longer expecting him to appear, he owed it to his niece to show himself. Some of the faces that had seemed featureless on his arrival now grew clearer in his memory. Not one was familiar. Most were closer to Gustchen's age than his own, many much younger – children.

Cautiously he crossed the rugs to the open door. The withdrawing room, ten steps to his right, looked a long way off. With one hand on the panelling, he finally reached its doorway and glanced in at the muted throng.

The guests looked ill at ease in morning suits and best dresses, nibbling from plates of cooked meats and truffle pastries and drinking small measures of a Swedish punch. To one side of the lacquer-floored room – near a grand piano that served as a plinth for a forest of silver-framed photographs – a stepped lectern held an unopened book.

Kummel was the first to notice him. Wide-eyed, he launched himself across the room to alert Gustchen. Her eyelids fluttered madly when she looked Grimm's way. Then to his surprise, as everyone else fell silent, she burst out laughing.

'Oh Apapa!' she cried, coming across and raising a hand to her hair which had long since begun to spill from its pins. 'But you have no shoes on!'

A cheer went up as Jacob appeared in the doorway. In his arms was a pile of twelve newly printed volumes, fresh from the binders. Sheepishly he scanned the withdrawing room, returning the smiles of the thirty people most dear to him, tightly packed in since the Christmas tree, brilliant with candles, took up a huge space in front of the far window. Candles burned on a number of other surfaces, but still the overall effect was one of warm darkness, broken by this sea of appreciative faces.

As was only right, the women outnumbered the men. Grimm's eye ran from Philippine Engelhard to the Hassenpflugs then on to the Haxthausen girls and the Wilds. Without their help, he and Willi would never have unearthed so many fine tales nor so many indispensable tellers. If this first volume had any success, then all of them deserved some share in it. But Jacob did not expect success. When he looked at the twelve books in his hands, he could think only of the remaining eight hundred and eighty-eight in

Reimer's Berlin warehouse and wonder how the stack might ever be whittled down. As for a second volume, he doubted now that it would ever see the light of day.

'Enough of this waiting!' cried Achim von Arnim, one of the few who was seated. 'Let us see the fruit of the labours!'

Willi appeared at his brother's side. Flushed with good humour, he winked as he relieved Jacob of six copies and began to pass them around. Noticing that Jacob was not doing the same, Dortchen Wild – who earlier that evening had given the brothers their regular monthly haircuts – swept quietly forward. 'Allow me,' she whispered, taking the half dozen other books to distribute among the guests in front of the towering, candle-lit Christmas tree.

A low rustling followed, punctuated by occasional squeals and giggles. Some of the guests had already seen manuscript versions of these *Tales for Young and Old*. Others, like Clemens Brentano and von Savigny, had long been consultants to the project. There were in truth few surprises now. To a greater or lesser extent these people would be gracious, but Jacob saw the disappointment on some of the faces – especially von Savigny's seven-year-old daughter's – because there were no plates, and observed some equally forlorn looks at the length and complexity of the footnotes.

Publisher Georg Reimer himself had complained that the book was neither flesh nor fish. Its transcriptions were too dense for children to enjoy, its contents too 'subcultural' to attract the serious attention of academics. And there were those in the room, Jacob knew, who believed that preserving the tales with their authentic rough edges – the book's great claim to originality – was bound to repel, not attract, casual readers. Friedrich Rühs, in one of several hostile early reviews, had already said that it contained large quantities of 'the most pathetic and tasteless material imaginable'.

Perhaps, after all, Willi had been right. The tales needed to be dressed up. If there were ever to be another edition, Jacob would gladly now let his younger and in some ways shrewder brother nip and tuck to his heart's content.

Dortchen returned to Jacob's side. For the first time since he had known her she took his elbow and squeezed it hard. 'It'll be marvellous,' she assured him, beaming. 'It'll bring you fame and fortune.'

'Fortune?' Jacob said with a thin smile, sorry that she had taken her hand away again quite so abruptly. Too busy to deal with Reimer himself, he had left Willi to negotiate the terms of publication. As a result they had secured countless protestations of editorial support but no written contract, nor even an agreement on when royalties would start to be paid. On the credit side, Reimer had hinted that he might be able to find work at his firm for Ferdinand, the most unemployable of the younger brothers. The household was crying out for another income to supplement Jacob's from their Corsican king; for this seasonal gathering he had gladly over-reached himself but under normal circumstances they were all making do with just two meals a day.

Dortchen slipped away towards the door, indicating to Lotte that they should head for the kitchen. Small, tireless, her chestnut hair attractively braided in coils on top of her head with curls hanging down at each ear, Dortchen was playing the part of hostess more diligently than Jacob's own sister. Minutes later they returned with salvers of steaming spiced wine in small cups that they handed to each of the guests. Jacob, holding his own warm cup in his fingertips, saw Dortchen nod to von Savigny, who from the back of the room called for order.

'You don't want many words from me,' he began, holding up the green-bound volume. 'All the words one could wish for are in here. All the eternally new facts that make these tales so vital to young and old alike.'

There was a murmur of agreement and von Savigny smiled

first at one brother then at the other, but for the remainder of this brief toast his eyes stayed affectionately on Old One.

'It was Schiller who claimed that the fairytales of his childhood had a deeper meaning than the truths taught by life. This book will make it possible for future generations of Germans to say the same – let us hope, in a new and unified Reich that stands shoulder to shoulder with Europe's other sovereign states. We Germans form a single body; its limbs demand one head. And even as we celebrate here the achievement of Jacob and Wilhelm, while our Corsican emperor sinks deeper in the Russian snows, we are surely moving closer to the conclusion for which we all most dearly wish. I believe that this book marks a large step along the way. I know that some have wondered for whom these tales are intended. Are they for the young? they ask. Are they for the learned? I say to them that they are for everyone – and they are for Germany! *Prosit!*'

Jacob's lip trembled at the solemn health-drinking that followed. Dortchen, back at his side, had to remind him to sip from his cup too. The way she looked at him was no longer shy. 'Your book will live,' she smiled up with a steadiness which almost managed to banish his doubts. 'I know that, Jacob. It will have such a life.'

She made it sound triumphant, not a consolation for any life that he had so far quite failed to live for himself. He nodded hard, looking straight ahead, and only afterwards wondered if she might have meant more, that with her beside him like this, he no longer *needed* to look for an alternative to a truly lived life. And if that had been her real meaning, then he was surprised and touched, but most of all he was glad. Profoundly glad. But to let her know how glad he was would mean crossing such a frontier, and still he was not ready for that.

*

Grimm could only pick at the slightly tough strips of mutton and pickled gherkins that Gustchen brought him from the sideboards. Seated by the window, where his family had once used to stand their Christmas tree, he dutifully sipped from a glass of peach brandy. Kummel had fetched his shoes but no one had yet laced them back on his feet. What were they afraid of? That if they did he might bolt?

Weaving, he thought, *we are weaving* . . . It was hard not to feel like a ghost at his own feast. The guests glanced his way now and then and on catching his eye they would anxiously smile and bow. But for the most part they gave him such a wide berth that he might as well have been in quarantine in his sunlit corner, especially after a string of sneezes that left his head feeling desperately thick.

According to Gustchen, the guests were either relations or former servants of old citizens who had contributed tales to the original collection. Several she identified by names that Grimm recognized, but he was glad he did not have to ask to see their credentials. In and around Cassel, over the past fifty years, there had been no shortage of folk claiming to have helped the brothers in their work. So many, in fact, that if they were all telling the truth then few of the helpers could have contributed more than a couple of paragraphs each.

The room's occupants all appeared to be waiting for something specific to happen, although Grimm could not think what. He sat in his well-upholstered chair for maybe no more than an hour, but it felt much longer. The cries from the street below often sounded louder than the rustle of conversation around him. The smell in here was predominantly of oranges but, as the afternoon wore on, he rather fancied that an odour of ether was growing stronger.

The apartment's owners, having generously given over their home to strangers, did not press themselves on him, but at one point their small granddaughter skipped up to the lectern, opened the book – which was Willi's first edition of the *Tales* – and charmingly if haltingly read *The Golden Goose.* Later Grimm noticed her playing on the floor with a familiar lead model, a quarter-century old now, of a carriage being escorted across the Hanoverian border by dragoons and students. How many of these things, he wondered, were still in circulation? She kept looking up from the little red-cheeked exile waving in the carriage to Grimm himself. Clearly she found it hard to believe that they were one and the same person. *Weaving, weaving . . . We are weaving your shroud . . .*

Another youngster, a boy of around fifteen, approached with a copy of Edgar Taylor's illustrated 1823 English translation of the *Tales.* On request, Grimm signed his name on the title page but still found his lower arm stiff, and afterwards he had to dislodge the pen from his right hand's fingers with those of his left.

Gustchen, spotting the awkward manoeuvre, grinned his way in a quiet kind of delirium. By and large she was manfully hiding her concern and embarrassment, although earlier when she had asked Kummel to fetch his shoes Grimm had heard her refer to him not as 'Apapa' but 'Papa'. He also saw her talk twice in the doorway with a tall, heavily bearded, balding man who was the function's sole cigarette smoker. From his well-cut coat and sombre manner Grimm took him for the doctor who had earlier examined him in the bedroom. He could equally well have passed for an undertaker. A thin little boy now attended him, and Grimm noticed that his fingers were stained a similar shade of yellow.

Gustchen and the maids began to usher the guests out into the corridor. As they filed away Kummel came across to stand beside Grimm's chair, almost as if to restrain the old man, should he try to abscond. The servant drew his hands from behind his back, revealing Grimm's shoes. 'Shall I, sir?' he asked, before kneeling and slipping them on to his master's feet.

Grimm studied the whorls of short hair at the top of the servant's head. His fingers felt icy, even though Grimm wore thick socks. 'In the bedroom,' he croaked, 'I called you Friedrich.'

'It's a name I answer to,' Kummel answered with a shrug, not looking up as he continued to tie the lace. When he finished he tilted back his head and looked into Grimm's eyes. 'But then, Herr Professor, what *don't* you know?'

Gustchen hurried across before Grimm could try to speak again. 'Apapa,' she explained in a rush, in case he should resist, 'I've arranged for a photograph to be taken. Of you, of us all, here in your old home. Apparently the light in this room is now too poor, so the photographer has set up his equipment in the parlour.' Grimm nodded, at last understanding the smell of ether and the yellowed fingers. 'The boy has prepared the plates, so if we could perhaps gently move you along now . . .'

She gave him no chance to protest. Her hand was at his elbow, squeezing a little as he rose. Grimm had no objection to a photograph. On the way out of the room he even clawed his hair into place across his forehead. His niece still held his left arm and Friedrich Kummel hovered close to his stiffer right, his hands poised to catch it if it dropped without warning from its socket.

Grimm went quietly. But in his mind he was on horseback again, and what he saw from the saddle was more vivid than anything he saw around him here in Hesse. It was as if this inner land where he rode was beginning to make more sense to him than the 'real' new world of double-entry book-keeping and night-lit factories through which he nowadays limped with such foreboding.

Weaving, we are weaving . . . went the rhythm of the hooves as he tore on up the valley. Soon, he told himself. Soon I'll be home.

EIGHTEEN

On his ride to the crag where the palace stood, the prince noticed many changes. Where before he had seen only isolated, long abandoned dwellings, now flourishing hamlets ran up the narrow valleys, and ribbons of smart cottages unfurled from working forest mines. Where earlier he had watched these cantons stretch and yawn at the dawn of their reawakening, now he saw a high noon of activity. And for every lone charcoal-burner or pedlar whose path he had crossed the first time, he found a dozen thriving families.

Doesn't every canton have its own kind of time? He could not say how many years had passed since his departure. All he hoped was that no one else had staked a claim to his princess. And all he prayed was that when she set eyes on him at last, she would know him and take him back. It never once crossed his mind, amid such industrious scenes, that she would still be asleep.

At his approach to the foot of the bluff he passed several companies of blue-coated soldiers firing fusillades at targets. But no one in uniform waved him down before he came to the switchback, where a sentry post the size of a gatehouse now stood in front of a dusty marching square.

He reined in his horse, dismounted and looked around for an officer to whom to present himself. It seemed unthinkable that he should pass straight through to the switchback steps, but he went unchallenged until a familiar voice spoke behind him: 'You've returned. I had not expected to see you again.'

He turned to find the chamberlain, looking more decrepit than ever, but his voice was even and his small smile wry. 'Don't you mean you *hoped* not to see me?' the prince asked. 'Why else did you leave me that horse, and prime it in the way you did?'

'How can a horse be primed? It responds to its rider. If it took you to your home, and quickly, it was because you wanted that. If there have been detours in your return, then they can be explained only by your own uncertainties.'

He smiled. 'So my being here now must speak for itself.'

The old man simply gestured that they should start to climb the steps together. The sentries let them pass with a stiffening of their already ramrod-straight backs. As they went up, under the hot afternoon sun, the aged chamberlain continued to speak comfortably, refusing an offer to pause and catch his breath. 'Much has changed since you were last here, as doubtless you have noticed.'

'I'm interested only in the princess. Will you vouch for me with her? You know it was I who came first. Have there been other suitors since?'

'Soon you'll have answers to these more personal questions. You need to know, though, that the Rose Kingdom is under threat of invasion. Preparations for a war of resistance are already well advanced.'

'But why should this matter to me?'

'If you are interested in the princess – who is now the effective head of this realm – then affairs of state must interest you too. The emperor whose armies are massing on our eastern frontier aims not only to seize the kingdom but to rule it as her consort. You'll have to fight for what you desire.'

'You've underestimated me before,' the prince laughed. 'If I need to, then I shall fight – and I shall win.'

The top of the steps came into view and they walked down the terraces leading to the palace. With every stride he felt more determined to become the man his mother had sent him out to be. The only remaining question was whether he would have time to marry the princess before he left again on campaign. And their wedding would be completed by a double coronation. *You are a prince, and you can be a king too.* The new Rose King.

He slowed to let the chamberlain direct him when they reached the palace courtyard. Even at twenty paces its dancing fountains speckled their faces with a pleasantly cool welcome. The old man did not point the way but continued to accompany him past the old garret tower into a secluded garden. On sandy paths bordered by box, they passed vegetable plots then came to a closely clipped lawn surrounded by acanthus and rhododendron bushes.

Up ahead lay a white-painted garden house, the kind of family haven where on winter evenings potatoes and apples would be baked on a stove's glowing top. Two children played quietly in front of it, wearing thin summer blouses and no shoes. Although one was fair and the other had hair the colour of tar, they were indisputably twins of around two years of age. When they jumped or squatted, even the awkward little movements of one seemed to be mirrored in those of the other. But the prince paid less attention to the children, at first, than to the unusual scarecrow they were dancing around.

He could see it only from behind: a well-cut coat draped over a wooden cross, topped by a white wig tied with black ribbon at the nape. A sword in its scabbard had been belted halfway down the cross and hung below the hem of the coat. He recognized each item. They had all once been his own.

As he walked on down the path, he looked across and began to see the figure's profile. The coat had been bulked out by a straw bale, the wig sat on what looked like a wax face-mask with features very much like his own. The children were now playing a game of tag, not so much around the figure as with it, calling to it as much as they called to each other, and the name they were crying was 'Papa'.

Pausing, he frowned across at them, then the chamberlain spoke as if from inside his own head: 'Yes, they're your children. They were all you left for their mother when you went away: them, the coat, the wig, the sword.'

'I went too soon,' he breathed, staring at them in wonder. 'I was confused. How could I have known she would wake and have babies?'

'She didn't wake and have them. It didn't happen that way. First came the babies, and still she slept . . .'

'But why, when everything around her had come back to life?'

'Because the poisoned splinter from the spindle was still in her finger. Only in trying to feed from her did one of the children put its mouth around her thumb, draw it out, and so at last free her from the enchantment.'

The prince stared on, as if he in turn were spellbound. *I'm proud of you. Very proud. I trust that you, in turn, will be as proud of your own children.* 'The face they've put on their figure – it's so like mine.'

'It *is* yours. Your likeness. The princess had a cast made from the impression you left in the flax in the garret. From that she takes a series of masks. As soon as one shows signs of cracking, she immediately makes another. You don't need me to vouch for you. Already she knows your face as well as her own.'

'And does she love it?'

'Why don't you ask her yourself.'

The chamberlain pointed at a high-backed chair next to the garden house where a young woman, her golden hair unbound, sat sewing in the shade, so busy that she had not yet noticed his arrival.

'I will marry her,' he declared to the old man, who had already begun to edge away. 'Please arrange for a coach to be sent to my mother's canton. She must be brought here for the wedding.'

'As you wish.' Before withdrawing he pursed his lips, tipped his head and clicked his heels. *The palace has always been beyond my reach,* he had once said. Yet here he was, playing the same role in its inner workings as – he had said on their first encounter – his father and grandfather had played before him. In his heart, even he must have been pleased. The prince watched him go then turned back to the garden house.

The princess, aware of him now, stood and set aside her sewing. The children stopped their game and stared his way.

And he smiled, widely enough to draw in not just the three of them but the palace too, its gardens and orchards, and this whole high forest crag to which he had finally come home.

NINETEEN

Auguste was surprised but pleased to find Grimm already in bed when she took up his nightcap. She felt his puzzled eyes on her as she crossed to his desk then sat facing him in the thin candle light. The day's events had discomposed her so completely that she now felt she had nothing to lose. And even if this talk came to nothing, she still had her prior arrangement with Kummel to fall back on.

'No Kummel?' Grimm asked, putting down his book, his hair fanned out on the pillow behind him like a drowned man's. 'He is still with us?'

'*Natürlich,* Apapa. He'll travel back to Berlin tomorrow too.' There was a new darkness in his eyes, and Auguste feared that he might have lost his bearings again. 'Then he'll return to the Dresslers, remember? He's with us only for a month.'

'Then why has he not come? To lay out my clothes?'

'I'll do that, Apapa. I want to do it. That's why I gave him some time off this evening. He's barely had an hour to himself since we left the Harz.' Looking down, she realized she was still holding his milky drink. She rose with an apologetic smile and put it on his bedside table.

'You take too much on yourself, Gustchen,' he said. 'Especially today – it must have taken you so long to organize the party.'

She smiled, drifting away from the bed towards the window, touching the back of the chair with its patch of worn velvet as if for luck. The party. How horribly pointless that had turned out. Perhaps it had been naïve of her from the first to think that a social gathering could catch him off balance, and so almost trick him into confiding in her. 'Your colour is better now,' she said, peering dreamily between a gap in the curtains. Out of sight, the small children were fighting again in the yard – did the two of them never just sit quietly? 'The doctor said a few days' bedrest is probably all you need, but I insist on a second opinion once we're home.'

If he replied, she did not hear it. Nor was she listening especially hard, not for that. She edged back to his desk, above which he had snuffed out the candle lamp. The green leather inlay was piled with the standard-sized cards he issued to his dozens of collaborators on the *Wörterbuch*. Most of the writing was not his own, except for the rash of minute corrections and cross-references in the margins. (He never corrected his own work. He used to be amazed that her father had ever felt the need to read over what he had written before sending it on to the publishers.)

This woodchopping was such a task. The uppermost entry was for the word *Frucht* – Fruit. Still he was no farther on than the letter F. Originally he had hoped to complete the well-paid drudgery within a decade, but even with assistance the first volume had taken fourteen years to appear. It ran from A to *Biermolke*. At the rate he was going, he would need an entire second lifetime to reach the end of the alphabet.

Auguste flicked up the lid of a small ornamental snuff-box and glanced dismissively at her reflection in the mirror on its underside. Then she picked up the fragment of crystal that had once sat on her father's Berlin desk. Holding it against her cheek, swaying her upper body, she turned back to the old man. There was a fringe of milk along his upper lip that she longed to cross over and smooth away. Noticing where her eyes were fixed, he smiled, reached up and smeared his lip clean. His own eyes, as she had hoped, were on his brother's piece of rock. Tomorrow the family would close in around them again, like a tide over a causeway. She would never have a better opportunity than this. 'How badly do you miss him?' she asked. And so it began.

Grimm took another sip from his glass then gave what looked like an involuntary jerk of his head. 'He cannot be replaced.'

The crystal's coolness steadied Auguste as the image returned of her Apapa stooping to scatter earth on the snow-covered coffin.

'Do you remember,' she said, 'when I was still a girl, I asked you why you never married?' He frowned back, but not in a discouraging way. 'And you replied, "What, when I have your father!" But then you also said, "Or, more seriously, when I do not have your wonderful mother." Do you remember that, Apapa? It was during a walk in the Tiergarten.'

Without taking his eyes from hers Grimm cleared his throat. 'No, it was before we reached the Tiergarten. We walked there afterwards. This conversation was in Unter den Linden.'

Auguste grinned, put the rock to her temple then replaced it carefully on the desk, glad that his phenomenal powers of recollection had lapsed only temporarily. His inability in Marburg to identify that snatch from Heine had afterwards made her very uneasy. 'I wondered what you meant by it.'

He took another sip. 'You know what I meant.'

'Tell me, though. The part about my mother.'

He shrugged. 'That if I had been as fortunate as my brother, and found myself a woman like your mother, then doubtless I would not have remained a bachelor.'

'Doubtless?' His eyes followed her as she stepped around the foot of his bed to the dresser where the two ceramic figures stood. She set the man's head nodding, just as Grimm had done the night before. Watching, she felt tears begin in her eyes. 'My mother was my age now when she got engaged.'

A long, thick silence followed. 'Tell me, *Fundvogel*,' he said finally, in a voice so small and remote that it could have been coming from another world, 'what is it you want to know?'

Fundvogel: foundling-bird – that came from a long, long way back. It was the name of one of the *Tales* that Gustchen had loved as a child, featuring a line that so caught her infant fancy that she had used to make him repeat it regularly: 'Neither now nor ever shall I leave you.' And once he had told her, without explaining why, that the line meant a great deal to him too, from even before she was born.

Tears ran down her cheeks. *Story, story, story,* she thought. With crushing self-consciousness she made herself smile, then said to the little man whose head stopped nodding: 'I want to know my own story. You used to say that everyone has a story.'

'Yours? But what can I tell you about that, *Liebchen*?'

She shook her head at her idiocy. The tears flowed faster. 'I'm sorry. I'm being feeble. My mother wouldn't have let herself down like this, would she, not when *she* was past thirty?'

'You're not feeble, Gustchen.' Kind words, but she needed him to struggle from his bed and come across and touch her with his kindness. And it was not really her mother she was comparing herself with.

'*You're* not feeble,' she told him. 'You've never cried.'

'Oh, I have,' he told her – so quickly that he seemed to take himself by surprise. He smiled. 'Just once that I can remember. But I've cried.'

'I'm frightened, Apapa,' Auguste confessed like a child, smearing both cheeks with the back of her hand, staring down now at the little woman.

'You worry so, Gustchen. Is there really anything to be afraid of?'

'Yes,' she answered abruptly. 'Not knowing.' Then she put out a finger to make the woman nod. The ceramic head stayed still. Again she tried. 'It shakes,' Grimm called hesitantly. 'You must tap it from the side. The man nods but the woman's head shakes.' Auguste let her hand fall, then her own head drooped before both figures as if she were standing before an altar.

'Marriage,' Grimm then said, startling her, 'it can't be the end for everyone.'

'The end?'

She looked at him but his expression told her nothing. She was not even sure which of them he was talking about. And now that he was speaking with obvious feeling, she was filled with both awe and embarrassment, although again she was unsure on whose account. 'Do you have someone, Gustchen?'

This was wrong. She had not come to talk about herself – not, at least, about the middle or the end of her story. *Someone* . . . She shook her head quickly, then checked herself and shrugged. What he said next confirmed that they were at cross purposes: 'When the time comes, you *will* know. You'll have to know – whoever the person might be.' There was a warning look in his eyes, and some disappointment too, she thought. Then the appalling idea that Kummel might have been indiscreet about their moment together bloomed in her head.

Suddenly it began to fit. She knew that Kummel and Grimm had spoken in the park on their way to the party. When she had asked the serving man about what, he had merely said, 'We told each other stories.' Horribly flustered, she found herself edging back to the door and reaching for the handle.

Grimm looked unnaturally stiff in his bed, as if he were bracing himself for fear of another spasm. But it seemed to Auguste that he was restraining himself from speaking out too. *Talk can always wait.* He had not talked to her for so long; coming here had made no difference at all. In his head, she suspected, he had never left his Berlin desk where he was safe behind that great tangled thorn-bush of all his books, watched by those huge dour portraits of his ancestors, worrying himself to distraction about Bismarck's blood and iron.

'I think we're very close, you and I,' she boldly, hopelessly declared. 'Perhaps, in spite of appearances, we are similar.'

'In the sense that we're both so committed to the family, yes—'

'No,' she dared to interrupt, 'I don't mean that. Not exactly. But in what we want from other people. What we need. How we choose to set ourselves in the world. In that respect, I believe, I have taken directly after you.'

It was as close as she could come. Closer than she had imagined possible only moments earlier. But for all his sympathy she saw behind his smile a mild contempt for her vagueness. This was, after all, a man for whom detail meant everything. And detail was what Auguste most lacked: hard evidence, chapter and verse, minute marginal annotations.

'I can't dispense wisdom, Gustchen,' he said. And she knew it. The dispensing of wisdom, such as it was, had always been more to his younger brother's taste. 'The future is a land of which there are no maps,' he would have been telling her now, or some other such *bon mot*. But Grimm's refusal to do the same only made him seem wiser. 'You have your life before you. It's too soon to speak this way.'

'Do you believe that people change, though? Truly?'

He looked at his glass. She could see how impossible this was for him and in spite of herself she pitied him. 'I think we can try to remake ourselves,' he said. 'I think that sometimes we have to. We all suffer from what you call "not knowing". But knowing, perhaps, is not always the solution.'

She clicked the door open then looked back. 'My mother,' she asked, 'when the time came – did *she* know? About my father?'

'That's something you would have to ask her.' His reply was not as curt as it might have been, but clearly he knew he was back on surer ground. Auguste's ferociously practical mother was simply not given to that kind of conversation. She would scarcely have recognized such a question, let alone been able to answer it truthfully, especially not now, from her safe haven of old age. ***My story, my story*** . . . They *were* two of a kind, her Apapa and her mother: both seeming desperate to deny that they had ever been young at all, together or apart; both affecting even now to be more superannuated, more set in their ways than they really were. So what exactly was it that they wanted to be too old *for*? In the end that was the only true question, and Auguste now accepted that she would never be able to put it to him.

Defeated by his decorum, she smiled. '*Gute Nacht,* Apapa,' she said. And she knew then, in the ocean of emptiness as she left the old mapmaker behind, that she had been right to ask Kummel to wait in her room: her steady, active single man; her newly arrived prince who happened to be on hand.

Jacob shook Wilhelm heartily by the hand, crossed to peck Dortchen on the cheek, then went back to his desk. 'A toast!' the Old One cried in a voice that sounded far too loud. 'We must have a toast! This is the most stirring news since the ending of the occupation!'

Smiling, Willi loped out, closing the study door behind him against the December draughts. It would take him several minutes to find a suitable bottle of wine, open and decant it.

Letting his eyes fall from Dortchen to the clutter of pages, Jacob shifted on his chair. Twice he picked up his quill then set it down. The echoes of what he had just heard seemed to be booming around him still. Three words in particular had snagged inside his head like three silk sleeves on a thornbush: *Nothing will change.*

'Willi insisted that we should tell you first,' Dortchen said, her piercing eyes continuing to look twice their normal size. 'We'll tell the rest of the family around the tree. I'm almost surprised he didn't speak with you before he proposed to me! Already he's insisted that we should name our first child after you.' Uncharacteristically, she simpered. 'He *didn't* speak with you first, did he?'

Jacob smiled back across the proofs of the second volume of his *Deutsche Grammatik*. She was sitting precisely where old Frau Viehmann had used to sit in their shared study, before the family's move here to Fünffensterstrasse. At the angle where the two walls of shelving converged she looked dwarfed by all the books. In seconds Jacob could have honed in on any title, but he could not for the life of him find the right words to greet the news which his brother had just broken, standing with a hand so lightly placed on his new fiancée's shoulder that he had seemed ready to take it away if Jacob should protest. 'No,' he replied. 'Willi said nothing.'

'But you knew, Jacob? You had guessed? This can't be a surprise after so long?' Although she leaned forward, she was still a great distance away.

'No – as you say – not a surprise.' With both hands he squared off the stack of papers directly in front of him. Beside it was the heliotrope plant in its shallow bowl, which Dortchen had given him only two days before. 'I'm really so pleased for you both. First Lotte marrying, now Willi. My only regret is that our mother isn't with us still, to share in such marvellous happiness. She loved you, of course, as one of her own.' He glanced up at her portrait, then turned and tapped the Family Book on the low shelf next to his desk.

Dortchen understood and tilted her head to one side, visibly touched. Four Christmases before, Jacob had had the family chronicle printed up as a household present. In it were recorded all the important events involving the brothers and their sister, with a preface in which Jacob wrote that the family's concerns were nearer to his heart 'than all the stuff that goes on in my head'. He had made a point of including Dortchen herself there, calling her *Schwester* and saying 'I love you as much as my own family'.

Jacob fully expected that now in her high excitement she might burst into tears. Instead, as he watched her fingers gently knead the reticule in her lap which matched the blue of her day dress, his own eyes moistened. His head too began to ring, and not just from the irregular hammer blows in the confounded forge below. *Nothing will change, nothing will change . . .*

'It will be a modest wedding,' Dortchen was saying. 'My inheritance is no longer large, and I know that you and Willi receive far less than your due at the library from the Elector. Not enough, certainly, to help support the other brothers as well. You really needn't worry yourself at the expense.'

Jacob smiled, but the cost of the wedding breakfast was not yet troubling him. She had been right: this was not a surprise. Despite his immersion in the *Grammatik* he had noticed a cooling in Willi's passion for Jenny von Droste-Hülshoff and his deepening interest in Dortchen. The affair with Jenny had never seemed likely to last. The Droste-Hülshoffs of Bökendorf, proud Catholic aristocrats, lived in a different world from the Grimms. A semi-invalid Protestant library secretary on a hundred thalers a year as a prospective son-in-law? Even Willi's degree of fame as the shaper of a surprisingly successful collection of fairytales would have seemed suspicious to people like that. Yes, of course Jacob had seen this coming. And yet . . .

'You do believe us, don't you Jacob,' Dortchen insisted, 'that nothing is going to change? *Nichts.* Here, anywhere. Whether you and Willi continue to work on separate projects or together outside of the library, none of your routines will be disturbed. I'll simply be here – with you both – rather more often than I am already. The last thing I want is to come between the two of you in any way. You will live with us. *We* will live with you. It's as it should be, Jacob.' She grinned awkwardly. 'And I'll go on cutting your hair, just as always.'

He smiled and dipped his head. 'Carl did say earlier that he thought it was looking a little scruffy just now.'

With two fingers she made as if to snip. 'Immediately after dinner then.'

Their gentle chuckles rang hollow. *Nothing will change . . .* It had begun to sound like a sentence. So little had changed – truly – since their mother's death, or even since their father's. Year on year Jacob had catalogued more books and published more of his own as his interest shifted from fairytales to folklore to philology and at last he had attained some financial security for them all. When he looked back on the first forty years of his life he saw himself scaling a shallow, stepped slope of volumes. *Nothing will change . . .*

The shallow slope rose on ahead. More words, more books, more steps, more honorary doctorates. Maybe in time he might even accept a professorship, provided that the teaching load were small enough. His own father's life had ended just four years on from here: a life of high achievement, reward, marriage, children. But now for Jacob, nothing would change. And he had always tacitly assumed that – one day – a change was going to come.

In a blur of blue he became aware of Dortchen rising from her chair and approaching the desk. He felt absurd to be sitting behind it, as if he were giving her a professional consultation. But whereas earlier his body had been so restless, now it was leaden. He was unable even to raise his head.

'*Komm*,' she murmured, '*gib mir deine Hand*.'

He remembered how as a girl she had told him and Willi her stories. She had told them so well, with such a quiet, maternal authority. After his own fashion he had loved her ever since hearing her first *Long ago, when wishes were still of use* . . . Dortchen's small hand closed over his own. Still he could not meet her eye. 'I love you as much as my own family,' he had written. She had not understood it then and she would not understand it now.

'Speak, Jacob,' she murmured. 'Tell me what you want to say. Say it to *me* if you can't tell Willi. It's not too late. Tell me.' Her hold on his lifeless hand tightened and he felt his fingers quicken. He watched their odd, almost independent movement as they became entangled with hers. 'Say it, Jacob. For my sake as much as for your own.'

There was a commotion outside in the corridor. Lotte had arrived with the tiresome Hassenpflug for the dinner they would all be sharing that evening. Jacob heard Willi warmly welcome them, then Carl's voice too as he came out to greet them; Ludwig's, Ferdinand's. The last brother was nearest to the closed study door, asking Willi why he was holding a decanter and only *three* glasses.

Jacob lifted his head. 'Nothing will change,' he assured Dortchen in a voice that threatened to break.

The door clicked open and swung in to reveal Wilhelm at the head of the rest of the family, just beneath the Christmas mistletoe. Jacob's fingers died again but Dortchen kept hold of them as she turned to the doorway and quietly, proudly, announced her news before sending off her fiancé to fetch more glasses.

She wanted him to be waiting in her bed. The time for talk had passed; the term was up, now she must wake. And for that she wanted to be back in his arms, coming back to life in the same way as she had imagined the princess's statue in Marburg becoming flesh. *Marriage can't be the end for everyone.* There was much to dwell on there. Too much. Stepping lightly along the uncarpeted corridor of the inn she began instead, as her Apapa had suggested, to remake herself.

Pausing outside her door, she straightened the sleeves of her dress and checked her chignon. In sending Kummel up to her room after relieving him of Grimm's nightcap she had given no explanation, nor had he asked for one. Her steady look had been enough. As she turned the crystal door handle she hoped more fervently than ever that he was already in the wide bed.

Only one candle burned inside the empty room, above the bureau to Auguste's left. She closed the door and her eye was drawn at once to the sheet of paper beneath it, a sheet not left by her, half covered by a clear, confident script in a hand that was not her own. An uncapped pen lay beneath the last line:

Sehr geehrte Fräulein Grimm,

I am sorry not to be here, as you requested.

I have arranged for all the Professor's requirements to be met in the morning by one of the hotel porters, who will at that time be off duty. He is trustworthy, and will ensure that your baggage is safely delivered to the station and stowed aboard the train. For these services, I have paid him in advance from my own wages.

Please forgive me for failing to complete the full four weeks of my commission with your family. For this, I will forego payment for the final seven days. I trust that you and the Professor will enjoy a safe journey back to Berlin.

It ended there and a tiny cry escaped Auguste's lips: half incredulous, half despairing. In that moment too, she realized she was not alone. Stealthy bootsteps from the balcony broke the silence, followed by the rustling of its curtain and a cool new breeze at her back. 'Fräulein . . .'

Auguste stiffened but did not turn. Her heart beat so hard that it threatened to burst through her bodice. 'I'm confused, Kummel,' she tried to laugh. 'You write that you've gone, yet in fact here you are.'

'I began the letter but couldn't continue it.'

'You're *leaving* us?' She pressed her thighs against the bureau's edge, glaring at the tears of wax that disfigured the squat yellow candle in its dish. He did not answer. She heard a heavy muffled sound, as if he had sunk to the floor. Turning, steadying herself against the bureau's surface behind her, she saw him standing at the foot of the bed, pale and tall. Her prince, here – because it was time – to witness her awakening from the sleep that had passed for a life.

The sound had been him setting down his own small valise. His hands now hung free at his sides, the fingers of the left flexing. '*Was ist los?*' Auguste asked, trying to smile. 'Where are you going? *Why* are you going?' And already, madly, she wanted to say, 'Let me come too.'

'The Professor hasn't spoken to you? About me?'

No Kummel? Grimm had asked. *He is still with us?* Dumbly she shook her head.

'He will.' He smiled, as if at some joke out of Auguste's range of hearing, and his shadowed face became quite beautiful.

'But now? Must you leave *now?* If something has happened between the two of you, there was no sign of any difficulty at the party or on the way back here. At least not to me. And we need you with us, Kummel. Tomorrow more than ever, with the Professor so fragile . . .'

'The Professor will not suffer,' Kummel cut in. 'He won't die – not here, not on your journey home.'

'You know this? You have it on some higher authority?'

His eyes narrowed and Auguste gripped the bureau behind her. He could not be humoured out of this. Nothing had changed but everything about him was different. Had he not been wearing her father's old coat she might even have failed to recognize him. He faced her like a cornered animal not known for its ferocity but ready to strike first if it had to. Auguste looked away. 'You're frightening me, Kummel. Why didn't you just write your letter and leave? What do you want with me now?'

She looked back to find him shaking his head slowly, rhythmically. She longed to step forward and take it in both hands, still it, soothe away the torment. But she dared not make a move. Out in the yard the two children were tearing at each other but Auguste's heartbeat – to her – sounded louder.

'You really don't know?' he said.

'Know what? Please, please tell me.'

'You don't know me, then?' It was like a wretched taunt. 'You don't know what I am? *He* knows, your Apapa.'

Auguste stared back, petrified, as the candle behind her began to gutter and the room appeared to be struck by its own tiny bolts of lightning. Then beyond the children's squabbling a deeper commotion arose: a goods train rumbling its way through the night. Despite the distance, by a fluke of the wind the faint, panicked lowing of the boarded-in livestock carried through into the room where she stood, mixed in with the locomotive's ghostly hiss and clank.

'I am a Jew,' he told her in a soft, strangled purr. 'I've tried not to be. I've tried to stop but I can't – not since I was ten, not since I lost everything.'

The train's noise was swallowed. One of the children screamed, then Auguste never heard either again. Her grip on the bureau loosened and the candle's flame began to burn more steadily. *I think we can try to remake ourselves. I think sometimes we have to.* Her instinct was to giggle, to laugh away the notion that this could matter. Instead she racked her brain for a reason why it might have been an issue for Grimm. 'You didn't wish us to know?' she stammered. 'And the Professor found out?'

Kummel's eyes flashed.

'And he minds? I really can't believe that he would mind.'

'Who *doesn't* mind? Here?' He flinched and waved an arm that might have been meant to signal Cassel, Hesse or every last German state. 'Would *you* marry me? Do you think your family would let you?'

This time Auguste did laugh. 'Marry?' If this was a proposal it was not her first but it was certainly the most unexpected and – if only Kummel had waited for an answer – the least easy to reject.

'I don't mean to offend you,' he said, 'Not you.' Again he was shaking his head, chopping the air with his hands. 'The Dresslers would mind. I know them. Their sort. It's happened to me before. Once they find out, they'll sack me anyway, so what good would it do me to return to Berlin? I'll move on again.' He smiled wryly. 'There are other worlds than this one.'

'But you think the Professor will tell the Dresslers? Why should he do that, if you don't wish it? If *I* do not wish it?'

'Because *that's what happens!*' He gave the last three words enormous emphasis. 'It's how it is now. But you're kind, Fräulein. You're good. And not just to me.' He glanced away. 'I admire you. That's why I couldn't just leave you a letter. I had to see you.' He looked up, past her.

'But what would you do? Where would you go?' Something made her hesitate. 'Do you have family?'

His eyes met hers. And in the first instance she was glad that the candle chose this moment to burn itself out. His expression had skewered her. *Lost everything,* she remembered. *Lost everything.*

'You can't go,' she babbled before he could say a word in that darkness as black as an ogre's heart. 'You can't disappear. I can't let you. Stay. We'll talk. I have to talk with you. Not just about you. About me too – about why I brought the Professor here . . .'

She would have gone on. But the room seemed to rear up in front of her and she was drawn forward as if into a void. She tried to cry out, more in relief than protest, but the hand at the small of her back propelled her face up into his.

Their kiss was passionate, but she felt still more driven as she tore her mouth away, pressed her head to his smoky neck and slid her palms up over both his shoulders. No talk, no words. This was the better way. The prince's way. Stirred, she was turning from stone to flesh. But still he held her against him with only one hand, and when she slid her own hand lower on his arm and came to his fist, she found it curled tight around the handle of his valise.

'*Nein,*' she pleaded, trying to fit her fingers between his and loosen the grip. '*Nein, nein.*' She kissed his quivering neck, his ear, clumsily his jaw, his chin. Her tongue flicked against his bulbous throat. But he did not put down the bag. In the blackness every sound was magnified. Another goods train rolled through in the direction of Göttingen, and she heard more animal cries, which then, unaccountably, turned for a short while into that eerie dry clacking that had been troubling her intermittently ever since they had left the Harz.

'Tell me now,' came his voice, filling Auguste's head. 'Say it. Why did you bring the old man here? What do you want from him?'

'It's insane of me.' She clutched at his coat with both small hands. *The most precious person in my life . . .* 'I can hardly say it to myself. It's only what I think, what I've been half guessing for so long.' *I was only ever looking after her for you . . .* 'I don't have the first idea if it's true but to me it *feels* so true.'

'Say it.'

And then she knew it was time. She had to hear it herself, and had to have it heard, partly because she knew she could not stop this man from leaving, partly in the hope that it might make him stay. But as soon as the words were out, loud and bright in that void of a room, his hand was gone.

He passed across her and the door opened on to the lamp-lit corridor, leaving her to whisper the words a second time as if they might answer or atone for the first: 'I think he's my father.'

TWENTY

In the week that followed, messenger after breathless messenger stormed into the palace precincts from the eastern frontier. Each wore a look on his face like five days of bad weather. The emperor's invasion forces were ready to move, but still he held them back until the princess gave a final reply to the ultimatum of his own marriage proposal. She delayed sending it, even as preparations were rushed through for the wedding to the father of her children and the double coronation.

Meanwhile each day the prince oversaw the training of the Rose Kingdom's troops and astounded his generals with his instinctive grasp of strategy. Each night he was reunited with his bride-to-be and children, slipping by second nature into the duties and delights of family life. All he needed to complete his happiness was his mother's arrival. He gazed out west across the treetops and wished her closer. This was the world where she belonged – her truest home. 'Surely she should be here by now,' he asked the chamberlain on the morning when the emperor's ultimatum ran out. 'You sent the coach to the right town?'

'I did, sir. And I would trust my life to the driver. But we can no longer delay the ceremonies. Perhaps your mother will appear in time at least for your crowning.'

The prince went to the princess in her sunny morning quarters and found her already dressed for the wedding. The children too wore matching wine-red velvet suits and had brought with them the blue coat which, until that day, they had left on their totem in the garden. On a chair behind them his wig and sword waited. With two kisses he sent the children ahead to the palace's main hall. Then as he dressed he noticed that although the princess watched him with a loving smile, there was anxiety in her wide eyes.

Those eyes alone had justified his return. Luminous and thick-lashed, they brought such new depth to her beauty that again he was glad to have seen her first asleep. That way he had not been numbed by the shock of discovering all her loveliness at once. He crossed to where she sat by the high, west-facing window, knelt and took her slender hands in his.

'What is it?' he whispered. 'Tell me what's on your mind. Is it that I must leave immediately afterwards to fight? You can't doubt that we shall win? The right is on our side – the good. That counts for everything.'

Still looking through the glass, she held his hands more tightly. 'It's foolish of me, but I keep thinking of the last feast day here, the one to celebrate my birth. While I was growing up, people spoke of it so often, and in such detail – about its lavishness and then its awful ending – that I started to feel as if I remembered every moment myself, that I *saw* the coming of the last dark guest, whom I *did* then briefly glimpse, years later, in the garret . . .'

He put a hand to her face, tilted it towards him and lightly kissed her lips. Now he understood why she had insisted earlier that the feast should be brief and frugal, why the coronations should take place with only the kingdom's leading officials present. He kissed her again and thrilled to her gentle response. 'Come,' he said, standing. 'This time it will be so different.'

An hour later, married and crowned, they emerged into the sunlight to cheers from the palace staff, from the troops already assembled for the march and from everyone who had come up from the surrounding towns and villages. So many packed the courtyard and surrounding terraces that the couple had to walk right around the palace to be seen by all the well-wishers.

Smiling, waving, the new king's eye was drawn to the eastbound road, down which all the previous week's messengers had spurred their flagging horses. A coach led by two grey geldings was approaching from the spinney above the defensive wall's eastern gate. The chamberlain, who was walking behind the royal pair, led the king aside at once.

'That's the coach I sent to fetch your mother,' he said, with a face to split a pitcher. 'The horses too. I would recognize them anywhere. But they are coming from the wrong direction. It's as if they've been circling the palace.'

The king shook off the chamberlain's hand and, with his wife behind him, took several steps closer to the road. The crowd parted in front of them to form a human avenue.

As the coach drew to a halt at the gatehouse, everyone else turned to watch the unexpected arrival. Two sentries challenged the driver, who remained up on his bench, while another armed man opened the coach door. After a long moment, its only passenger clambered down.

'Oh, tell me please, tell me,' breathed the young queen to her husband. 'Tell me that *she* is not your mother.'

But the prince did not hear. Already he had broken away into a run to greet the woman to whom he owed everything.

Ten Days Later

TWENTY-ONE

After lunching with the Stenzels at their house in Bellevuestrasse, Dortchen suggested a walk home through the Tiergarten. At first Auguste said no. Apparently she had promised Jacob that she would be gone for only two hours. But Dortchen decided to be firm. Both Rudolf and Gisela were on bedside duty at Linkstrasse, she reminded her daughter, and prepared to stay until evening to regulate the stream of well-wishers, friends, university colleagues and even – latterly – contributors to the *Wörterbuch*. Besides, Auguste needed the fresh air: she had left the apartment only three times since returning to Berlin from Hesse.

'Your Apapa won't be going anywhere before you get back,' Dortchen said as they joined the large crowd of Thursday afternoon strollers. 'I don't think he would dare.' And when Auguste flashed her a mortified look she could not help flying at her: 'You heard the doctor yesterday, as well as I! He's a tough old warrior and he's pulled himself around. A few more days in bed and he'll be back at his desk woodchopping for fifteen hours at a stretch.' And immediately she regretted adding under her breath, 'Just like old times.'

They took a meandering route across the park towards the city centre, keeping the dome of the Schloss in sight but using the narrower paths to avoid gangs of students and the usual flock of flower girls. Uniformed soldiers were everywhere, and from the wooden podium near the beer houses the sound of a military band gusted through the autumn air. Dortchen, unlike Jacob, did not especially mind that Berlin had become a glorified barracks where one's legs were in constant danger from officers' swords. As Bonaparte had said, Prussia was hatched from a cannonball. And at least they're *our* soldiers, she would think whenever her brother-in law set off on one of his *sotto voce* rants.

Auguste took little interest in anything she saw. Once her attention was caught by some open-cupped wild mushrooms that had broken through the sandy soil in such straight lines that they could have been on a drill square. And she smiled at a svelte woman's dachshunds rubbing their backs into the pathway's gravel. Otherwise in all but body she was still back in Hesse, presumably blaming herself all over again for pushing Jacob past the limits of his physical endurance.

Dortchen had long since stopped trying to argue her out of that. Crises had always affected them in different ways: Dortchen would grow tetchy, while Auguste was prone to melodrama. Even in the best of times the girl seemed to live her life against its own grain – and she scarcely made matters easier for herself by insisting that she would marry only *after* finding love, not as a step towards achieving it. Their western trip seemed not to have been strenuous. A persistent cold followed by inflammation of the liver could hardly have been brought on by so gentle a jaunt. But if her daughter was simply terrified of Jacob dying, then that was something else again – and rather unexpected.

During Willi's long last confinement she had been dutifully attentive and, at his death, as sad as either of her brothers. But she had never been as *consumed* as she appeared to be now. For all Dortchen knew, it was a fashionable affectation to mope in the manner of the widow of Balmoral, rather like those silly society girls who drank vinegar to give themselves an 'interesting' pallor. For his part, Herman believed Auguste had too little to keep her otherwise occupied. It was he who had suggested taking her along to the Stenzels to break her mournful vigil at Jacob's side. But two glasses of cherry wine and a mouthful of smoked goose had brought about no obvious change for the better.

Dortchen found her own appetite was returning in the open air. At the canalside she bought some hot garlic sausage from a boy vendor and while she ate Auguste stood apart, watching two men in fishing boots toss buckets out into the brackish water, then pull them in full of eels. Although dusk was still hours away the sun was now obscured by a smoky off-white pall through which only a few scraps of blue showed. The silence between them was starting to irk Dortchen. 'Soon,' she remarked in a voice louder than was strictly necessary on resuming their easterly route, 'we shall have to plan for Christmas.'

'Christmas. *Ja*.'

'Perhaps Gisela will have an announcement to make to us by then?'

She said it purely to provoke her daughter, to incite an outburst against what Auguste called her obsessions with marriage and babies. But the younger woman merely tilted her head, and they walked on again without speaking. Dortchen resigned herself to letting this mood of hers run its course. Gustchen would come round. She usually did. Then they would go on much as before, lively enough companions, very probably sharing a smaller home when, in the end, Jacob went the same way as his younger brothers and sister. Truly, Dortchen sometimes thought, they were going to need each other then. Life without the man she had known for sixty years was still scarcely conceivable.

On leaving the Tiergarten, her eye was drawn to a skinny male figure passing behind a street clown who was performing with two wooden dogs on strings to a rapt, mainly adult audience.

'There!' she breathed, grasping Auguste's forearm. 'Our man! Crossing the road between those carriages? There! Yes, I'm sure it's him!'

At first Auguste could not see who she meant. '*Isn't* that him?' Dortchen pressed. 'With the close-cropped hair? Our Flying Dutchman? There! There!' She felt her daughter's arm quicken, then almost at once go limp in her grip.

'No Mother, calm yourself. The person in the road is taller, and broader too about the shoulders.' She sounded almost offended by the anticlimax.

Dortchen took away her hand. It was the third false alarm that week. Gisela said she kept conjuring up young Kummel because she so badly wanted to box his ears for deserting in Hesse. Perhaps that was it. And she still had to explain his loss to the Dresslers when they returned from Italy. God alone knew what had got into the boy, passing up a week's wages just to avoid a train trip back to Berlin. It made no sense. Any suggestion that Jacob had taken against him for being an undeclared Jew was too absurd for words. And up to the minute of his disappearance Kummel had been so reliable. Dortchen had fully intended to ask the Dresslers for further short-term loans. Now she was left with this acute embarrassment.

Suddenly the clatter of the traffic took the wind out of her sails. 'Gustchen,' she called, resting against a circular advertising pillar as her daughter wandered ahead to watch the street clown from closer. 'Do you think you could hail a carriage to take us the rest of the way?'

Auguste turned, immediately anxious.

'Oh I'm not unwell,' Dortchen assured her, putting a hand to her breast and smiling. 'Just short of puff, that's all.' And although she would never have said so, she was also a woman of seventy who – just now and then – would have appreciated a little of the cosseting that seemed to be handed out so freely to this family's older men and younger womenfolk.

As Auguste went to find some transport, Dortchen watched her pretty, preoccupied profile and wondered again how she was going to bear up to the eventual loss of her Apapa. But her concern was not entirely selfless. Wondering about how her daughter might be affected at least saved Dortchen from worrying about the impact that Jacob's death was sure to have on herself – a loss which would, in its way, match the shock of losing Willi.

'It's over. Jacob has died.'

'It was peaceful, God be thanked. He slipped away in his sleep.'

'Poor Jacob. Poor dear little child . . .'

He heard his brothers' hushed voices behind him in the parlour as he slipped out of the bedroom and down the darkened corridor to the study. He could stay no longer with Willi and Dortchen in their grief. He needed time at his desk: a few moments alone after twelve unbroken hours by the cradle, virtually breathing into his tiny namesake's mouth to keep him alive. Now the vigil was over. The child had not even reached his first Christmas. Jacob had to gather himself, pray, and find a way to accept what already felt like the cruellest death of all.

With a cold but steady hand he managed to light a candle on the shelf just inside his study. Then he went to the window, closed the curtains over the latest swirl of snowflakes and turned to his desk. Instead of sitting, he shut his eyes, rested both hands on the back of his chair, and tried not to think base thoughts. And for the first time in a life lived in his brother's almost constant company, that was not easy.

For eight joyful months he had looked on the child almost as his own. Jacob, *der kleine* Jacob. There had even been physical similarities. Dortchen had said so: his darting eyes, his smile, the way his nose was curving. But now in death he was indisputably Willi's. Oh how – *how?* – could a man whose own life had always hung by so slender a thread hope to father a thriving child?

Jacob reached out and took up the Family Book. He could not open it at the page where the boy's birth had been recorded eight months and twelve days earlier – less time than it had taken for him to grow out of his mother. His cheek twitched. He could not stop it from twitching again. His breath came in sharp, irregular gusts, choking out of him in knotted little clouds in the dark, unheated room. He felt large, strong, ludicrously fit and well. He would have hurled the book at the facing wall but the door clicked and slowly opened inwards.

Dortchen entered as if the door handle were leading her. She clung on to it, staring at the corner chair, then took another step, her arm becoming taut behind her. When her fingers came free she paused as if waking from a sleepwalk and rested back against the door which clicked shut behind her. Only now did she turn her eyes on Jacob. Quietly he put down the book and stared back.

'Where has he gone?' she asked, with an odd, incredulous smile.

Jacob came from behind the desk. He did not know if she meant Willi or her lost son. Either way, he had no answer. 'Where is he?' she asked again, her dry eyes fierce with what looked like fury. She slumped lower against the door and it was almost too painful for Jacob to look at her: ruddy-cheeked, sternly lovely in this grim extremity, brimful of *life* in her combative little frame.

He was aghast at the way intimacy could inflict such suffering, appalled by an anguish so much denser even than his own. And although he tried not to, he remembered his own mother's despair when his father had died. Then he knew beyond all doubt that he would never have the stomach, let alone the heart, to marry and be so close to another mortal soul. It was not so much death that harrowed him, but having to live on like this in the midst of it.

'Our mother,' he began, trying to console her across the width of the study floor, 'our mother lost her first child too. Then there were *six* that lived . . .'

Dortchen knew this. Jacob had probably told her himself during the endless days of waiting. He glanced away from her crazed, hungry gaze to the heliotrope plant she had given him just before her engagement two years earlier. Its spiky purple flowers looked harsh and cold in the single candle's light. Dortchen too must have found them impossible. Launching herself off the door, she swiped out and sent both plant and bowl crashing to the tiled floor.

As she darted back Jacob, who half expected her to strike him next, tried and failed to catch her wrist. Back against the door, she winced and bit her lip but still no tears came, as surely they had to. Jacob prayed for her to cry. She had to move past this. She had to take him with her, quicker than the clock could show, to somewhere further on, where they might both be safer, out of reach.

'Jacob, Jacob,' she muttered at the mess of dashed-down leaves and soil and earthenware fragments. 'Why did you go? Oh Jacob, my Jacob . . .' Then without raising her eyes she lifted both her arms as if she were being sucked down where she stood, and at last he had to stalk across the floor into her embrace.

'Jacob,' she murmured again as he felt her arms close on his back, her fingers bite into his shoulders. *Cry*, he roared at her in silence, *Cry now*. But instead of sinking into him she was stiff against his waistcoat, shuddering, her breath ferociously hot on his throat, his neck, his stubbled cheek. His own hands met at the small of her back. She smelled different. A summer scent of apples. *Ich liebe dich*, was all he could think – and then the line from *Fundvögel* that had always conjured up her quietly smiling face in his mind: 'Neither now nor ever shall I leave you.'

Silently he turned his head aside and her cheek was against his. They both looked in the same direction. He saw all the books marching away like guardsmen on their shelves and not one word spilled out of them that he could use for her here.

Their heads turned back together, as if two layers of a single skin were being peeled apart. And when they were joined by only the tips of their noses, their mouths met and opened.

Day by day Kummel's features grew vaguer in Auguste's memory. Perhaps the figure crossing the road near the Brandenburg Gate the day before *had* been him. Her mother thought she had seen him twice before as well.

Curious now, Auguste left the apartment again after lunch on Friday, not, as she had told her mother, to tend Wilhelm's grave in Schöneberg. Instead she walked east of the Gate, up through Montbijou and finally amid a swirling wind into the tenement zone of Scheunenviertel. Berlin was not a city, Heine had said, only a place where people come together. Or completely fail to do so, Auguste thought.

The impressive new synagogue on Orianienburgerstrasse looked misplaced above the street flotsam of prostitutes, poor students and pawnbrokers' shops. In the streets around it she glimpsed unshaven fathers hanging out of upper-storey windows to smoke, since the rooms they shared with several different families were so cramped. Some of the hovels made her gasp, and she could barely believe how many raggedy infants packed themselves into minuscule courtyards barely big enough to turn a fire-hose in.

In the Harz and again in Hesse Auguste had missed the city badly. In her mind it was a solid haven, far more real than that other fairytale world. But now – even beyond these scenes of destitution – it seemed shockingly temporary after the great sweeps of forest, as if it could all be smashed to rubble tomorrow.

There were few obvious Jews with their beards and black velour hats. None of the other faces bore any kind of resemblance to Kummel's. And why should they have? If he had not told her, she would never have thought him an 'Israelite', to use the slang of some in her social circle. Grimm too claimed only to have *suspected* this, certainly not to have accused him. 'I mentioned to him only that elements in his story were unconvincing,' he had protested on their sombre rail journey home from Cassel. 'I had guessed, I'll admit, that he was not a Christian, but nowadays that would hardly be conclusive either way.'

'Then why should he have said you knew?' Auguste asked. 'And why should any of it *matter*? To him, to you, to anyone?'

'To me, it does *not* matter.' His clouded eyes fixed her and she dipped her head, unable to let it go but desperate not to seem too interested.

'But it doesn't matter, does it? Not now? People convert and no one cares what they used to be. But what he said was he couldn't *stop* being a Jew, ever since he was ten. How could he have failed to convert?'

Grimm looked away at the passing Hanoverian countryside from which he had once been so famously expelled. 'To some now, Judaism is a question of race, not religion. A Christianized Jew is therefore still a Jew – and perhaps *more* of a provocation, since he pretends to be what he is not. Our man may have met with such prejudice. Or even outright persecution.'

'He said that at ten he lost everything.'

Grimm turned his eyes back on her. Auguste could not read them. Or rather, she could not be sure why they looked quite so disappointed. 'His family may not even have been German,' he said. 'They could have come here to escape from pogroms, further east.'

'But haven't Jews suffered in Germany too? Not as terribly, but it has happened?'

Again he had looked away. 'As you say – not as terribly.'

This was dangerous ground. Auguste knew that some crusaders for unification – a few tavern rabble-rousers, according to the incontrovertibly liberal Grimm – saw no place for Jews in any future German nation-state. She also remembered, years before, a smooth-cheeked young pastor at a salon describing the Jewish 'nation' as a parasitic plant that wound around the healthy German tree to suck out its life juices until finally it would moulder and decay. She knew that Kummel had not necessarily come from abroad to suffer. And now, she thought, she understood that sorrowfully forbidding look in her Apapa's eye.

On returning home she was glad to hear laughter coming from his bedroom. The talk there with his visitors was normally so hushed and dour. Even with the *Wörterbuch* contributors, it dwelt on the so-called Realpolitik of that accursed 'minister of conflict' Bismarck: his contempt for peace, his reported readiness to find unity through force of arms. Bonaparte and Bismarck, she thought, they stood like bloody bookstops at either end of her Apapa's long, troubled life.

She looked in the letterstands in the hall and on the kitchen dresser but still her photographic prints from Cassel had not arrived. If they failed to appear on the following morning, a Saturday, she would wire a stiff message.

The two voices along the corridor were familiar, both professors from Berlin's Academy of Sciences. Dortchen, unusually, was sitting in with them. This gave Auguste an opportunity that she decided was too good to miss. Leaving her parasol on the kitchen table she slipped down to her mother's bedroom, shut the door behind her and made directly for the cupboard where old clothes were kept. There were plenty inside. Little that had come into this once penurious family's possession had ever been thrown away.

Auguste's eyes fell on a dark framed photograph lying under a rack of dresses. She leaned closer but saw it was a portrait of Wilhelm, wearing the coat that had been altered for Kummel, and did not stop to pick it up. Squatting to dig through the heaps of folded blouses, she gave a start as a train inched its way into the Potsdamer Platz station.

I think he's my father . . . Every time this happened, she recalled the magnified din of those cattle trucks in Cassel as Kummel held her close and made her say the unsayable. As soon as she had let that genie out of its bottle, it had seemed both more and less plausible than before. *My father . . . My father . . . My father . . .* And then he had simply run out on her.

She could appreciate that just as Kummel's Jewishness mattered not a jot to her, so her own parentage was of no interest to him. She could see that. But he *had* asked. And on that last night in Hesse, falling asleep with her lips still stinging from his prince's kisses, she had not been ready to believe she would never see him again. Nor, in her heart, was she ready now. If he really was the prince for her, then he would have no choice but to come back.

At last she found what she was looking for. With her heart beating faster, she tugged the garment out from under the pile, hurried from the room, and did not unfold it until she was perched on the side of her own bed. She had been thinking about it ever since Kummel had mentioned her Apapa looking at shawls in Marburg. But this was not just any shawl.

She wanted to find it pretty; she knew that this French style had been fashionable just before she was born. It looked funereal, a sable ground with green and red floral edgings. Yet its linen was fine and it could not have been cheap. Her mother would never have chosen it for herself, but she had treasured it as a gift. She had been wearing it in so many of Auguste's earliest memories, to the extent that as a child she had thought her mother's favourite colour must be black.

Weaving, we are weaving . . . surged into her head, like a child's mocking cry. Heine: one more Israelite. Those few words of his were all her Apapa had given her in Hesse, all he had passed on and left for her to hold.

She smoothed out the shawl's creases on the counterpane, lifted it in a gentle, gingery breeze of preservative and draped it around her own shoulders. And when she turned to look at herself in her dressing-table mirror, first she smiled with a frisson of recognition, then all at once she burst into tears.

TWENTY-TWO

At sundown the king was scheduled to leave at the head of his troops. Every moment till then was precious. He had never been so happy: to have his mother, his wife and his children under a single roof was the fulfilment of all his wishes and also – he felt sure – of his mother's longest held dreams.

'Had it not been for her,' he told his queen as they undressed in the bedchamber before consummating their marriage, 'I would never have come to you. I would never have known of this palace. It was she who spurred me on, she who sent me out to find you, she who made me believe that I could win you.'

'I know,' she answered, looking as haunted as she was lovely. She had perched on the edge of her bed to unbraid the single scintillating rope of hair that hung over her bare left shoulder. He came to her from behind and kissed the tan flesh at the nape of her neck, then turned her to face him. Although she tried to smile, her eyes were moist.

'Trust me,' he whispered as he put his arms around her. 'You don't have to be afraid. This feast is nothing like the last. No evil can come of it, nor from the war I must fight for our kingdom. Only more joy awaits . . .'

They made love with tawny, late-afternoon sunshine spilling down through the high west-facing windows. He was so keen that only when they peeled apart did he realize that she had been as dead to him as she had been on the spinning-garret's floor. And while he dressed again and buckled on his sword she stayed on her back, as if numbed by some new poison. If she had not been furiously blinking away tears, he would have crossed to check that she was still alive.

Voices rose from the courtyard below the chamber: the twins, giggling and shrieking in delight. He looked down to see his mother sitting on a wrought-iron chair in the last corner of sunlight. She had his face-mask on and was comically waving her arms like a monster. One after another the children raced up and crashed against her great bosom.

His own eyes filled with tears as he watched. It was so long since he had seen her free to enjoy herself. He would make sure now that she never suffered again.

'Come and see,' he called over his shoulder. 'It's as if they have always known her.' But his queen did not stir, just as she had neither spoken nor returned his mother's kiss when they had met. 'Tell me what's wrong,' he said, returning to her side. 'You can tell me anything.' He touched her wrist, which was so still and cool that he briskly pulled his hand away again.

'She frightens me . . .' she began, then she shook her head on the pillow. 'It's as if *I* have always known her . . .'

'But how? Why? How could you?'

Again she could only shake her head, screwing up her face, either because she did not know what to say or did not dare to put it into words. Suddenly piqued, he glared down at her. 'The children love her. Why can't you?'

She stiffened and lifted her head a little way from the pillow. 'But where are her own children? You said there were five as well as yourself: the "babies", where are *they?*'

'She told me they're being looked after while she's away. Do you *want* them here?' He certainly did not want them himself, even though he had been expecting them. One reason why it thrilled him so to see his mother in this special place was that she was alone and unencumbered.

His queen glanced back, not accusingly but as if she sensed some kind of collusion with his own mother. Then her head sank back down and she closed her eyes. The children's squeals below grew more raucous.

At a loss, he repeated what he had told her earlier: 'Without her, we would never have met.'

'But why did she want that?'

He watched her tremble, her eyes still shut tight, before turning towards the door. 'Sleep now,' he suggested. 'You're tired. When you wake you'll see all this differently. And when I return we shall never part again – any of us.'

He left without kissing her, and waited in vain for her to call him back as he paused at the head of the main staircase. He strode through the shadowy feasting hall, counting up the eleven bejewelled cutlery caskets that had still not been moved from their places on the dresser.

The chamberlain fell into step with him when he beckoned. 'Watch my wife closely,' he said. 'She's not herself: full of dark imaginings. I doubt if she will rise from her bed for some time.'

'Your word is law, highness. But as regent she must supervise the affairs of state in your absence.'

The king's step did not falter as he left the palace. Nor did he even look at the chamberlain after he said again, 'Highness, the affairs of state must be supervised.'

'Then my mother shall be regent.'

'Your mother?'

The king's horse was brought up from the stables. The groom stood aside to allow him to mount. 'My mother shall be regent,' he calmly repeated before urging his stallion up the road to the east, where his armies waited. 'Let *her* word be law.'

TWENTY-THREE

Grimm woke late on Saturday morning with a strong, sad impression that his face had just been touched. His cheekbone felt cool, possibly damp, as if a pair of lips had grazed it. His eyes shut tighter as vivid light fell on him from high to his right, accompanied by a ratcheting back of the curtains along their rail. Blinking, he rocked himself on to his elbows and immediately suffered a rush of nausea.

'*Guten Morgen,* Apapa.' Gustchen's voice. 'You've been threatening to wake for over an hour. Twitching, mouthing. Can you remember your dream?'

Dream? Was she blind? Could she not see the streaks of mud all over him? The clods of earth on his eyes, in his mouth? And then at last he came fully awake, freshly irritated that he was not alone. It made him so uneasy to be overseen. But nothing he said could have removed Gisela, Dortchen, Herman, Rudolf and – by far the most regular sentry – Auguste. He had lost count of how often he had woken (usually from fanciful dreams of riding: first up to a palace, then away to a war) to find her poised in the chair by the wardrobe, just like a parent about to tell a bedtime story. He wished at times that she *had* told him tales. Anything but these long, anxious, guilty looks of hers.

Hoping she would not come to help him, he eased his legs from under the bedcovers and planted his feet on the cold floorboards. It required a huge effort but, for her, he managed not to grimace. He ran a hand across his stubbled jaw then pushed back his hair from his forehead. His fringe seemed shorter. Dortchen must have trimmed it at some time over the past fortnight. He remembered her shaving him several times, but not the haircut. 'Would you be so good as to bring me water?' he asked Auguste, as he reached for his dressing-gown. His mouth still felt caked with soil; forest ground, a distinct taste of pine needles. 'I'll shave myself today. And put some clothes on too.'

'Clothes, Apapa? Isn't it a little soon for that?'

His hackles rose. 'I don't plan to perform gymnastics! I wish only to be in a shirt and trousers. I can't fester here indefinitely. And please, Gustchen, no more visitors today. It has been endless. Should my condition deteriorate again, then they can all re-form their queues if they so wish.'

Nodding, he eyed the stack of Berlin newspapers and journals that the maid had been keeping ever since he left for the Harz. 'I'll do a little light reading. It's been too long since I read.' He pushed himself to his feet and did not have to grip the bedside table with its ewer. Then he nodded across at the pile of publishers' proofs on the window seat. 'A little reading can do no harm now. And you must go about your own business too, *Liebchen*. You've been devoting far too much time to me.'

To his surprise she left the room without further protest. And it was Dortchen, ten minutes later, who brought his water, with a newly ironed shirt and undergarments, followed by a tray of rolls and weak coffee. On neither brief visit did she speak, for fear of disturbing his concentration. She did not have to utter a word. The knowing smiles they exchanged said it all: her continuing concern, his determination not to be pestered, her amusement at his incorrigibility, his long-standing gratitude to her simply for being the woman she was. Then he was left alone for almost the whole of that bright afternoon, distracted only by the city birdsong and the occasional judder of trains drawing into the nearby terminus: one of the true new gatehouses since all the city walls had come down.

The proofs were an edition of Greek fairy tales that he had promised to look over for a fellow member of the Academy of Sciences. He found them charming, and a welcome alternative to returning at once to his infernal woodchopping. But the longer he read, the less likely such a return became. He could not help feeling that he had reached the end of a line, that like the trains arriving in the Potsdamer Platz he had travelled as far as he possibly could and that now he could move off again only in some new direction.

Soon after five o'clock there was a tap at the door. Hoarsely he called out, '*Herein.*' Gustchen appeared, carrying spiced tea and ginger biscuits, with a short brown tube under her arm. As she put down the tray on the floor at the foot of the bed and took the tube into her hands, Grimm noticed something unusual. She was wearing an old black shawl he had once bought for Dortchen – years ago, while she was pregnant with Auguste. It astonished him that his sister-in-law had kept it. She had certainly not worn it for decades.

Auguste did not pour the tea, although she had brought two cups. Instead, smiling, she crossed to the window seat where he was perched, holding the tube in one hand and tapping it on her free palm as if she were about to strike him. Stopping just short of the window, she drew out a paler roll from inside and unfurled it in front of him without saying a word.

'*Heh*,' he exclaimed. 'The Cassel group portrait. *Ach*, yes.' She was actually holding it too far away for the faces to be clear, but he had no wish to study it any more closely. His mouth had become very dry again and more than anything in the world he needed his tea.

'You look exhausted in the photo, Apapa. I'm sorry I made you sit through it.'

'Not at all. I'm glad we have the record. Our hosts were extremely generous. Will they too be sent a print?'

She nodded, still apparently absorbed in the photograph. The shawl hung loose from her right shoulder, close to his face. The smell of ginger made his lips feel all the more parched, and his nose cavernously hot. She pointed to a tall figure standing at the far left side. Her finger trembled. 'He has vanished completely since Cassel,' she said, 'although Mother keeps thinking she sees him in the streets around here.'

'*Heh*.' The servant again. It seemed obvious to Grimm now that she had set her cap at young Kummel. In truth he had half suspected it before. He only hoped she had not compromised herself too deeply, if at all. But even if he had not begun to feel so flushed and light-headed, he would not have been eager to discuss Kummel again. There was no telling why he had bolted. He might even have slipped off purely to avoid an entanglement. These things happened – and who was he to cast the first stone? It was the way some men behaved: men for whom – as Grimm had clumsily tried to tell Auguste before they left Hesse – marriage could not be even the beginning. *Tea*, he thought, gesturing limply towards the tray.

'Have you thought any more about him?' she asked, oblivious.

The ragged images on the photo now seemed to be floating.

His shoulders burned, his heart seemed to slow, his breath became fitful. Dear Willi, he thought, must have felt like this for so much of the time, yet he always made so light of it. And then for a senseless moment he toyed with telling her the untellable: that more than once in his own sorry recent state he had *envied* the runaway Kummel: young, free, unencumbered. (Tea. *Tea.*)

'About his reasons for not wanting to be Jewish?' she prompted, as if the question had only just occurred to her. 'Since he was ten? What could have happened then, do you think? To him, to his family?'

Grimm knew she would not let this go. He had to speak, but fast. Satisfy her, move on, drink tea, then maybe he would find himself on horseback once more, beyond all this. 'Yes, since he was ten,' he croaked. 'And his age now is – what? – twenty-five? That would take us back to 1848: the year of revolutions. And yes, there *were* excesses during that period.'

'Excesses?' Either her hand was shaking now or his vision was blurring further.

'Attacks on Jewish communities. Burnings. Lynchings. And his accent maybe did suggest Baden-Baden – where some of these atrocities took place . . .' It all seemed so remote: another world that he scarcely knew, let alone one that he had helped to shape. A world of trains, not horses; stone cities not forests. A world whose limits he had reached, and on which he no longer had the heart to look back. 'The world must become romanticized,' Novalis had written under Bonaparte's yoke. 'That way one finds again the original meaning.' Perhaps that was now the only way left to Grimm of looking at this world at all.

Auguste lowered the photograph, and the ginger stink all but overpowered him, shooting through his head like flames from a fire. 'Tea, Gustchen, *bitte*,' he panted, his eyes shut. 'I really must drink something now.'

She moved away but his head continued to swim. To stop his cup from falling when she handed it to him, he had to concentrate hard on her pretty cuffed and lace-edged boots, with their low heels. She held her own cup but appeared to be waiting for him to invite her to sit. The last of the afternoon sun seared his back. He tapped the seat cushion and she was next to him, but he wanted no more talk of Kummel. Enough of that. Already other, more arresting images were seeping across his mind: vistas of battle seen from high on the back of a horse, where he himself was involved in the maelstrom, cutting about him with a sword.

'That shawl . . .' he began, his cannon-voice banging and echoing so deafeningly inside his head that he could not go on. And although he craved the tea, he could not lift the cup to his lips.

'You remember this shawl?' There was a quiet leap in Auguste's voice.

Immediately he regretted having spoken. This, too, was plainly of intense interest to her. So much intensity! Yes, he remembered, however hard he wished not to. The autumn of 1831, his research tour of the libraries: Strassburg, Frankfurt, Switzerland. Meanwhile back in Göttingen Willi went on losing ground: asthma, his heart, pneumonia. The university had already promoted him to professor to give Dortchen access to a more generous fund if, as seemed inevitable, she should shortly be widowed. Grimm had found the shawl in a rather superior Frankfurt boutique and sent it back under separate cover from his next letter to Wilhelm.

'Tell me,' Auguste's voice rang through his head. 'Please tell me . . .'

What did she want to know? Tell her what? About himself and Dortchen? *Neither now nor ever will I leave you* . . . He became aware of how close they were, that his head had sunk against her sloping shoulder. Tell her . . . Now, after so long. And why, in the last resort, should he not? As the horse beneath him bucked, he felt an unexpected surge of triumph: pressed in a single saddle against this sweet, oversensitive young woman, as if he had snatched her up to safety from all the smoke and carnage. This was how he would travel on now. Westward through the forest, once the battle was won. Already he could glimpse a new path opening up ahead. *Neither now nor ever . . .*

He heard his cup crash down against the floorboards followed by her shriek of alarm. And then, once again, he was fighting on alone.

Jacob found her where her mother had said she would be: curled up on the ottoman next to the tree. The only light in the parlour fell from the candles on its branches. Dolefully she watched him enter in his winter greatcoat, but then she turned her eyes to the scatter of wrapped gifts like gaudy indoor mushrooms in the Christmas tree's needly shadow.

It was late and she looked pinched. He was glad, though, to see her tears had stopped. When he knelt to bring their faces level, she moved her head and smiled back bravely at him.

'It's time now, Gustchen,' he told her. 'You know I have to go.'

'Won't the king even let you stay for Christmas?'

'No, my dear *Fundvögelchen*, not even for Christmas.' He took between his fingers the length of dark material that she lay wrapped in. 'What's this you're wearing?'

'Mother put it on me. It's her favourite shawl. She said you bought it for her in Frankfurt, before I was born.' Quickly he let his hand fall. Just six years earlier – yet it felt like his own lifetime ago, not this tiny girl's. She shuffled herself in the swaddling but left her head on the ottoman's upholstered scroll. 'But where will you *go*, Apapa?'

Jacob had to tilt his head to meet her eye. 'Oh, there are plenty of places beyond Hanover. Plenty of other Germanies – you remember what I used to tell you?'

She nodded. 'Will you try to find the realm that fell out of its ruler's pocket and live there?'

He smiled, letting his fingers run again across the shawl's folds. 'No, Gustchen, I'll find somewhere better than that. Somewhere I can work and earn money, and then you can all come too, and we shall never part again.'

'Will the work be teaching students still?'

Jacob pursed his lips. In truth he hoped not. There were surely better ways of chopping wood. He was no teacher; even eight hours a week here in Göttingen had taxed his patience to the limit. In addition to the thirty-six hours he was obliged to devote to the university library, it had left precious little time for real work. 'I'm thinking of making a big book of German words, Gustchen. A *Wörterbuch,* so people would know where all the words come from and what they all mean. Your father could help me perhaps – and we could do that anywhere, *ja*?'

Her snub nose puckered. He could see her fighting back new tears. 'But what if you went to that other land?' she asked. 'Where there are the dark forests and stories, and all the good and the evil? Would we come to be with you there?'

'Wouldn't you want to live there, *Schatzi*?'

'No!' She shuddered, not entirely theatrically. 'I'd be frightened.'

'Then I'll keep well away from that land, I promise you.'

'But what if you went there by accident – if you just slipped through a crack in the map?'

'*Ach,* that can't happen. You have to want to go there.'

'And the evil people? If they want to come here – can *they*?'

'Well,' he smiled, 'we must pray not.' Then he raised his hand to her cotton-reel shoulder, squeezed it and stood. 'I must go,

Gustchen. The king says I have to leave by midnight, and I don't want to make him any more angry.'

She twisted her neck to gaze up. 'Will you be on your own?'

'No, I'll have company. The two other professors – you remember? – Dahlmann and Gervinus, they're waiting outside now. We shall travel together to Witzenhausen on the border, then over into Hesse. That's our true home, Gustchen. You'll see it soon, I'm sure. Then I'll show you where we grew up when *we* were children. All the places, all the people.'

'But can't you just tell the king you're sorry – all of you? Can't you do the swearing now and then stay?' Her eyes at last had filled.

Sighing he knelt again, but this time at more than an arm's length from the ottoman. How much could a five-year-old understand about the abuse of constitutional rights by a would-be tyrant? How much of it, indeed, made sense to the tyrant himself? 'Eight hussars are more valuable than the whole university,' Ernst Augustus was reported to have said in expelling the academics. It was said of him in turn that he had committed every sin save suicide. But in all conscience, neither Jacob or his six fellow-protestors could have stood by while the new king unilaterally revoked the old, liberal constitution. They were bound to it by a sworn obligation, and no mortal man could release them from that. As Jacob had written to von Savigny, the honour of the university, and indeed of all Hanover, was at stake; this was a matter of principle for Germans everywhere.

'What the king has done is wrong,' he tried to explain. 'Very wrong. He wants to rule without listening to any of his people, but the people have a right to speak, to advise him, to say what *they* want. That's why we professors won't swear to obey him, do you see? And he is surprised by that. Professors don't usually say things that their kings don't wish to hear – not, at least, in the German lands. But Gustchen, we're doing a good thing . . .'

'Not an evil thing?' she interrupted, grasping at least this distinction.

'No, not at all. The three of us and the four others – including your father – who must leave their jobs but don't have to leave the country: we're all doing what we *must* do. And even if there aren't many people in Hanover who see things our way, there are plenty outside who will help and support us.'

'Mother said you're famous now. Much more famous than before, when you were writing your books.'

He stood. 'Is that what she says? Now I do have to leave you. But see, I've put your present under the tree, Gustchen dear. Think of me when you open it.' He began to back away but she lifted her head.

'May I have it now? Tonight? So you can see me opening it?'

'No, that's not right, is it? We must keep on doing things in the proper way.'

She fixed him in her gaze. 'Apapa?'

'Yes?' He was in the doorway now. He could not keep the carriage waiting in the street under its escort of dragoons for much longer.

'Don't go to the land beyond the map.' Her voice broke, her eyes glistened in the candle light. She wanted more from him than he thought he had to give. Her need almost irritated him. He had to say something to silence her.

'I swear to you, Gustchen, that if you won't come with me, then I won't go to the land beyond the map. You are far too precious for me to leave behind – *the* most precious person in my life. Have I ever told you this before?'

Wide-eyed, she shook her head.

'Well I'm telling you now. Good night and Merry Christmas

to you. We'll be together soon. And then we shall never part again. *Neither then nor ever shall I leave you.* That's my promise.'

Auguste's mother left very hesitantly for St Matthew's on Sunday evening, along with Gisela and Rudolf. After Grimm's shockingly sudden stroke, she clearly feared another – possibly final – turn for the worse while she was away.

Auguste herself insisted that she could be left alone in the apartment. Having worshipped and taken another extended walk that morning – this time towards Moabit, north of the Tiergarten – she welcomed the chance to sit quietly with the invalid and maybe write some letters. Besides there was the maid, and any number of neighbours on call, should she need their help.

But only as Auguste was saying goodbye from her seat at the kitchen table did her mother remark on what she had been wearing since the previous tumultuous afternoon. 'Why on earth did you fetch that old thing out?' she asked under her breath, sounding more offended than amused.

Auguste gathered the shawl at her throat. 'I'd been thinking about it,' she smiled. 'I like it.' Their eyes met. 'Do you mind?'

'Why should I mind? Are you hoping that it might come back into fashion?'

Auguste smiled again but her mother had turned towards the hall lamp to check the contents of her bag. Suddenly she looked very young, much as she must have looked when she had told those tales to the brothers back in Cassel. And perhaps for the first time it did not seem impossible to Auguste that, decades before, so profoundly practical a woman should have taken time out to recount passionate stories in a summer house. 'He's awake just now,' she said, pulling on her gloves. 'It might be sensible to try to keep him that way until the doctor's next call.'

'Keep him awake? But how?'

'Rudolf has given him a little writing block and pencil. He can communicate after a fashion by writing with his left hand. It's not perfect, but it allows for a kind of conversation. And his hearing, of course, is no worse than before.' She looked up as Gisela patiently called to her from the front door. 'You *will* be able to manage here on your own?' she asked Auguste.

'Yes!' The younger woman saw how badly her mother needed that answer. Her face looked so tense, her usually piercing eyes begged like a child's for reassurance. Grimm's stroke, which had paralysed his tongue and left the right side of his body immobile, had hit her hard too. After church that morning, Auguste had stayed out of the apartment partly to let her sit alone with her dear Jacob. Now the older woman in turn needed to be out of the invalid's hushed and stuffy room, if only to pray for him in a different place.

When the outer door closed, the silence suddenly seemed so dense that Auguste wondered if she would be able, after all, to rise and go through to Grimm's darkened bedroom. The moment passed. She set aside her pen and the photograph that she was about to parcel up and send to Cassel, stood up, and stepped out into the corridor.

Grimm's door was ajar, and by approaching on tiptoe she could observe him for a short time without being seen. He sat propped up in bed with pillows behind him and to his sides. With the fingers of his left hand he was gingerly touching his right forearm and elbow, frowning now as if he had expected his stricken side to spring back to life but been disappointed. Then he stared at the fingers themselves, distastefully, as if they were dirty. He had told her that he had cried. Once. But when? Who or what could have made such a man cry?

Rudolf's writing block and pencil lay on the counterpane that was stretched across his lap. Her Apapa appeared to have made no marks. The ironies cut Auguste to the quick. The tongue with which he so fluently spoke so many languages: now stilled. The hand with which he had written so elegantly throughout his scholar's lifetime: petrified.

'Thought is the lightning,' he once said, comically waving his arms for her like a spoof shaman, 'words the thunder, consonants the bones and vowels the very blood of language.' Auguste folded her arms under her breast and held her elbows. But this silence was not really new. He had always had it with him. Earlier that evening she had looked through his letters to her during the two years between his expulsion from Göttingen and the family's move to Berlin. 'I have drunk at the silent springs of the Middle Ages,' he lyrically wrote in one of them, 'and sought to enter the rude forests of our ancestors. I feel that I am a part of all that exists.'

He was ten steps away, but it could have been ten centuries, and the worn rug on the floor could have been the whole unfurled land mass of Europe. The stillness did not reach very deep in him; she saw that clearly now. Inside he was still fighting battles. The air over there was clotted with the intensity of his struggle. A clotting she had also sensed in the streets around Moabit that morning, as if the city itself were slowly falling silent out of respect for the great little man. Nothing would be the same once he was gone. A door to the past would be closed forever.

His eyes turned her way and narrowed, as if she were giving off a light that he found too dazzling. For so long he had lived in a country that was teetering on the verge of itself: a fatherland in fragments, which he had loved above all else. And maybe on account of his writings its appreciative *Volk* had, after all, come to love him back, and would go on loving him even after his death.

History would surely know of this man, who had known so much of history himself.

'*Hier*, Apapa, I'm here,' she called into the room without pushing herself off the door jamb. 'Are you feeling a little better?'

He nodded. Then he resumed his distant stare. *Ours is the cloudy realm of dreams,* Auguste thought, *where there's no rivalry* . . . That realm had always been his truest homeland, and now he was on his way back there. Not talking, but dreaming. Talk could always wait. The kind of talk Auguste herself was fated never to have with him. And yet at the crucial moment on the afternoon before – when she felt his gentle pressure just before his cup fell and she realized that he was actually collapsing – her heart had risen so high. He's touching me, she had thought, hardly daring to believe it. He's really going to tell me . . .

And perhaps, after all, he *had* been about to tell her. And now she could just as easily ask him. She could simply ask and he could nod or shake his head – if only she, in turn, had not been struck as mute as he.

But there was, of course, that writing block.

The first knock at the apartment's outer door was too soft for her to hear. On noticing the second, she presumed that her mother must have left her prayer book behind and sent up Gisela, keyless, to fetch it. The doctor was not due for at least another half an hour. 'A moment, Apapa,' she said to Grimm when it appeared that the maid was not going to answer.

She glided down the corridor with her head so full of clotted silence that when she pulled back the door, and the waiting Kummel began to speak at once, she watched his lips move but heard not a word of what he said.

TWENTY-FOUR

The king rode back through the night at the head of a small detachment of guards. As the horses flew down the darkened westward paths, he planned to bring first news of his effortless victory in person. Lovingly he would then describe to his mother, wife and children how the mere sight of his army, ranged beneath the flags of all thirteen cantons, had been enough to make the emperor's forces melt away after only a few skirmishes.

At the time, he had felt almost cheated of the chance to spill more blood along his new kingdom's frontiers, to mark its limits in a way that every future aggressor would understand. Now he was glad to be returning all the sooner, to seek new success in peace as well as war.

Waving to his fellow riders to rein in their horses, he cantered ahead as the forest path gave way to the straight stone-surfaced road that led down to the palace gatehouse. Smoke coiled into the night from the western range of buildings, its sharp meaty smell warmly welcoming. The sentries, recognizing him, rushed up for reports. But on dismounting he pressed a finger to his lips, then paced stealthily across the gravel to the back of the palace where, in the dead of night, only two of its many windows showed lights.

He entered through the kitchens, taking care not to rouse the cooks, maids and scullions who slept in corners or with their heads on folded arms at the tables. But as he passed into the feasting hall he heard a louder echo to each of his careful footfalls. He turned to find the chamberlain walking just behind.

'You return in victory, highness?' he said – rather than asked – in a strangely broken voice.

'How do you know?'

'I know that if the outcome had been any different, you would not have let yourself return at all.'

He nodded, touching the hilt of his sword under the flap of his unbuttoned coat, and turned to go on to the stairway.

'You have been acutely missed here, highness.'

He paused on the first step, smiling. 'In so short a time?'

'With respect, it's seemed long. Especially, highness, to your queen.' He searched the chamberlain's uptilted face. His expression was haunted, troubled, even guilty. 'I fought with my conscience,' he whispered, 'but in the end I had to maintain my sworn allegiance to you and – because of that – to your regent.' He swallowed awkwardly. 'You will find that no one at the palace has strayed in any way from that allegiance.'

The king looked puzzled but wanted to hear no more. Talk like this could always wait. Gripping the oak banister he took the stairs three at a time. He cared little now if his wife heard his approach and was alerted. All he wanted was her arms around him, her smiling face against his breast; then they would consummate their marriage as true partners. But in the shadows at the head of the last flight he saw two halberdiers stationed to either side of the master-bedroom door. Quickly they crossed their weapons to keep him out.

'You fools!' he hissed, striding closer. 'Don't you see who I am? Who put you here?'

'The chamberlain, highness, under orders from the regent.' They looked appalled but continued to make an angled cross with their weapon shafts.

'Tell me then who has tried to force an entry! I'll hack the man's limbs off!' Thrusting up an arm, he broke the barrier. 'Speak!'

'We're here to prevent an exit, highness – not an entry. These are the regent's orders. We disobey on pain of death. But now that you are returned . . .'

Driving his way between them, he forced back the doors on to a dimly lit scene. At once he wished he could see even less of it. Too aghast to be outraged, he could hardly believe that a room could be reduced to such squalor so quickly.

No windows were open and plainly, scandalously, his wife had been forbidden the latrines. Except for the wide bed, everything that had been whole now lay in fragments and tatters. The queen lay in virtually the same position as at his departure, but on sheets torn to ribbons in a debris of smashed statuary. Gaunt, spent, her incomparable hair slashed down to a ragged pelt, she breathed fitfully at the ceiling but would not look his way.

'She has been alone in here, highness,' one of the halberdiers protested before he could be blamed. 'She went into a frenzy when the children were taken. She did all this herself.'

'The children?' He took a step into the fetor, towards the inert woman. '*Where are my children?*'

She twisted herself over and with eyes that had aged by decades she glared at him from under her savage crop. 'Your mother had them,' she said in a soft growl, almost a purr, of profound despair.

'What are you talking about: *had*?'

'You brought her here,' she bayed on, oblivious. 'You wanted her here . . .'

'Where is she now? Tell me where she is.'

'Where do you think?'

He raised his eyebrows, panting himself now. But he knew. And he knew more too. More than he had ever dared to dwell on.

Footsteps sounded on the stairs: the chamberlain, following him up. 'She took them to the old tower, highness,' he called from the doorway. 'To the old spinning-garret.'

Slowly the king turned to face him. 'You've seen them since?'

He shook his snow-white head, his gaze as firm as a buttressed wall.

'It was her. I knew it was her,' the queen moaned from the bed. 'I wasn't wrong. She was there. She called to me and made me touch her spindle . . .'

He could not swing around to face her again. 'What do you mean? Speak.'

Hoarsely she began to weep. 'I thought I knew her when she stepped down from the coach. I should have spoken then, but what could I have told you? That I thought she was familiar – though I'd only ever seen her from behind?'

'Who? *Who?*'

'The spinner in the garret, at the wheel with the poisoned spindle! It was her. *Her*. It must have been her too who came to the palace feast to lay the curse that would have killed me.' She took a long, grating breath. 'I thought she had come back now for me but no, it was my children. She's evil, pure evil. Not a woman at all, not a *person*! She can be any shape she likes!'

'She is my mother.' He said it softly, not to her but to the chamberlain.

'Go to the garret, highness.' The old man passed across a small golden key. 'I believe you'll need this.'

'And ask yourself what happened to her own children,' his wife sobbed and coughed, rising. 'Even your father too. She's an evil, evil ogress . . .'

Closing his ears to her din, the king grasped the chamberlain by his spare upper arm, so hard that he almost raised him from the ground. 'How did this ever happen? How can you all have stood by?'

'The regent's word is law.' He quivered bodily as he spoke. The king thrust him aside and strode to the top of the stairway. As he went down he heard his queen follow, dogging his footsteps and breathing the same rhythmic incantation each time his boot found a lower stair: 'Destroy her! Destroy her! Destroy her!'

When he crossed the courtyard to the palace's western quarters, billows of the smoke he had smelled earlier gusted in his face. It was belching, he saw, from the top of the old tower, which now looked more like a gigantic chimney.

TWENTY-FIVE

The Fräulein looked so deep in thought that Kummel wondered if she had not recognized him. Very few lights were on in the apartment behind her. From the street, after watching the spry old mistress and her daughter-in-law leave for church, he had not even been sure that anyone else was still inside.

'You should come in,' she murmured finally, stepping aside and making no attempt to take back the coat that he was holding out. She closed the door as if she were listening closely to its panels. After a pause she turned and beckoned him down the corridor behind her. He followed, staring at the old black shawl she wore over her dark blue, pagoda-sleeved dress even though the air in here was as warm and fusty as ever.

To Kummel's surprise she slipped inside the first room: the Professor's study. Her manner was so odd that he thought she might have mistaken it for the parlour, but he went in after her. He had been in here only once before leaving for the Harz, to help pack the *Wörterbuch* papers. Books in cases lined three walls, interspersed by cupboards filled with manuscripts and, directly ahead of him, two high eight-paned windows that overlooked the Linkstrasse.

The curtains were open, letting in just enough street light to pick out the Fräulein's profile. She had perched on a large, leather-upholstered sofa to his left. At her side was a presentation salver engraved with the faces of the Professor and his dead brother. As Kummel stood waiting, the coat still slung over his linked hands, she rocked to her feet, stepped up to the Professor's desk chair and gripped its back. The desk consisted of three heavily loaded tables arranged to form three sides of a square. The Fräulein, having put the width of the nearest of these tables between them, at last turned to face him.

'We weren't expecting you back,' she half smiled, her voice still hushed.

He raised his arms as if in explanation. 'The coat, Fräulein. I thought it wrong of me to keep it. It belongs to your family.'

'The coat,' she echoed, looking past him. Carefully he went to the sofa and draped it over the nearer scrolled arm. Watching him, she put a hand to her throat where she wore a small blue brooch inlaid with silver. It made her neck look very delicate; flimsy enough to snap with one hand. He returned to his original position in front of the half-opened door.

In the poor light it was hard to be sure, but the study looked remarkably similar to the way it had looked five weeks before. The desk itself was as tidy as the Professor had left it on departing for the mountains. No work seemed to be in progress in front of the chair that the Fräulein still clutched. Even the plants on the windowsills looked neglected. And suddenly it struck Kummel, as he looked at the mourning black of her shawl, that he might have come too late.

'I've spoken to the Professor about what you said,' she said in a different register from before. He opened his mouth to try to speak but, snatching glimpses of him, she continued to address the doorway. 'About losing everything. When you were a boy.'

Faintly, only faintly, he felt the old heat, saw the silent figures moving through the bonfire haze, tasted the stench, first of the holy books, then of their readers.

'Did you lose your family then? I know there were riots, burnings. Was that what happened? You lost your people, yet you managed to escape?'

Her voice was so uneven that she could have been talking about her own blood relatives. She spoke in little more than a whisper, as if for fear that the portraits lodged on top of all the bookcases might hear and cry down at her to hold her tongue for shame. Kummel wished he still had the coat to fiddle with. This was not at all what he had come for. His eye was drawn up to the portrait that stood alone between the windows; a full-bosomed matron with fleshy, rounded, almost taunting features.

'It was years ago,' he said. 'It's behind me. I want it behind me.'

The Fräulein glared at him and seemed to sink inside herself. 'But you've been without family all these years? *Allein?* You've been on your own?'

He looked back pointedly. 'No more so, I dare say, than most.'

'You believe that?'

'Sometimes.' He looked up again, then back at her. Her hand fluttered to her brooch. He had not come here to talk about himself, but she was too far away from him. If she had still been on the sofa he might just have dared to go and sit beside her. The barrier of the desk was too forbidding, as forbidding in its way as the gaze of the fleshy woman in the portrait: vulnerable but black-eyed, caustically knowing, her lips pursed in disparagement. He could see why she had been given pride of place in here.

She had an almost regal air, a hungrily presiding quality even though she was only a few streaks and dabs of paint.

'That lady,' he indicated by tilting up his face. 'Who is she?'

'The Professor's mother.' She did not twist around to follow his line of vision. 'I never knew her.'

He could not deflect her. She was still dwelling on the family *he* had barely known: father, mother, sister, uncle. She was breathing in the smoke of that bonfire, flinching at the stink of seared flesh. Yet to him now it was truly distant, a land where he no longer had to go unless he chose to do so. He saw nothing, heard no screams, smelled nothing, felt no heat. It was as if she had drawn it all away from him. And for that, if nothing else, he was in her debt.

'Where is he?' he asked. 'The Professor.' It was not enough. He swallowed, to prepare both her and himself for the next two words. 'Your *father*?'

Briefly she glared again, then shook her head in defeat.

'You still don't know?'

She bit her lip. 'I can't ask. It's not in me. He's been in bed ever since our return. And yesterday . . . yesterday afternoon he had a stroke.'

'*Bitte schön*, Fräulein, may I see him?'

'I'm sorry?'

'The Professor? May I go in to him?' The tick of a clock above one of the cupboards seemed to sound louder. Again Kummel felt the eyes of the sour woman in the portrait on him. And, when the Fräulein finally answered, the words seemed to float down to him from *her* lips.

'He can't speak. He can barely move.' She stole a last glance at him and then, perhaps, she understood what he was wanting. Wrenching herself around from the chair, she came out of her little refuge.

The clock's ticking seemed to grow louder still and then, just for several strikes, irregular, turning into that odd, dry clacking that had seemed to dog Kummel back in Hesse. Only now it did not sound so much like the dull peal of bone on bone as the loud, even resonant clashing of teeth. Yes, surely: teeth. Beyond everything on display in this darkly draped and pleated Biedermeier interior, it was as if he could hear someone biting, champing. And he quailed at the thought of what such an eater might look like.

The Fräulein paused on her way to the door, as if she too were listening. She was close enough for him to take her wrist between his fingers if he chose. 'Do you hear it?' he whispered instead. 'Or is it just in my head?'

She half turned her head to him but already the clock's unobtrusive tick had resumed. Kummel saw her hair was too tightly fixed at the back, as if she had furiously stabbed all the pins into place. Her voice, when she spoke, barely carried to him and a sudden terror came into her eyes.

'What is it you want?'

'Take me,' he murmured back. It was all that was left. And when she frowned, he quickly elaborated, 'Please, take me in to him.'

Jacob slipped unnoticed out of the Frankfurt Paulskirche and crossed the empty Römerplatz. The din of the debate rang on in his head. So many voices but so little sense. Now at last on this mild September evening he knew that the dream was over. The first National Assembly of all the Germanies was floating into oblivion on gusts of its own liberal wind. And as the member for the 29th electoral district came to his quiet, half-timbered hotel he knew that he would not be going back. For all the effect that his impassioned addresses had made – including his motion to guarantee freedom, not only to all German citizens but also to those who came to live on German soil – he might as well have kept his mouth shut since arriving in May.

He had, as ever, a perfectly good excuse for returning to Berlin: his brother's poor health. His two sickly nephews could be mentioned as well. At the age of sixty-three he had probably not even been expected to endure the damp, cold Frankfurt winter. But he had planned to stay; months before, nothing could have stopped him from seeing through this year of revolutions to an epoch-making end.

Here on the hallowed soil of Hesse he had hoped to play the midwife at the birth of a proud new Reich, peacefully unified, constitutionally governed. But week by week, session by session, he had realized that his ideals had no place in this grubby political arena, that no state would surrender its sovereignty save at cannon point, which was probably, catastrophically, what would happen in the end.

Quiet now, he told himself. He needed silence again, to chop wood regardless and see out his days that way. He fetched the key to his rooms and tramped up the hotel stairs. He was finding it hard to swallow. Several times he tried to clear his throat but the tightness remained. His hands shook too, and, as he went straight through to the room he had fitted out as a temporary study, his right cheek twitched even though his face felt almost entirely numb.

He had placed three tables and his chair under the street window, recalling the arrangement back in Berlin. The table to his left was smothered in proofs for his *Geschichte der deutschen Sprache*, a history of the German language that was scheduled to be published in two volumes before the turn of 1849. He picked up a pencil as his eye caught two printer's errors in a single sentence of its preface, penned in a flood of patriotic fervour just weeks before. Instead of trying to insert the missing words he wrote the corrected sentence in the margin:

> *This book teaches that our nation, after the Roman yoke had been thrown off, brought its name and its fresh freedom to the Romance people in Gaul, Italy, Spain and England, and decided through its great power alone the victory of Christianity and set itself up as an impenetrable dam against the violently pressing Slavs in the middle of Europe.*

He stared at what he had written for a very long time. Dusk fell and he lit no lamp. Turning from the proofs he looked down at the letter to Gustchen that he had been trying to write for most of that week.

She had written to him so often during his increasingly forlorn stay in Frankfurt. He kept her letters piled in their envelopes beside his bed, weighted down by a fossilized shell. The most recent described a dinner Willi and Dortchen had given to mark her sixteenth birthday – '*but without you there, Apapa, it was barely half a party*'. She tried so hard. He owed her a letter back now, but what he had written was not what she wanted to hear: '*We fear further outbreaks of crude violence, particularly as ever against the Jews . . . the failure to unify Germany makes all other accomplishments seem insignificant . . .*' He had never quite been able to tell her what she wanted to hear, and he doubted now if he ever would. Like mother like daughter, he thought and a tremor passed through him.

He looked across to where he had stacked the latest set of submissions for the *Wörterbuch*. Then he pulled out his chair and slumped into it, his head drooping on to his chest. Beyond the window, his eyes ranged over the silhouettes of the noble rooftops of what Goethe had called Germany's secret capital. But how could it *not* be secret when the country itself did not exist, when

'Germany' was still no more real than the realm that had fallen from its ruler's pocket?

And then, without warning or preparation, Jacob wept. Tears swam down both cheeks, his chin bobbed on his collarbone. It was so long since he had cried that it made him feel like another person, simultaneously younger and much, much older. There was nothing he could do to stop himself and nothing he wanted to do.

Images massed in his head of the dead at the barricades of Berlin and Vienna earlier that year; of blameless 'usurers' from the south-west to Hamburg whose homes had been murderously burned by benighted opportunists whose minds would never cease to be medieval. He cursed himself for ever thinking that the wind of history had been blowing his way. Wind was all it had been: words, noise, subtly deceptive sound. How could they build borders out of sound? How would noise hold back the next Napoleon, the next invading emperor from east or west? Frankfurt's failure would haunt the generations. Only those cannons remained: the Prussian way. *Ach*, the Prussian way. Jacob closed his eyes and he glimpsed a map of *that* future – and it was such a dirty, bloody scrap of nothing.

On he wept, a tired old man in a rented evening room. Tear stains blurred the ink on his letter to Auguste. He took up the page, balled it in his fist and bit on it to staunch the sobbing. And slowly, very slowly, as the streetlamps' light from outside crept across him, the necessary silence descended again.

Grimm heard voices from the hall before he saw movement in the doorway: the blurred male figure first, then the smaller female. They could have been Willi and Dortchen; von Savigny and Kunigunde; his own beloved parents. Almost any couple, fluent in the intimate, playful language of marriage, with lines of children tailing away behind them, good, quiet children, dutifully continuing the family name.

They stood close together, looking in on him, maybe thinking he could not see them back. He had sunk down in his pillows, his chin now resting on his chest. The stubble on his unshaven jowls pricked the fabric of his bedgown. When he moved his head it rasped against the crisp linen sheet. Directly in front of his nose lay the old writing block. The pencil had rolled to the floor. But not before he had struggled to etch out a message with his left hand.

It was hard now to remember for whom he had written it. His mother, perhaps? He had felt so like a child, fighting to write – freed of all responsibility, pleasantly like an infant who could not even be expected to speak. It was good to be like this, as if he were travelling back towards a birth, another new beginning.

'It's Kummel, Apapa.' The voice was as loud as it needed to be. Gustchen. Only Gustchen. Gustchen and her man.

'*Guten Abend,* Herr Professor. I'm so sorry.'

Grimm did not know if he spoke in apology or commiseration. Either way it sounded sincere. They had drifted up on both sides of his bed, Gustchen to Grimm's right, young Kummel to his left and standing closer. Grimm took hold of the writing block and offered it up to him, almost dropping it. Gustchen meanwhile stooped to pick up the pencil. He felt her place it again on his chest. 'What has he written?' she asked Kummel across him.

He hesitated before answering. 'Three words – I think all the same. Would they be "Story, story, story"?'

'*Ach so,*' exclaimed Gustchen, and Grimm thought he heard her chuckle. 'It was the way we asked for a tale when we were children. The way that Apapa and his brothers and sister used to ask before us. "Story, story, story!" Is that what you mean, Apapa? Do you wish to be told a story?'

Grimm reached up to take back the block, resettled it, and

picked up the pencil to scratch out more words. Gustchen perched on the bed's edge, steadying the block and leaning over to decipher as he wrote, but she waited for him to finish before speaking the sentence aloud: "A story of your people."' She had not seen the 'K' he had written at the end. To emphasize it, Grimm again passed the block up to Kummel.

'You want me to tell you about my family?'

As vehemently as he could, Grimm shook his head. He patted the counterpane, inviting Kummel to sit too, since the effort of looking up was threatening to snap his neck. The dark young man obeyed, coming into closer focus.

'I think,' Gustchen suggested, reaching across to touch Kummel's sleeve, 'that he means a tale – a story – that's told *by* your people.'

'A Jewish story?'

Grimm sank back. It was done. For what seemed like a long while he had to close his eyes and the room became remote. Gustchen and Kummel, he knew, were speaking to each other but nothing they said sounded. He felt as if he were sinking, falling in a shower of crumbled earth, not only him but a whole miniature realm around him. He continued to fall but soon the motion became so natural that he noticed it no more than a weekend stroller notices the earth turning.

And he too, dismounted, was walking in this other realm: hurriedly, fearfully, across a darkened palace courtyard, his footsteps followed by those of others – lighter, more erratic. The air in that enclosed space smelled singed. The fatty stench was so strong that his stomach turned. The entrance arch to an ancient tower loomed in front of him, a tower that doubled as a chimney. Stairs wound up through the smoke inside. He wanted to turn and run. Instead he had to step in. The voices behind him grew more insistent and finally some words came clear:

'. . . so long ago now.'

'But surely you remember something? However small? It would mean so very much to him . . .'

Grimm opened his eyes and saw Kummel gazing down, close enough to his own face that he saw where his arched eyebrows merged above his nose. The servant shrugged and straightened his back. He had been persuaded. Grimm would have his story. The room rearranged itself in readiness. Grimm closed his eyes but all that he saw now, from the beginning through to the end, was what Kummel chose to show him:

'A pious Jew could not support his sons and daughters. All he would do was study the Torah in the synagogue until one day his wife said to him, "How long will you sit idle? Go and look for work, near or far, that will save us all from starvation." So he took his staff and tearfully set out beyond the city gates.

'In the first city he came to, at every corner he heard voices studying Torah. He was generously welcomed and went to worship in the synagogue. But as soon as he was inside, the whole congregation revealed itself to be demons in disguise.

'Taking fright, the pious Jew tried to leave and return to his home, but the demons wouldn't let him. "You will stay here with us," they said. "You will marry one of us and have children with her, and you will have great riches and anything else that your heart desires." "I have a wife and children already," pleaded the Jew. "Please let me go back to them." But they took no notice. And all he could do was take one of the she-demons for a wife, and with her he had many sons and daughters . . .'

'Apapa,' came Gustchen's voice close to Grimm's right ear. 'Are you hearing? You look so sleepy. Can you hear what Kummel is telling you?'

Grimm nodded once, and although he could no longer open his eyes, he managed to nod again.

'Then one day,' Kummel resumed with the same even, almost monotonous but highly effective delivery, 'the pious Jew begged his demon-wife to let him go and visit his wife and children. "If you promise to come straight back and not spend a single night there," she replied, "then yes. And I will give you a great sum of money for them, so they will no longer live in need. I'll even give you a special horse that will take you there in no time at all." "Whatever you say," he answered.

'So the horse was brought and the money was brought and the pious Jew set off and soon he found himself in front of his own house. "Thank God you're home," his wife and family cried, weeping for joy. "Where have you been for so long?" He told them nothing of what had happened, but when night came he couldn't bring himself to leave. And he lay down beside his wife, crushed with sorrow. "Tell me what's the matter," she begged him tearfully, "or I swear I'll kill myself." At that, he could stay silent no longer and he told her everything.

'"Husband," she said when he'd finished, "go to the synagogue and study Torah. That way you'll be protected from all harm." So in the morning he rose early, went to the synagogue and sat there studying all day and all night. And after the she-demon realized he wasn't going to come back, she went to the synagogue herself and found him deep in study. She went to the rabbi and said, "Master, I wish to file a complaint about that man who reads there."

'The pious Jew overheard, looked up and said to her, "You have nothing to complain about. You're a demon." "But I am your wife," she pleaded. "You married me lawfully and I had your children. You promised to return to me and you've broken your promise. I demand that you fulfil your duties in accordance with Jewish law." "You are no Jewess," said the man. "You have no right to be here at all. Get thee behind me, Satan!"

'When the she-demon saw that she couldn't move him, she

said, "Then I have one last request. Grant it and you'll never see me again." "What is it?" asked the man, sensing an end to all his trouble. "Kiss me," she said, "and that will be the last thing I ever ask you." So he went to her and he kissed her. And with that kiss she drew his soul right out of his body.'

Kummel coughed, his duty done. The repugnant smell of burning fat swept over Grimm. His feet were on the tower stairs again, but the higher he rose, the greater the heat in his face became and the more his eyes stung and streamed from the smoke.

'Apapa,' Gustchen could not refrain from adding. 'That's his story, he's told it, and in your hands he leaves it.'

Grimm felt a touch at his shoulder. Kummel's hand – drawing him closer, mercifully guiding him back down those awful circling steps. He felt comfortable in Kummel's grip, safe. Then their hands were linked too.

'Herr Professor, can you hear me? I know you can hear me – you heard my story. That was what you wanted. Now, Herr Professor, will you give to Fräulein Gustchen what *she* wants? An answer to a question. Just nod your head, or squeeze my hand . . .'

'No, no!'

Grimm felt the bed shake under him as Gustchen must have leaned across to grab at Kummel but he seemed to be disregarding her.

'A nod or squeeze will be enough, Herr Professor. So say if it's true. It's all the Fräulein wishes to know. Are you ready to answer now, sir? This is the question: are you the Fräulein's father?'

'Oh, *Gustchen!*'

The bed quaked again as both sprang to their feet, although Kummel was careful to lower Grimm back down into his pillows – back into that fearsome palace courtyard – before letting him go.

'Mother,' Auguste breathed in the direction of the doorway.

TWENTY-SIX

At the foot of the tower he turned back to face his queen. The thin ashy smoke curling down from above made it hard to see beyond a few footsteps. She came on like a pale, lopsided blur, almost on all fours, whimpering, gagging, turning her tufted head from side to side as if to shake out a nightmare.

Although there was so much smoke it was cold at the tower's entrance arch. He had to stop her from following him in. Whatever was waiting inside was not for her to see. Stooping, he raised her with a hand on both shoulders. 'Let me go up alone,' he said, unable to look in her face. 'Please let me do it.'

'She's killed your children . . .'

'We don't know that. Not yet.'

'It's what she *is*. Her nature, can't you see? She's killed before and she'll go on killing. You can't let her live. Wipe her out forever.'

She slumped again in his grip. Ferociously though she spoke, he knew she would follow him no further. He too quailed at the prospect of climbing the circular stair. If there had been any other route, he would have taken it. A route away from this palace, this kingdom, this world. He longed to load the blame on someone else's shoulders but all he could remember were the warnings he had ignored. He was here because he had chosen to be here. It was between him and his mother now. There had never truly been anyone else.

'Wait for me?' he asked, pulling his near-demented queen to him and kissing her cold temple. 'Don't lose hope.'

She leaned against the tower wall and turned her face to it. He kicked the low door and it swung back without his having to use the chamberlain's key. With a last glance back, he took the stairs quickly, three at a time.

The smoke eddied down so thickly that he took his sword from its scabbard as if to chop a path through. But no blade could have cut away the acrid swirling stink. He covered his mouth and nose with his sleeve, but still it swept through him. On the night when Friedrich died, his mother had used to tell him, the house caught fire and burned down too: two disasters that had driven her close to committing a third, she said, by taking her own life. He prayed as he climbed higher that, if anyone now had to be dead, it would be her.

But he prayed for the sake of his wife, only her, and the tears in his eyes when he opened them were caused only partly by the storm of smoke. She was his mother, after all; she would always be his mother.

He came to where the steps all stopped. To his right he could barely see the window he had looked through after his first ascent. Again he saw the face of the woodman who lived beyond that crack in the map where, had he chosen, he could have stayed. He knew it was possible to slip between worlds. His mistake perhaps had been to stay in a world already mapped out by others, and not gone on to chart one of his own.

The smoke thinned a little, though the smell was like five

fingers invading his face. It was the smell of meat, but no flesh he had ever tasted. Down the short passage, the door to the spinning-garret was ajar. Again he would not be needing the chamberlain's key. Holding his sword before him but dropping his sleeve from his face, he stepped down to it, wincing as waves of heat broke over him. The loudest sound he heard was like the clack of a spindle bobbing.

With his boot he edged the door back. He saw her only from behind, sitting on a spinning stool, blocking from his view all but the right-hand extremity of an open fire that she had set in the floor's centre. The glass in the oriel window high above had been poled out and, although most of the smoke escaped that way, streams poured back through the doorway too. The low clacking went on, too irregular for a spindle; and its ring, besides, was not truly wooden.

Still she wore the dress in which she had arrived late for the wedding feast, filthy now and too small for her shoulders as she hunched towards the fire. He could see one prop for a spit standing beside it. The meat on the spit was hidden by her back, but the fat dripping into the low flames made the room echo to its hiss and crackle.

He had the sword in his hand. He could have plunged it into her back without ever seeing her eyes. Already he knew that was his duty, but he could not do it. Instead, as the clacking continued, he looked away to the room's corner. A tarnished iron cage stood on the tiles, the kind used for bringing apes or lions to the palace menagerie. In a scatter of sawdust and half-gnawed joints of mutton and bitten wedges of bread lay one of the twins, curled up on his side.

Rushing across, he understood at last what the chamberlain's key was for. Thrusting it into the lock – alerting his mother, if before she had been unaware that he was there – he joyfully saw the child shift in sleep even before he wrenched back the cage door and bent to scoop him up with his free hand. He kissed his matted hair as his fattened arms came up drowsily to embrace his father's neck.

Then as he swung around to step out of the cage, he had to see the trussed-up corpse of the other twin roasting on the spit.

Shamelessly his mother shifted herself on the stool. She reached forward and with a familiar jewelled knife shaved off a curl of blackened flesh. Then, holding it to the blade with her thumb, she drew it back into her grease-stained mouth and began to chew. And the sound of her great clacking teeth behind those opened lips made him stagger where he stood.

'No!' came a cry from the doorway.

He looked past his crouched mother to where his wife suddenly stood. She had braved the stairway after all. From there she could still not see the spit and its terrible load. Her mortified eyes were on the child he was holding to his shoulder, and clearly she thought him dead.

'He's safe,' he assured her, crossing to the doorway and passing him into her shaking arms. 'Here, you see, we have him back. Now take him down. Please, take him.'

She pressed the sleeping baby to her face like a wet sponge. But he knew why she cried even harder, less from relief that one child was spared than from the certainty now that the other must be lost. 'Go!' he yelled, turning wife and son away. 'You can trust me to do this, I swear!'

She stared at his sword blade and dug in her heels. 'Wipe her out,' she barked and sobbed simultaneously. 'Wipe her out or she'll haunt the generations.' She clasped the child's head. '*His* children. *Their* children. Because *she* won't die, she'll never stop. You have to end it now.'

He urged her out, then half closed the door behind her. And when he turned back to his mother, she swung around on her spinning stool to face him.

TWENTY-SEVEN

'Please see this person out. I shall wait for you in here.'

Auguste watched her mother enter Grimm's bedroom and stand like a sentry next to the washstand. For some reason she had picked up the rolled Cassel photo from the kitchen table and was gripping it now like a cudgel.

Briefly Auguste stood her ground, glaring across the bed at Kummel to make sure he did not move either. There was no doubt that the older woman had heard his question to her Apapa. She looked spirit-white in her navy church coat, with a look on her face as acidic as a glass of Grünberger wine. 'Kummel isn't to blame,' Auguste stammered.

'Blame? For deserting his post in Cassel? Or for persecuting a sick old man?'

Auguste's hand rose to her brooch. Feverishly she fingered its sharp edges. 'Hardly persecuting,' she said, but the wretched word was already chipping at her.

'Frau Grimm . . .' Kummel spoke up.

'I'll hear nothing from you! You have gravely disappointed us all.'

'No, Mother. He means no harm. He simply brought back the coat.'

'Hoping to claim a last week's wages? They are forfeit, as he must know.'

Auguste gripped her brooch tighter. She could only shake her head. Even her mother, she knew, was speaking more from misery than conviction. She looked so small, smaller than Auguste had ever seen her. Their eyes met briefly across the room's dim expanse and both women flushed.

'This is unworthy, Gustchen.' She brought her hands together in front of her as if to warm them, and the room did feel icy. She looked from her daughter to Grimm and then at the hapless Kummel. 'Unworthy.'

Kummel bowed and strode directly from the room. Still Auguste did not move. 'You know what to do,' her mother said, perhaps a fraction less implacably.

'But why are you here?' She sounded like a fraught child. 'Why are you back so soon?'

'I saw him in the street. Waiting for me to be out of the way. It's furtive, Auguste. I won't have furtiveness.' Her eyes levelled with her daughter's.

'Perhaps he has to be furtive. Perhaps he has no choice. Among us – among people like us. Don't you think we might have *made* him like that?'

'He is what he is.' She turned her bonneted head away, then said more softly. 'And you are what you are.'

'And what's that? Tell me what I am!' She launched herself to the end of the bed, stopping only just short of her mother, whose voice quaked when after a pause she answered:

'You are, it seems to me, confused. This is a hard time for us *all.* See him out, Gustchen, then come back to us. Clearly we have to talk.'

Auguste might not have moved even then if she had not heard the distant click of the outer door opening. Passing her mother, she saw Kummel at the end of the hall, leaving the apartment. 'Wait,' she called.

He looked back as she came to him. Thankfully Gisela was not there too; her mother must have sent her on alone to church. So no one saw her seize Kummel's arm in both hands, drag him back in and push the door to. He did not resist, except to stop the door from clicking completely shut. And when she reached up to kiss his mouth he did not pull back his head, but his lips were not alive. It was as if, like the man in his story, he was afraid she might drag out his soul.

Unworthy: the word seemed to stab Auguste repeatedly in the back. He was shaking his head even before she found the breath to ask, 'Will I see you again?' He continued to shake his head as her grip tightened on his arm. His arm was all she could cling to. She stopped herself from saying, 'Where will you go?' Where he would go mattered so much less than where he was from. But that was not why she no longer thought, *Let me come too.*

She wanted to say she cared for him deeply, which she did, especially now. But he was not her prince, and her heart was not at home on this map. This was not love. Even for him she could not stretch the caring and the undeniable excitement that far. Love was another realm again. A country whose borders she guessed she would only ever cross for visits, just long enough to satisfy herself that it was there, but whose climate and constitution were no more suited to her than they were to the man she had always been most like. And now, after this, she had to go back in to him.

Her left hand slipped down Kummel's arm, found his fingers

and entwined them with her own. '*Danke*,' she whispered into his shoulder. His fingers stiffened around hers then relaxed. He knew what she needed him to tell her. Disengaging himself, he answered before she could ask, 'I don't know, Fräulein. I felt no response. I'm not even sure he heard what I asked.'

She pressed her forehead into his sleeve. It smelled of tobacco, but not in the old way. Mustier, cheaper. This coat's fabric too was coarser. Her head whirled as she wondered if he had calculated it all: shown himself to her mother, held back his question until he knew that she would have followed him up.

She let him go and he looked down at his sleeve as if she had left traces. He left the apartment without fully opening the door on to the landing. Circumspect, she thought, not furtive but circumspect.

She smiled when he half turned to bow before disappearing down the street stairs. Neither of them said *Auf Wiedersehen*. Then Auguste shut the door, leaned against it, and stared down the length of her home's dark corridor.

Jacob bustled out into the corridor, fiddling with the belt around his dressing-gown. Herman, who had rapped on his bedroom door, was backing away in his street clothes into the arc of lamp light just inside the apartment's outer door.

'He's feverish, Apapa,' he called breathlessly. 'I'm going for the doctor. I'll fetch Rudolf too.' Jacob nodded. Obviously his nephew thought Willi would not survive the night. He heard the outer door open and close as he battled on with his belt until he had it fastened. Then, after taking several moments to compose himself, he made his way down to the master bedroom.

Over the years there had been so many scares, but Jacob too felt in his blood that this would be the last. Willi's autumn vacation in Pillnitz with Dortchen had seemed to invigorate him. But for the past three weeks, even before the carbuncle's lancing had failed to clear his infection, Jacob could tell that even his brother sensed he would not live to celebrate his seventy-third Christmas.

At times in the last week he had caught himself imagining Willi already gone. When the strain of this threatened to become too great, he turned his mind to more practical considerations. Twice he had sat in the smaller study adjoining his own, assessing how much new shelving would be needed to convert the room into a library for their combined collection of books and manuscripts. The second time, Auguste wandered in and sat down on the sofa before noticing him at the desk. A slow smile then spread across her face and Jacob could only smile back, but oddly it felt more like collusion than mutual consolation.

The billowing warmth from Willi's room hit him before he turned into it. Dortchen and Auguste stood shoulder to shoulder at the rear wall to the right of the doorway, as if the stove's heat had driven them back from the wide marital bed. Again Jacob had to steel himself without letting the other two see his momentary unsteadiness.

'He's delirious with the fever,' Dortchen sighed, her eyes on the gaunt, panting figure lodged at an apparently precarious angle amid a sea of pillows. 'If one of us goes near, he rants.'

'He seems to think we're paintings,' Gustchen added in a louder voice, and when Jacob glanced at her she arched an eyebrow.

'We thought you should be with him, Jacob. We thought he would want you.'

He went into the sweet, blooming stench of his brother's sweat and decay. It made him think of that old mix of wine and water he had been made to bathe in as a boy. Wilhelm did not see him until he was very close. 'The likeness!' he wheezed at once. 'Such a likeness! Oh, this could *be* my dear Jacob!'

'Hush, Willi, hush.'

The sweat-spotted face clouded over. His sunken eyes darted first to one side of Jacob, then the other, as if the voice had come from some dark corner of the hallucinatory picture frame. His hair was plastered down over his left ear but flew loose above his right. And his skeletal hands lay poised on the counterpane, as if he were sounding the concluding chord of one of his favourite passages from Bach.

'Hush now, Little One,' Jacob said. The student name came from nowhere, and made Jacob's own eyes sting.

Wilhelm heard and smiled in recognition. The demon slid deeper inside, if only temporarily. He rested back, closed his eyes and let his jaw drop, beyond exhaustion. Only the demon, it seemed, had been giving him the energy to see and speak. But then he surprised his brother, who had sat in Dortchen's bedside chair.

'I dreamed, Jacob,' he began in his thin rattle. 'I dreamed I was in Steinau . . .'

'Hush now, Willi. Save your breath. The doctor is on his way.'

He shook his head. It seemed very loose. 'Steinau. The Amtshaus again, after all these years. I went back to visit. And it was all so neat in there. Neat and tidy. A beautiful house. A lovely house. As it always was, you remember?' He paused, needing an answer.

Jacob cleared his throat, then smiled. Not this again. Not now. 'I remember, Willi. This is your old dream. For fifty years you've been having it. Be still now. I know your old dream. You've told it to me so often.'

Edgily Wilhelm smiled, his eyes shut tight, his hands still sounding that last resonant chord on the counterpane. He was hearing no one any more. No one here. 'But everything was so dusty. Everything was covered with a layer of fine dust. And Mother and you were sitting across from each other. At the little table, you remember it? She sewed, and you were reading.' Again his mouth flickered with a smile. 'And it was as if, Old One, with my dusty boots and my brightly coloured travelling clothes, I did not *belong* there with you.'

Unable to speak, Jacob shifted forward in his chair, then eased himself back again. Away to his right he heard his sister-in-law turn in choked-back tears to her daughter. Dortchen knew. She would always have been the last one to admit it, but now she knew too that Willi was slipping away – from him, from her, from them together.

'You're here,' the sick man said in a flatter, more confidential tone. 'I'm glad to have you here, Jacob. I could never live without you, and now – it seems – I can't die without you either.'

'*Genug*, Willi. You've said enough.'

His voice sank lower. 'But they're both yours now.' Jacob saw from the corner of his eye that Dortchen, loosely held by Auguste, had taken two steps further into the room. Wilhelm saw them too and leaned closer. 'She's yours,' he gasped with a ghoulish imitation of his old heart-warming grin. 'Take her back now, won't you?' He closed his eyes as if in self-defence. 'I was only ever looking after her for you.'

Closing his own eyes tight, Jacob put a hand over his brother's. After an age seemed to have passed, he looked up at Dortchen. Her face was buried again in her daughter's shoulder. But Auguste looked straight back at him. She was pressing her lips together to stop herself from crying – or much more probably, Jacob later thought, from smiling.

Dortchen watched Auguste reappear in Grimm's bedroom doorway.

Her daughter's expression gave nothing away. The shawl that she must have deduced to be a love token now hung from the crook of her right arm. She looked both defiant and crushed and, until she began to speak, far older than Dortchen had ever seen her.

She shifted on the bedside chair, bonnetless now, with her left hand placed over Grimm's right on the counterpane. In her other hand she held the scrolled-up photograph of the group from Cassel. While Auguste had been in the corridor, she had looked at it to steady herself. Of the three sitters known to her, only Kummel, hovering at the portrait's edge in Willi's old coat, was immediately recognizable. Lithe, eyes askance, he seemed already to be halfway out of the white border.

Her daughter, in the front row's centre, looked almost shockingly similar to herself at that age, her smile disguising nothing. Grimm, hunkered down next to her, had moved his head at the wrong moment. His face was not badly blurred but his ivory mane looked wilder than it really was and seemed to sit at an odd angle, as if it were a wig or he had just removed some kind of headgear.

The longer Dortchen looked at his image, the more she was reminded of what a Göttingen pupil had once appreciatively written: that although her brother-in-law appeared slight, even delicate, he had in him something akin to the warriors of old who would pause to remove their helmets and cool off in the air, then return to the fight with renewed vigour. And just as the old warriors gained strength in battle, so Grimm gained it through his work.

Dortchen glanced at his still yet somehow unquiet face on the pillow. *Nothing will change . . .* But that was not true, and perhaps it never had been. She felt new tears starting. Tears she was not yet ready to let Auguste see.

'How is he?' asked her daughter, this girl who wanted love before marriage, as if love could be brought in from the outside like a bundle of firewood.

'He seems to be asleep. It can't go on much longer.' She paused to adjust her grip on him, and so give herself strength. 'But he had his story. He will have appreciated that.'

'Mother . . .'

Dortchen laid the photograph in her lap and raised her hand as Auguste came in. 'I meant it. I saw what he wrote on the block. "Story, story, story." And it was a good story.'

Auguste, slowing, reached the side of the bed. The rucked-up counterpane showed where Kummel had sat. Biting the inside of her lip, Auguste bent forward to smooth it out in one long sweep.

'Sit, Gustchen,' said her mother and she obeyed, stiffly, with more of her back than her profile to the other two. She started to wind the shawl around her forearm. They sat in silence for several minutes, then Dortchen spoke again. 'It seems to me now,' she said slowly, as if she were paying out the words like a rope of her own hair from a high turret window, 'that you thought too little of Wilhelm. Underestimated him, perhaps, in comparison with your Apapa.'

'*Mother* . . .' Auguste half turned towards her, frowning at the man who may or may not have been asleep between them. 'He may be listening.'

'He heard the question,' Dortchen almost snapped back, briefly her old self again. 'He would want to hear the answer.'

Auguste swung her face away, her shoulders crumpling.

'They were a pair,' Dortchen resumed. 'Like twins. I knew that from the start. They breathed the air out of each other's mouths. It was never easy, for either of them. You think perhaps that Wilhelm took more than he gave. But you can't know how they sustained each other over the years. Even I don't know the whole of that, although I do know, for what it's worth, that without Willi's more common touch the *Tales* would never have become so successful.'

Auguste shook her head – heavily, unconvinced, speechless.

'You think your Apapa made many sacrifices, and he did, but his duty was also his desire.' Dortchen's colour abruptly deepened at the accuracy of her own phrase. 'His duty *was* his desire. His duty to Wilhelm, to his mother, to you children. To his fatherland. There was nothing else for him. Can you not *see* that?'

Auguste shook her head at the floor. Dortchen knew she was speaking of him as if he were already gone, but that was the only way she could do it, the only way to keep any kind of steadiness. And this now was her own duty. 'There is little, I believe, that he's missed in this life, little he has had to go without.'

Her daughter turned. In her exquisite embarrassment, she seemed to be grinning.

'I mean in his private life,' Dortchen forged on. 'Of course on the public side there were disappointments. You don't need me to tell you that. If unification had been achieved – peacefully, as he always dreamed – he would surely be looking back now in complete fulfilment.'

Auguste pursed her lips. 'He said years ago,' she managed to murmur, 'that he never loved anything as much as his fatherland.'

Dortchen remembered. She remembered wondering even at the time if she pitied or resented him for having said it. 'I think,' she said, 'he found it safer that way.'

'Safer?'

'Nobody made him take the path he took, Gustchen. He had his choices. We all, in the end, have choices.' She saw Auguste eyeing Grimm's limp hand, the hand that had gripped Dortchen so many Christmases ago to console her as she had needed to be consoled – in bereavement – for just those few wild moments. And how many times had Dortchen relived those moments over the years?

'You too?' the younger woman asked. 'Did you make your choice?'

Her eyes at last filled. Tentatively, as if to ask his permission to give her answer, she looked at Grimm, this man who had sought to enter the rude forests of his ancestors and who surely now had succeeded. 'There has only ever been one man. I love Jacob, but as he himself wrote in our Family Book, "as much as my own family". Not as a husband.' She could say that with impunity now. Half a lifetime ago, it might have been different. But that was behind her. She wanted it behind her.

Auguste dipped her head. Dortchen could not tell if this was what she had hoped to hear. Very possibly it was not. To her own surprise it had been easy to say. Her daughter stiffened and stared again at the far wall where the summer's journals still stood stacked, unread. A long moment passed, but Dortchen had taken the conversation as far as she could. If anyone were to break this silence, it had to be Auguste. But instead of speaking she stood up, as if to find a new perspective on what she had just heard.

'Tell me one thing, then,' she said sharply. 'On Papa's last night – when he thought we were all paintings – what did he *mean* after Apapa calmed him down? When he said, "Take her back now. I was only ever looking after her for you." What did that mean? Was he talking about you? Or me? Who?'

So this was a part of it. '*Ach*, Gustchen,' her mother sighed. 'He was delirious, you know that.'

'Even so. It meant something. And Apapa looked shaken when he heard it.'

'It isn't what you think.' Dortchen closed her eyes and put the back of her hand to her lips. But if she had turned, her daughter would still have seen her smiling. It was almost too absurd for words.

'You see that curtained walnut cabinet by the door, just above the boot rack?' Auguste nodded. 'Go over to it.'

Auguste crossed the rug to the cupboard from which, at different times, she had seen her Apapa take cuff-links, matches, collar studs, shoelaces.

'Pull back the curtain,' said her mother. 'I think you should look on the middle shelf.'

Two candles lay horizontally across that shelf. They were fixed with a seal of their own wax to prevent two old but well-preserved figurines behind them from tumbling out accidentally. They stood back to back: a tricorn-hatted man and a high-coiffured woman in a pale blue gown that predated the Empire period.

Immediately Auguste understood, and although she smiled she shuddered too, as if someone she loved very much had not just stepped over her new grave but paused to dash down an extra, quite unnecessary, handful of earth.

'Tap her head very gently,' said Auguste's mother. 'On the side.'

'I know what to do.' Auguste reached in and made the woman's head shake. Unlike the little man in Cassel, the motion was not silent. The room echoed to a low clack-clack-clacking, when the ceramic stick intermittently struck the inside of the body. It seemed to Auguste that she had been hearing the echo inside her addled head for weeks. And only then did she wonder if Kummel had meant *this* when he asked in her Apapa's study if she 'heard it too'.

'They had them as children in Steinau. One each. Willi had the little lady, who said no.' There was a catch now in her mother's voice that she could not disguise. 'The man was always Jacob's. At the end he wanted Jacob to have them both . . .'

Auguste stepped back towards the chair where she sat. She twisted around just before reaching its arm, her fixed smile lighting up a face full of tears that she in turn was determined not to cry. *We must keep on doing things in the proper way . . .* In a single smooth movement she drew out the old black shawl and draped it ceremonially around the older woman's shoulders.

'Thank you,' they said together.

Then Auguste took a step back towards the door, as if to bring her singular Apapa more closely into focus. He was beyond her reach, as he always had been. But still as he lay there, having come as far as he could in this land that had finally failed him, she sensed him going on. As he himself had told her so often, there were other worlds, further journeys.

'I'm sorry,' she whispered, to no one who was there with them. Behind her the clacking of the ornament slowed down and became even more fitful: *No . . . no . . . no . . . no . . .* She wanted to go closer then, take his hand, reassure him of her love as her uncle, her father, whoever. She still could not be sure who he was. Perhaps she had never dared to hear the question answered. Certainly not by her mother. What else, after all, could that good woman have said? Auguste could no more expect to hear the whole truth here than she could expect to see the whole of a tree above the ground.

'In Göttingen,' she said because she had to say something, 'when he was exiled, he promised me he would never go to the land beyond the map. I was so afraid I would never see him again. I asked him if he would go to the realm that fell from its ruler's pocket. Do you remember how he used to talk about that?'

Her mother nodded. '*Natürlich*.' Blinking hard, she held up his hand and shook it as if he were an incorrigible infant. 'And if he'd gone there, you know what he would have done at once, don't you? Made a collection of all its oldest stories, then written the history of its language.'

Auguste tilted her head.

Like the pious man at the end of Kummel's story, the life had somehow gone out of her. Her soul had flown; she was stone, pure stone. She went back to the wall cabinet, and just as the little lady's head came to rest, she reached in and tapped it once again.

TWENTY-EIGHT

Clack – clack – clack . . . Even though she had stopped chewing, the king's mother ran her tongue around the inside of her mouth and went on making the loathsome sound with her teeth.

'Enough!' he cried, reaching forward furiously to strike the side of her large head with the flat of his free hand. The blow drew blood from her ear. She stilled her tongue and stared up at him, impassive. When he said no more, she passed a sleeve across her lips and chin to smear away the grease. All the while she looked at him, steady, unrepentant, an abomination who had no place in this world, but also the mother who had brought him into it.

'Stand up,' he said. As she obeyed he looked away from the ghastly spit and the flames that flared from the fat. He knew he should have stabbed her in the back. Skewered her on his sword then fried her in her own fire. He stepped aside and pointed to the door. He had to get her out of the garret, get himself away from its heat, stench and hideousness. Her look became quizzical but not defiant. She was not going to plead with him. He wished she would. That, at least, would stir his anger again. Instead she was almost flirtatiously passive.

'I don't want your blood in here,' he told her, still pointing his sword at the door. 'You'll dig your own grave outside. No one else should have to do it.'

Blinking at him lazily, a half-smile twisting her lips, she heaved herself across the floor, pulled back the door and left. He was behind her at once, nudging her on when she took the steps too sluggishly, then again as they crossed the back courtyard towards the gatehouse.

Ogress, Mother, Ogress, Mother . . . The two words thundered in his head with each pair of her steps. But if she had the power to lay so grim a curse on his future wife all those years ago, then surely she did not have to accept her punishment so meekly now? Perhaps the fact that he was her son as well as her executioner was weighing just a little with her.

The sentries at the gatehouse came alive when they saw her lumbering ahead of him across the chippings. Each man took a blazing torch from the walls and held it in front of him like a talisman at her approach. If the king had ever imagined he could turn her killing over to them, or to anyone else in his kingdom, their petrified expressions told him otherwise. Besides, this last task was his. It had been waiting for him from the moment he first set foot on the steps up the bluff to the palace.

But already he was thinking of displacing her, not wiping her out entirely. For there were, he knew, other worlds than this. 'Bring me a spade,' he called to the sentries before his mother reached them.

One of them had it ready for him to snatch as he pushed her out of the palace precincts. Then, sheathing his sword, he seized the man's torch too. 'There,' he directed her, off the military road down a convex slope to the left towards a thin, broken streak of tree-tops that stood dark against the paler, moonless sky.

Tramping through the ferns and grasses, they came sooner than he had anticipated to a grove of dwarf oaks, most of them no more than twice his own height, their branches oddly leafless and inextricably intertwined. The ground they surrounded was dank, crumbling to humus. 'Stop,' he cried out, and when she did, he tossed the spade to land with a thud near her foot. 'Dig.'

Although she had walked slowly there was strength in her arms. Soon she was standing knee-deep in a trench wide enough to take her. The only sound in the grove was the clang of iron on root. No birds sang, no forest creatures rustled in the undergrowth. The torch in his hand had ceased to spit and crackle as he left the palace behind. Occasionally he would glance behind him to make sure its nearer buildings were still there. From that angle all he could see was the outline of the oldest tower beyond the top of the iron gates, still belching smoke.

Ogress, Mother, Mother, *Mother* . . .

Again he thought: displacement. Vividly he remembered the woodman Friedrich. For him, the whole Rose Kingdom had been nothing but a story. And somehow he himself had passed through a crack in the map to find that other world, with all its inverse truths and meanings. The dead were alive in his lost brother's fatherland. There, straw could be gold. And there, perhaps, his mother need not be this principle of evil incarnate.

She asked for no respite. When she was visible only from the waist up, he stooped to plant the torch in the rotting ground and said, 'Enough.' Apparently unwearied, she held out the spade to him. He stepped up to the pit's lip, took the tool and threw it down at her feet. Then he drew his sword.

She did not flinch. The look on her face had not much changed since he first saw her in the garret. *Ogress* . . . His blood had to be hotter for this, and he guessed that she knew it. Before her, he was neither a king nor a prince, but simply Old One again. In the stillness of the grove, with her head at the level of his thighs, he could not wipe out all his love for her. And he believed he had found a way of not needing to. In her own fashion, she may even have been guiding him: leading him here to another crack in the map.

Before he could speak, she sank to her haunches, then laid back her head and straightened her legs. Fussily she adjusted the skirt of her soiled feasting dress, clasped her hands over her belly and closed her eyes.

There are other worlds, he told himself as he began to circle the pit, sliding in piles of crumbled earth on top of her with his boot. Round and round he went. Other worlds. He knew he would never see her in this one again. He let himself look only when the first layer had covered her, half expecting her stiffened arm to shoot up in farewell, or salute, or even contempt. Already, in a sense, he had done his duty. Then with a surge of energy he threw in his sword, dropped down, and loaded in all the rest of the earth with both hands.

After tamping the ground flat he stretched himself out on it and stayed prone until the torch guttered across the grove and the sun began to rise. At times in the night he thought he could hear the tramp of marching boots, glass smashing, the echoes of faraway screams.

When finally he rolled over on to his back, the tangled oaks seemed to be applauding him, hugging each other at his triumph. Beyond them in the distance the pines looked heather-blue, soaring away from the palace like a vast tilted ocean. He remembered how, when he was a child, his mother had forbidden him to go far into the forest, although often he went to gather brushwood at its fringes. Briefly the new sun's fireball brilliance was trapped beneath the canopy, but the golden glare was too great and when he narrowed his eyes tears snaked thinly down both his cheeks.

He stood, thought for a moment, then knelt and began to scoop out great handfuls of earth. It took him longer than it had taken her. By the time he caught a glimpse of the blue dress he could hear the outriders of his returning army hailing the sentries at the gatehouse. He scuffed away more strenuously. The sword was gone. The dress lay flat and uninhabited. He found the spade close beside it. No flesh, no bones.

Other worlds . . . She had passed through and that was enough – for him, for his wife and surviving child, for his obedient, delivered people.

After refilling the pit he climbed back up to the palace where the white-haired chamberlain stood waiting, flexing his right arm as if he had recently taken a blow but was no longer troubled by the pain.

As the king approached the gatehouse, trailing the spade behind him, he paused and almost looked back. He thought he heard the clacking again – more vigorous than before, then quickly fading. But not here. Never again here.

With a forlorn smile the chamberlain shook his head, then beckoned him on.

At 10.20 pm on Sunday 20 September 1863 Professor Jacob Grimm died at 7 Linkstrasse in central Berlin. He was seventy-eight years old. His brother's widow Dortchen and niece Auguste subsequently moved to Schellingstrasse. The former died of pneumonia in 1867; the latter lived on until 1919 when she died, unmarried, at the age of eighty-seven. Grimm's work on the *Deutsches Wörterbuch* was continued by others until its completion – in thirty-two published volumes – in the early 1960s. Of Friedrich Kummel, there is no historical record.

Within eight years of Grimm's death, Prussian Prime Minister Otto von Bismarck proclaimed a unified German Reich after a series of victorious national wars against Denmark, Austria and France. Known as the Second Reich – the medieval Holy Roman Empire had been the first – it lasted until its dismemberment by the Allies after the First World War.

In 1933 Adolf Hitler established a Third Reich. His Nazi Party encouraged German families to use highly selective editions of the Brothers Grimm's *Tales for Young and Old* as 'housebooks' promoting the traditional values, strengths and unity of the German folk community.

Intended to last for a thousand years, the Third Reich fell within thirteen. During the Second World War, Hanau, Cassel and Berlin were all laid waste. Afterwards the country was divided again, until 1990.

This is my story, I've told it, and in your hands I leave it.

AUTHOR'S NOTE

Anyone wishing to take a closer look at the stories which inspired this novel might begin with *The Complete Grimms' Fairy Tales* (Routledge & Kegan Paul, 1975). As for the 'meaning' of the tales, Bruno Bettelheim's controversial *The Uses of Enchantment* (Thames and Hudson, 1976) first raised my own interest in this area, while among more recent studies Maria Tatar's *The Hard Facts of the Grimms' Fairy Tales* (Princeton University Press, 1987) is accessible and interesting. *Paths Through The Forest* by Murray B. Peppard (Holt, Rhinehart and Winston, 1971) provides an excellent introductory biography of Jacob and Wilhelm, and Christa Kamenetsky's *The Brothers Grimm and Their Critics* (Ohio University Press, 1992) places the brothers' folktale research within the broader context of their scholarly work.

According to the German Romantic writer Novalis (1772–1801), novels arise out of the shortcomings of history. In creating this fiction based on the lives of the Brothers Grimm, I have tried to write a novel that is not in itself another shortcoming.

If I have failed, it is not the fault of the following people, all of whom I would like to thank for their expertise and assistance over the past three years: Kim Cole, David Fickling, Jamila Gavin, Dr Dakota Hamilton, Antonia Hodgson, Dr Tim Holian, Stephanie van Leeuwen, Christopher Little, Nick Szczepanik and Deirdre Counihan, Dr David Stacey, Simon Trewin, Andrew Wille, Hilary Wright and – last but not least – my dedicatees.

Haydn Middleton
March 1999